Falling
into Grace

Also by Michelle Stimpson

Last Temptation

Someone To Watch Over Me

Published by Kensington Publishing Corp.

Falling
into Grace

MICHELLE
STIMPSON

Kensington Publishing Corp.
http://www.kensingtonbooks.com

DAFINA BOOKS are published by

Kensington Publishing Corp.
119 West 40th Street
New York, NY 10018

All Kensington Titles, Imprints, and Distributed Lines are available at special quantity discounts for bulk purchases for sales promotions, premiums, fund-raising, and educational or institutional use. Special book excerpts or customized printings can also be created to fit specific needs. For details, write or phone the office of the Kensington special sales manager: Kensington Publishing Corp., 119 West 40th Street, New York, NY 10018, attn: Special Sales Department, Phone: 1-800-221-2647.

Dafina and the Dafina logo Reg. U.S. Pat & TM Off.

ISBN-13: 978-0-7582-4691-2
ISBN-10: 0-7582-4691-9
First trade paperback printing: June 2012
First mass market printing: July 2015

eISBN-13: 978-1-4967-0398-9
eISBN-10: 1-4967-0398-7
Kensington Electronic Edition: July 2015

10 9 8 7 6 5 4 3 2 1

Printed in the United States of America

For everyone who labors in the name of Christ.
Your toil is not in vain. You will be rewarded.
A thousand years from now,
you will still rejoice that
you did things His way.

ACKNOWLEDGMENTS

Thank You, Jesus, for the grace of complete surrender that came to me over the course of writing this book. Nine books and almost forty short stories into this writing career, You never cease to amaze me. Thank You, thank You, thank You.

To my family: I know, this particular book took me quite a while to write. Thank you for giving me the space to write. Every writer's, every teacher's, every minister's family loses a part of their loved one while he/she is out there loving on other people. Just so happens I am all three. So, thanks to my peeps for "sowing" me.

Several folks lent their expertise and thoughts to this book. I kept track this time! To my writing group, Lynne, Pattie, Kellie, Janice, Jane, Dana—thanks for reading the outline and giving me feedback. And to Lynne again for consulting with me throughout the drafting process. Tia McCollors and April Baker, thanks for being available to talk me through plot points without any notice. Rev. Rodney Carter, pastor of worship at Oak Cliff Bible Fellowship in Dallas, TX, thanks for sitting down with me between services to talk about life as a minister of music. Lisa Lin, THE cat lady, thanks for telling me everything I ever wanted to know about cats. Sharon Jenkins provided information about how "big churches" run—thanks! To my uncle, Fred Williams, and my cousin, Myron Williams, thanks for answering my questions about the gospel music world and offering time in your studio. Mom, thanks for the medical information. Finally, thanks again to Howard for walking me through all the practical police matters.

A shout-out to all the book clubs who continue to support my works. Few of us get to write this many books, and those of us who do owe you great big hugs! Your dedicated readership ministers to me, reminds me of why it's important to write the words He has given.

Thanks to my agent, Sara Camilli, and Selena James at Kensington for working with me and believing in these characters and stories that keep arriving in my head. You have made these tough literary times a pleasure for me. God bless you.

To all of my fellow writers—read the dedication again. And to all the writers who are sitting on works that are ordained to bless the body of Christ—read the dedication again. I urge you to allow Him to finish the work He has begun in you (Philippians 1:6).

In His Love,
Michelle Stimpson
September, 2011

CHAPTER 1

Your account is overdrawn.

Camille Robertson unchecked the e-mail notification box on her cell phone. No need in setting herself up for even more depressing announcements. Bad enough she was turning the big three-oh today. She didn't need to be reminded that she was also broke. Below broke, actually, because by the afternoon, her account would be charged another thirty-four dollars for insufficient funds.

She closed her eyes as the phone's screen dimmed and then went blank. *Insufficient.* A good word to describe Camille's life for the past eleven years.

The dull beep of her neighbor's alarm clock added another level of ridiculousness to her life. Cheap rent always came with thin walls and bad layout, i.e., adjacent bedrooms. No privacy. Not that Camille needed it. Her life was as uneventful as they came.

She listened to the beeping awhile longer and decided that this fellow tenant must have already left the apartment, or maybe she was dead. Either way, the clock had another fifty-nine minutes to blare unattended.

With the last moments of sleep now forfeited, Camille slapped her dry feet onto the cold tile. Pedicures got laid off a long time ago. She couldn't remember the last time she'd been pumped up in a hairdresser's chair. Boxed perms, homemade hairstyles, and do-it-yourself French manicures had become a way of life now.

Camille steadied herself on the edge of the bed, thinking about her plans for the day. Her father would probably call and wish her a happy birthday in one breath, ask for some money in the next. He still believed that Camille had some kind of money stashed from her brief but profitable R&B run a decade earlier.

"I know you didn't go through all that money that fast, baby girl," he had practically begged at Christmas-time. "All I'm askin' for is a couple thousand dollars to put a new engine in my car. Dang! Hate to see what happens if I need a kidney!"

A couple of thousand dollars would have been like ten dollars when Camille was riding high. But now, in the real working-class American world, a few thousand dollars might as well have been ten million dollars, because, either way, she didn't have it.

Three months had passed since that depressing Christmas conversation. Camille had made attempts to contact her father, but he hadn't been too receptive. Probably just as well, though, because she was within an inch of calling it quits with Bobby Junior, as everyone called him. Fathers were irreplaceable, Camille knew. But what good was a father who constantly reminded her of her biggest failure?

Heavy footsteps overhead caused the white, frosted

ceiling lightbulb cover to clank. Camille pictured the woman upstairs plodding across the floor, her chunky frame swaying with each flat-footed step. The old Camille would have sworn at the fat woman, said, "It's about time she turned off that alarm, with her fat [so-and-so] self." The new Camille experienced stuffing an extra thirty pounds into her Spanx daily. She literally had no room to resent big girls, because, right about now, Camille might make a good Lane Bryant model.

She stood and opened the center section of the eighties-style French closet doors. Her closet offered varieties of only black and gray. Shades for the self-conscious.

She pulled a knit dress from the closet and grabbed undergarments from her drawer on the way to the bathroom, side-stepping the areas where carpet had worn thin enough to expose the staples.

The bathroom mirror added insult to injury. The under-eye circles could be softened with concealer, discolorations with bootleg MAC foundation. Those off-white teeth, however, required a professional. If she could afford dental insurance, she might even be able to replace the "temporary" crown she'd been wearing so long she'd probably need a porcelain veneer at this point.

After plopping her clothes onto the toilet seat, Camille further surveyed herself at thirty. Nothing was the way it used to be. The whites of her eyes, once bright and shiny, had lost their glimmer, thanks to crooning in smoke-filled nightclubs trying to get rediscovered. Patches of dry skin lightened some areas on her otherwise caramel brown complexion. Her lips, which had actually been mentioned once in *People* magazine for their "perkiness," seemed to have taken a permanent downturn at the corners. They reminded Camille of her deceased mother's lips. Momma was always concerned. Worried.

Maybe if Camille worried more, she would get more done with her life. But as it stood, she wasn't concerned enough to worry. Wouldn't make much difference anyway.

Once out of the shower, Camille made a half-hearted effort to make herself presentable for work. Somehow, men didn't quite view Camille as the washed-up ex-beauty she knew she was. A trip to the corner gas station brought a misguided suitor toward Camille's ten-year-old Lexus coupe. Try as she might to dissuade him by avoiding eye contact and pretending to dial numbers on her phone, the tall, thin brother approached her nonetheless.

He took the liberty of resting a closed fist on the trunk. Way too close for a first encounter. Camille might have made a run for the store if he hadn't been wearing obnoxiously loud cologne and cheap transition glasses that barely reacted to the early-morning sunlight. Sure signs of a harmless wannabe player.

"Your man ought to be out here pumping gas for you," he remarked, his silver grill exposing the fact that he, too, resisted the thirtysomething years racking up on his life calendar.

Camille knew her response was supposed to be either, "I don't have a man," or something to the effect that her man was sorry, which would, of course, give this amateur an opportunity to step in for an unhappy-chick rescue mission. Instead, Camille replied, "He's out of the country handling business."

Undaunted, this smooth operator examined the pump panel. "He must not be handling it too good, got you putting cheap gas in this luxury car. Gonna mess up your engine, you know that?"

Camille dared not reveal her special remedy for saving on gas: alternate regular with premium. She looked the stranger dead in the eyes. Were it not for Miss Norris's super-scary Sunday school warning that we should always be nice to strangers because they might be angels in disguise, Camille might have flat told this guy to leave her alone. Really, why waste his time when Mrs. Loud Cologne might be down the row at pump number seven?

Camille chose a condescending rebuttal. "*Well*. People handle things *well*, not good."

"Whichever one it is, sweetheart, he ain't doin' it." He raised an eyebrow. Stood silent. Then his facial muscles jumped an inch. "Wait a minute. I know you."

Thump-thump in Camille's chest as the attitude slipped away.

"You were the lead singer with that group!" He snapped his fingers. "Aw, man, I can't think of the name."

"Sweet Treats," she helped him out, nodding all the while.

"Yeah!" He hollered and covered his mouth as though he'd just witnessed a monster slam dunk in a basketball game. "Man, that CD was the jam back in the day. And you still lookin' good."

Suffocating a smile, Camille thanked him for the compliments. "Meet me, baby, meet me in the hot tub." He crossed his arms across his chest in slow-dance grinding formation as he sang the familiar lyrics from

Sweet Treats's debut compilation. "Girl, I think I lost my virginity to that song. Everybody did!"

Camille seized the opportunity. "You want an autographed CD?"

"Yeah."

Camille pushed the trunk icon on her key fob. The trunk popped up. She ripped open one of three identical boxes and pried a CD out of its row. She slammed the trunk closed, then fumbled through her purse for a pen.

"What's your name?" She had to get personal before springing the price on him.

"Gary."

"Gary, that'll be twelve dollars."

"Whoa! Twelve dollars?"

Camille smarted off, "Retail was thirteen ninety-nine."

"Yeah, back in *nineteen* ninety-nine," he matched her wits.

Camille rolled her eyes. "Music never gets old. Plus, this will be autographed to *you*, Gary."

He pursed his lips. "Eight."

"Eleven."

He countered, "Nine."

"With tax, ten."

Gary reached into his back pocket, pulled the bill from his wallet. "This economy ain't takin' no prisoners, I see."

Camille signed quickly, before Gary could change his mind. They exchanged, CD for cash, just as the hands-free gas pump latch snapped, signaling a full tank.

"Shoot!" Camille stomped. Fooling around with Gary, she'd accidentally filled up the car.

"You okay?" Gary asked.

"Fine. Hope you enjoy the CD."

"Straight. Good to meet you. You think we can, you know, get together some time?"

Camille had almost forgotten Gary's original intent. Back to the game. "My man wouldn't appreciate me cheating on him."

"Looks to me like your man doesn't appreciate you period. But I don't want to break up a happy home. Unless . . ."

"No, Gary, I'm fine."

"Suit yourself."

Gary went his way as Camille trudged into the store to surrender the ten dollars she'd just hustled out of Gary, plus nine more that she had hoped to use for lunch money the next couple of days. She'd have to brown-bag it now that she'd unintentionally flushed all her cash down the gas tank.

Come on, Friday.

CHAPTER 2

Camille clocked in, digitally, seven minutes past her official start time. She calculated she'd already been late by a total of nineteen minutes. Her boss, Sheryl Finkowich, had threatened to start docking them if they were more than half an hour late in any one week. Though her warning was probably meant to encourage timeliness, Camille took it as a license to rack up exactly twenty-nine unaccounted-for minutes between Monday and Friday. She had two more days before the game started again.

Worse than her boss's threat, however, were the watchful eyes of coworkers who would throw one another under the bus for a nickel more per hour base pay. Camille had ratted out her fair share of employees, but not for a nickel. A quarter, maybe, but not a nickel.

The maze of cubicles provided some margin of ambiguity about what time everyone came in to work. Only the electronic record could tell the whole truth.

Camille tucked her purse behind her elbow as she breezed past desks, only offering, "Hey, Bob," and, "Hi, Rene," because "good morning" would give her away.

She made it to her space without much eye contact or being spotted by Sheryl. Camille pressed the power button on her computer, threw her purse into the second drawer of her file cabinet. The start of yet another meaningless day at Aquapoint Systems. *Really, does the world need another water-filtration company? Why were these losers so cheap they couldn't just fill the office refrigerator with bottled water? No one likes to use stupid paper-cone cups.* And beside all that, Camille had read a statistic somewhere saying the only water most people drank in a day's time was what was left over after they brushed their teeth.

Of course, Camille never shared these sentiments with her potential clients. "Yes, Aquapoint Systems provides a less expensive, earth-friendly alternative to bottled water for your employees," she spouted off the sales pitch while responding to birthday posts on her Facebook page in a separate window.

No matter the caller's response, Camille was determined to set an appointment for a field representative to demonstrate the superior quality of Aquapoint System's product. Newer businesses, especially, liked to give the underdog a chance. "We're a small business just like yours, and we would really appreciate the opportunity to grow right along with you." That line was Camille's secret weapon.

By noon, Camille had managed to set up seven appointments with office managers. Not bad, considering she'd made only about a hundred calls. Any telemarketer would be proud of a 7 percent closing rate. Plus, she'd earn ten dollars on top of her eight-dollar-an-hour base pay if the appointments didn't cancel.

Sheryl performed the kind of bad congratulatory routine only seen in chain restaurants, where all the workers lined up and clapped for someone who was celebrating a birthday or anniversary. "Yaaay! Everyone, Camille's almost reached her quota for the day, and she hasn't even gone to lunch! Let's give her a hand!"

Halfhearted applause stumbled through the area.

"Great job, Camille." Sheryl then slapped a puppy dog sticker on the back of Camille's hand.

Is she serious? A sticker? "Thank you."

"You're welcome," Sheryl chirped. "I got them at a dog show last year."

"Mmm." *You just gave me something you got at a dog show?*

Sheryl gave one last thumbs-up and walked away. Camille removed the sticker, folded it in half, and tossed it in the trash.

Stickers wouldn't help. What she needed was some cold, hard cash, because she had only enough change in her purse to buy a candy bar for lunch. Camille wished, for once, that she was a coffee drinker. People feel *entitled* to coffee, and everywhere she'd worked in the past few years always provided free java. Maybe, one of these days, orange juice drinkers would rise up and revolt. Until then, Camille was stuck with plain old Aquapoint water.

The break room quickly filled with other brown-baggers. Some health conscious, evidenced by their multiple plastic containers filled with salads and fish. Others were dieting, eating foods that probably tasted like plastic. Janice, a woman Camille recognized from training class only three months ago, pulled up a chair at Camille's two-seater table.

Janice couldn't have been more than forty, but she always looked like she was in the wrong decade. Regardless of clothing or hairstyle, Janice just had that throwback 1970s, *Charlie's Angels* look.

Janice opened with small talk. "Tell me your name again?"

"Camille."

"That's right. How's it going for you?"

"Okay, I guess." Camille shrugged. "You?"

Janice leaned in and whispered, "Awful. I've been looking for another job."

Another one bites the dust. If enough people left or got fired, Camille might actually be in the running to become a supervisor, then all she'd have to do is push paperwork. Still, she needed to appear sympathetic. Janice might be trying to feel Camille out so she could rat her out. "Why? I mean, the pay isn't too bad."

Janice countered with a hint of sincerity, "It is if you don't make any appointments."

Camille had to nod in agreement. "Have you talked to your supervisor?"

"Patrick?"

"Never mind."

Even people who didn't work for Patrick knew he wasn't the helpful type.

No sense in leading Janice on. Maybe she just didn't have what it took. She sure didn't have Camille's killer closing line, and Camille wasn't about to give it up. "Good luck in finding something else."

Janice unfolded the foil covering her bologna and

cheese sandwich. She took a slow, contemplative bite, then asked, with a bit too much food in her mouth, "Don't you ever want to, like, do something that really matters with your life? Something really big and great?"

A laugh escaped Camille's grasp. "I did do something really amazing, back in the day."

Janice's eyes widened. "Really? What?"

What could it hurt to tell Janice? "I used to sing with a girl group. We sold millions of CDs, toured the world. Limos, fancy hotels, all that."

"Oh my gosh!" Janice took another bite, her eyes begging for Camille to go on.

"I mean, that was it. We did it." Camille shrugged, balling up her candy wrapper.

"What do you mean, that was *it*? What happened?"

Sore territory. "We broke up."

"Why?"

Camille pursed her lips. She'd asked herself that question countless times. Why did Sweet Treats break up? The answer depended upon which Sweet Treat responded. Since there was no one to refute Camille's version, she replied to Janice, "Jealousy. I was the lead singer, everyone was after me. You know how that kind of thing goes."

"So, you all were like Destiny's Child?"

She had to give it to Janice. Maybe she was in this century after all. "You know your R and B groups, huh?"

Janice smiled. "I watch a little MTV now and then."

"Well," Camille continued, "we were *better* than Destiny's Child. We sang better, we looked better, we had better music. The only difference between me and Beyoncé was that her dad watched out for her and made sure his daughter was always in the spotlight. If

I'd had a dad like hers, I sure wouldn't be working here right now."

"Wow." Janice beamed in amazement. "You could have really been somebody."

Camille smacked. "Yepper."

"I mean, you *are* somebody. Everybody's somebody in their own way. You know what I mean?" Janice tried to backtrack.

"I know what you mean." Camille sighed. "But you're right. I could have been, like, a *real* somebody."

"I always wanted to be a teacher," Janice confided.

For the rest of the lunch break, Camille pretended to listen to Janice's secret career aspirations that would probably never come to pass, because, according to Janice, she was too far in debt to consider paying for college. Plus there was some nonsense about a boat that she and her husband had purchased with three other couples.

Camille nodded dutifully, asking trite questions whenever appropriate, but Janice's problems were regular-people problems—issues Camille wouldn't have had to deal with if Sweet Treats were still together like Destiny's Child. Okay, maybe Destiny's Child wasn't really *together* together anymore, but at least they weren't working alongside the general public, eating candy bars for lunch under the buzz of a bad tubular lightbulb.

No, those girls still had a lot going for them. It wasn't fair. Why did they get to keep making music when Sweet Treats, Brownstone, En Vogue, and SWV were out of business? Especially when Tom Joyner himself had said that Sweet Treats was the "best total package." And he wasn't the only one to point out Sweet Treats's potential. So why weren't they still on top?

Camille stewed over these nonstop questions all afternoon in her work space. All the shoulda, woulda, couldas replayed themselves in a matrix of never-ending possibilities, none of which resulted in Camille working as a telemarketer for Aquapoint Systems.

Bobby Junior finally busted through Camille's flashback by calling her cell phone.

"Hey, Daddy."

"Happy birthday, Camillie. This is the big one. Thirty. You grown now," he teased.

"Thank you. You got a present for me?"

Of course, Camille already knew the answer before he responded. "Naw, your daddy's got some bills to pay. I was hoping maybe you could send me some money."

"But it's *my* birthday." Camille laughed to mask her disappointment.

"The way I see it, you wouldn't *have* a birthday if it wasn't for me."

For all his drinking, Bobby Junior was still fast with his sharp replies. "So, you gonna let your old man hold twenty dollars?"

"I would if I could, but I can't so I ain't," she threw one of Bobby Junior's favorite excuses back at him.

"You still driving that Lexus, right?"

"Yeah," Camille affirmed, wondering where her father was headed with this line of inquiry.

"Ain't nobody who's driving a Lexus broke."

"My car is ten years old. Almost two hundred thousand miles on it," Camille spelled it out for him.

"All I know is, I ain't never had leather interior in none of my cars," her father reiterated. "You gonna help your daddy out or what?"

"I can't. You and I are in the same boat right now."

"Aw." He tsked. "Don't give me that. You forget

you're talking to somebody who knows the music business inside out. I know Lenny's still got royalties coming in." Bobby Junior never failed to reference his one musical connection—Lenny Williams—who allowed Bobby Junior to sing backup on one song. Depending on how far Bobby Junior took the story, Lenny was also a distant cousin.

"Lenny's still getting checks because people are still playing 'I Love You' and using it in new ways," Camille reasoned. "If somebody wants to use one of our songs for a commercial or a movie, I'll get a cut, too. But until then, I'm a regular person living from paycheck to paycheck just like you, Dad."

Actually, in Bobby Junior's case, it was more like woman to woman. Since her mother died, leaving Bobby Junior a widow, he hadn't been able to hold a relationship or a job steady. Lucky for him, there was never a shortage of foolish ladies who would take her father in, feed him, and make sure he had a decent pair of shoes in exchange for his good looks and company. The woman would usually buy him a cell phone, too, so she could keep up with him. But the relationship wouldn't last long. Sooner or later, Bobby Junior would get busted fooling around with his next victim. Then he'd move in with her, get a new phone number. Beg Camille for money until he built up enough trust with the new beau to get the ATM code.

"Humph," he chided. "Well, happy birthday anyway. You talked to your brother?"

"Nope."

"Don't make no sense, brother and sister grew up in the same house with the same momma and daddy don't even talk to each other no more."

"I don't have a problem with Courtney. He has a

problem with me." Camille said the same thing every time Bobby Junior broached the subject.

"Just don't make no sense. Look like to me you ought to want to hold on to whatever family you got left, 'specially after what happened with your momma. But y'all grown. I can't make y'all play with each other."

"All right, well, I've got to get back to work." Camille pressed the red "end call" button before her father could launch a campaign for ten dollars . . . five dollars . . . something he could pawn.

She threw the phone back into her purse and put her headset back in place for the last fifty calls of the day. Glad for the sales script, Camille plodded through the afternoon with her mind only half engaged in work. The other half was in LA. London. On stage with a microphone taped to her body. Four women standing six feet behind her.

Or should she go solo? That way she wouldn't have to split the money. If the group's second manager, Aaron, hadn't convinced the record label to keep Kyra in the group despite her blatant drug problems, Camille might still have some funds left in the bank. Dividing by three instead of four makes a huge difference when millions of dollars are on the line.

When Camille really thought about it, she could almost strangle Aaron now for saving Kyra's butt. All Kyra ever did was moan on most of the songs anyway. Granted, it was a sexy moan—one that she'd probably practiced many a night in Aaron's hotel room. Yeah, there was a reason he wanted to keep that butt around.

And Kyra was . . . slow. Not slow like she was born with a medical problem. Slow like she'd been smoking weed since the seventh grade. She just could not process information well, let alone read people.

Camille paused the dialer and maximized the Facebook window on her screen. She searched for Kyra Copeland and scrolled down until she found the familiar face. Jealousy pinged through Camille's chest as she explored Kyra's open photo albums. She was obviously married, living in Phoenix with three boys in a two-story brick home with a pool. *A pool!* Dozens of mobile-uploaded pictures documented family gatherings and vacations. But that pool took the cake.

Not to mention the fact that Kyra looked like she hadn't gained an ounce. In fact, she looked better than back in the day. Kyra always had that handsome beauty. She was probably one of those girls who was the spitting image of her father, which, at a young age, was a huge problem, but as she grew older and filled out (and shaved the moustache), her features actually came together well. Yep, that was Kyra.

She seemed happy. But who can really tell by Facebook? Camille checked Kyra's info page and nearly busted out laughing. Kyra was a photographer? Seriously! Who would entrust Miss Moan-a-thon to capture precious memories on film? Camille copied and pasted Kyra's alleged Web site address into the browser. A barrage of bridal photos and graduation shots paraded across the page. And they looked like someone who might know what they were doing staged and edited the shots.

How could this be? *Kyra Copeland is better off than me?* "I don't think so," Camille whispered to herself as she closed the extra window on her screen. No way was she going to let Kyra, of all people, have the upper hand. Tonya, Camille could understand. Her parents had money. Even Alexis might be understandable because she went back to college and finished her degree.

But not Kyra. If that man-looking Kyra was making it in this world, living in a nice house, going on cruises, Camille didn't have an excuse.

She slammed her headset on the desk. Took a look around her stupid, gray cubicle. *Useless waste of the earth's resources.* She could still hear coworkers talking, still see through the cracks and smell when someone burned popcorn in the microwave. The only thing those partitions actually did for her was cover up tardiness.

But what did it matter if she was late? Who cares? As long as she came in and made her ten leads for the day to keep the manager away, what time she got there should be irrelevant. This whole job was stupid anyway.

Worse than this depressing train of thought was the fact that she actually *needed* this job to pay rent in an apartment she was too ashamed to have anyone visit. Maybe she shouldn't have been ashamed of her place. I mean, at least she did have a roof over her head. Running water. Air-conditioning.

Her mother taught her to be grateful. Yet, Camille always figured the "grateful" thing was something you did on the way *up*. Like, if you had nothing and then, all of a sudden, you got rich, you were supposed to thank God for taking you from bad to good. She had a hard time showing gratitude after being robbed of the queen-of-pop-sopranos crown. Well, maybe that was taking it a little too far—like the time Whitney Houston said Bobby Brown was the king of R&B when, really, he wasn't even on the radar.

Camille still remembered the day Sweet Treats's last manager, Priscilla Longoria, called and gave her the news that Sweet Treats's song had beat out Kelly Price,

Dru Hill, and Toni Braxton for the number-one slot on the R&B charts. It was, to date, the best day of Camille's life.

If she didn't get something going, the best part of her life would always be in the past. What better day to start than her thirtieth birthday?

CHAPTER 3

This was probably a bad idea. Her hands shook as she waited for Kyra to answer the phone, *if* this was the real Kyra Copeland. Six degrees of separation had been reduced to three, thanks to a mutual Facebook friend. The whole thing was one big quirky coincidence. A coincidence that might change her life forever.

"Hello."

"Hi, Kyra. It's Camille."

"Camille? How do we know each other?"

"Camille *Robertson*?"

"From Sweet Treats?"

Camille tried the we-go-way-back approach. "Yeah, girl, it's me. How you been?"

"Fine. How'd you get my number?" Kyra's cautionary pitch caught Camille by surprise.

"We have a mutual friend named . . ." Camille reviewed the screen. She didn't realize she would have to reveal her source so soon. "Yolanda Wesley."

"Oh." Kyra's voice fell. "She's one of my husband's

cousins. She's an author, always trying to build her fan base."

"I ain't mad at her," Camille drawled.

"Well, *I* certainly am. What do you need or want or whatever?" she gushed with a sigh.

Apparently, Kyra had gained a few points in the thinking category. Camille couldn't remember ever hearing Kyra string that many words together so fast without at least three takes in the studio. Camille would have to up her game.

"I was just sitting here reminiscing. Thinking about what a good thing we had going in the nineties. And yesterday, I was reading something in a magazine about Xscape, and you know we were *way* better than them. So—"

"Are you trying to put Sweet Treats back together again?"

Might as well cut to the chase. "Yes. That's exactly what I'm trying to do."

"Count me out."

Camille gasped. "Why? Kyra, you were like . . . the voice of . . . sexiness in our group."

"Please. You sang so loud and took over every song in concert. The audiences thought me and Tonya and Alexis were backup when we performed."

"It's not my fault that Priscilla put me front and center."

"No, but it is your fault we broke up."

Camille challenged, "How can you say that?"

"Because you made the decision to betray your brother and Tonya."

"Betray is a very strong word, Kyra. Besides, Darrion was a free agent."

"Oh my God, you're still in denial," Kyra accused.

"Everybody knew Tonya had a thing for Darrion. He was pretty much her man."

Hearing Kyra voice Darrion's name suddenly jogged Camille's memory. She'd almost forgotten about all those piddly details. Or maybe she'd blocked them out. Kyra hadn't purged her files.

"That was a long time ago, Kyra. We've all grown and matured. I was hoping we could get past our differences and make a run for it again," Camille said calmly, deeply, the way she imagined Maya Angelou spoke. Who could deny a seasoned black woman's wisdom?

"You're right," Kyra agreed. "We should all be more mature now than we were then. Let the past stay there. Move on with your life, Camille. Sweet Treats is over."

I'm losing her! "It doesn't have to be, Kyra. We can do it again. Look at Tony! Toni! Toné! They're still together. I just saw them on BET the other night."

"I'm sure they still actually like each other because they've never messed one another over," Kyra summed. "Let Sweet Treats go, Camille; the rest of us have."

Camille sucked in her breath. "You all keep in touch?"

"Yes. Alexis and Tonya are still close. I talk to them from time to time. Alexis is teaching in St. Louis. Tonya's back home in Houston, but she travels all over the country singing backup for Liza Sticcoli. We're all happy, busy doing things we enjoy."

Resentment flattened the smile Camille had been holding in place to enhance her pitch. So much for closing this deal. "Okay. Don't say I didn't ask you, Kyra."

"No sleep lost here. More power to you, but don't call me anymore."

Camille held on to the phone for a second, hoping

Kyra would say, "Psyche!" She used to pull that lame attempt at sarcasm so often, Camille had a pink and black T-shirt made for Kyra with the word applied across the chest.

No joke this time, though. T-Mobile brought the conversation to an official end with a soft beep in Camille's ear. She couldn't allow herself to process Kyra's less than desirable response. The rejection rolled off Camille's back like water on a duck. If there was one good thing she'd learned as a telemarketer, it was how to get over people's negative reactions.

On to the next one. "Hi, Alexis. It's me. Camille. From Sweet Treats."

"Hey, Camille," Alexis nearly sang. "How are you?" Alexis's uniquely raspy speech always sounded like she needed to cough a few times. At their first re-hearsal, Camille had been shocked by the strong alto hiding under the wobbly speaking voice.

So far so good. "Great! How are you?"

"I'm fine. So good to hear from you. What have you been up to?"

"Girl, just working, tryin' to make it. You?"

"I'm good. Wow! I haven't heard from you in ages. Wait 'til I tell Tonya I talked to you!"

Camille ventured, "How is Tonya?"

"She's great," Alexis caroled. "She just bought a house in Cedar Hill out by some kind of lake."

"Tonya lives near Dallas?"

"Yeah," Alexis crooned. "I thought you knew."

"It's a small world."

"So, what's up?" Alexis asked. "How's your dad?"

"He's fine."

"Your brother?"

"He's fine, too," Camille guessed.

Then she took a deep breath, her pulse racing. "Okay. Brace yourself. I was thinking—"

"Wait a second," Alexis interrupted. "Ooh, that's Kyra on the other line. Lord, I wonder if lightning is about to strike. Hold on just—"

"No, Alexis let me explain—"

"Just let me tell her that I'll call her back."

Alexis forced Camille to hold, and the longer Alexis stayed on the other line, the more anxious Camille became. This new, improved Kyra was also quick on the draw.

Finally, Alexis returned. "So, you want to get Sweet Treats back together?"

Darn that Kyra. "Yes."

"No can do, my sister."

"Come on, Alexis. Don't let Kyra make this decision for you. Give me one good reason why you can't do this with me."

Alexis replied, "I can give you three. First of all, I'm a teacher. I work at least sixty hours a week as it stands."

"If we get back with the right producers, you won't *have* to teach anymore," Camille countered. "Plus, I know teachers don't make any money. You're probably just as broke as me, and I don't even have a college degree."

"I don't know about the money part, but you're missing my point. I *love* teaching, and I'm dedicated to my students. I don't *want* to change my career, thank you very much."

"Must be nice to actually like what you do," Camille pouted. "But, hey, I know you've got the summers off, Alexis."

"Summers off? Please. School gets out the first week of June, I have staff development for, like, three weeks, and then we're back in mid-August. I'm lucky to have July off, which is not nearly enough time to pull a band together and pop up in the studio. Do you know how much we'd have to practice to pull this together? I'm nowhere near you and Tonya."

Camille interjected, "Ever heard of Southwest Airlines?"

"And the last thing is, my parents aren't in the best of health. I can't go anywhere until they get stable or whatever . . . well, you know," her voice tapered.

"I'm sorry, Alexis. I didn't know. I wouldn't have bothered your parents for your number if I'd known."

"It's okay. They can *talk*. They're just getting older. We have to watch Daddy's diabetes," she explained. "My mom used to keep an eye on him, but now she's got her own blood-pressure issues, too. I swear, their bathroom is a pharmacy."

Camille empathized all too well with Alexis's concerns. "I hope you're able to help them get things under control."

Alexis sighed. "Girl, me and God and maybe a personal plea from Barack Obama, 'cause that's what it's going to take to get them to listen. They are so hardheaded sometimes. They question everything the doctors tell them."

Camille remembered how many promises Priscilla had to make before Alexis's parents agreed to let their only daughter tour all over the world. The Nevilses were old-school parents who'd been pleasantly surprised with a bouncing baby girl in their late thirties. Even though Alexis had been, legally speaking, old enough to make the decision about touring with Sweet Treats, she wouldn't step on the bus without her parents' blessing.

Alexis's life, good and bad, clearly wasn't conducive to singing again.

And then there were two. "Do you think Tonya would consider reuniting with me?"

"I'm gonna say, um, H-E double hockey sticks no."

Camille laughed. "Why don't you go ahead and say the word?"

"You know I don't cuss. Never did."

"Anyway. Is Tonya still mad about Darrion?"

"Girl, naw," Alexis squawked. "She knows he was just a dog sniffing out the first one he could find to give it up."

That would be me. "Alrighty, then. So why do you think she won't do it?"

"'Cause she's already got a good thing going with Liza Sticcoli."

Camille pointed out, "Can't be that good. I listen to music all the time and I've never heard of any Liza other than Liza Minnelli."

"Liza *Sticcoli* is a Christian artist," Alexis stated.

"Oh." The realization hit Camille and she mused, *"Christian?"*

"Yep."

No recourse for that one. "Well, if she's only singing Christian backup, I'm sure she could use more money."

"Probably so. But trust me on this one, Camille, she's not going to sing with you. You burned a lot of bridges when you left the group, you know?"

"Fine. I'll just have to do it solo," Camille snapped.

"I'm not trying to be funny, but you should have marketed yourself as a solo artist in the first place," Alexis concurred. "That's what you really wanted to be anyway. And, for what it's worth, I think you could have been good."

"Thanks, Alexis. Hey"—Camille fumbled for the words—"do you think, maybe, we could keep in touch? I know this will sound crazy, but I don't really socialize with too many females, you know? Too many divas."

Alexis laughed. "You know you're the queen diva, right?"

Camille had to agree. "I'm just sayin', it's nice to talk to someone who's not into the jealousy thing."

"I don't think I follow you. I mean, what are they jealous of?"

Camille huffed. "Don't you watch those real house-wives shows?"

"Nuh-uh. I mean, every once in a while I might see an episode, but I have better things to do with my time than sit up and watch grown women argue," Alexis said. "Work, Momma, and Daddy keep me all tied up. But I've got your number now and you've got mine. No excuses."

"While you're recording information, write down today's date. It's my birthday," Camille sassed.

"Aaah! That's right! March twentieth!" Alexis added a quick rendition of the happy birthday song.

Camille listened in wonder of Alexis's low melody. Simply beautiful. What a shame they couldn't blend vocals again.

"Thanks, girl. I haven't had anyone sing that song to me in a while."

"Well, text me your address so I can send you a pre-sent."

"Awww, you don't have to do that," Camille purred.

"I know, but I'm thinking if you haven't had a birth-day song in a while, you sure haven't received a gift in a while, either."

She didn't know the half of it. After her mother's

death, Camille's family seemed to have disintegrated. Jerdine Robertson had been the Robertsons' glue. Without her, no one knew how to hold the family together. So when Camille hit it big with all that fame and money, things naturally got worse. Money only magnifies relationship problems.

"I gotta go, Camille. Text me your address. And call me when you get the package."

Strike two and three at the same time. If she couldn't talk Alexis, who was by far the most forgiving of the Sweet Treats, into rekindling the fire, she sure wasn't going to be able to get through to Tonya, even though she lived less than twenty miles away and was in the best position to meet.

Camille set her phone on the coffee table and focused on the nightly news. A reporter blared the misfortune of an old man who'd lost his lottery jackpot to a store clerk who stole and cashed his winning ticket. Camille had seen his story on television before, but now, after talking to Kyra, she could feel his pain. Her own future had been stolen by . . . well, according to Kyra and Alexis, by Camille herself.

In their version of the split, Camille was to blame. Could she help it if the fans wanted her upstage? And how could Darrion have been Tonya's man if he didn't agree?

"I'm not going out like that." Camille closed her eyes, leaned over, and laid her head on the couch's pleather armrest. She pulled her feet under her behind and grabbed the remote control. She flipped to her favorite cable channels, courtesy of someone in the building's box-rigging skills.

Where would she be without all the hookups available in the hood? Humph. Probably someplace better, in a position to afford the authentic versions of all the free, reduced, and slightly inferior products she haggled for just outside the iron-barred beauty-supply house.

Enough, enough, enough.

Camille jumped off the couch and fixed herself a bowl of cereal so she could think. Plan A, the reunion scheme, hadn't worked. She needed another idea. Well, actually, Alexis had already given it to her. A solo career. Yes, she was dirt old as far as the industry went, but every once in a while, a miracle happened for an older singer. It happened for that British woman, Susan Boyle.

Somebody had to break the age ceiling in American music. Might as well be Camille.

Cap'n Crunch hit the spot, and the recreation center's Wi-Fi would soon light the way toward an agent. Camille grabbed her no-questions-asked laptop she'd traded for three autographed CDs and a hundred dollars cash at the barber shop. The serial number had been completely scratched off, and she could sign on to her laptop only as a guest. Truth be told, she didn't tap into too many systems because she wondered if, someday, the computer might get traced through an Internet connection and she'd have to surrender it to authorities for prosecution purposes.

The Medgar Evers center, however, was probably a safe place for tapping in. Dallas police officers had far better things to do than chase down hot laptops. She hoped.

Camille claimed an empty table near an outlet and logged on. She googled B-list artists' names along with the word "agent." She guessed most industry professionals who were already working with famous clients didn't need her. They weren't desperate for real talent.

They'd already discovered their cash cows. The B-listers, however, were still hungry. They were wheelin' and deal-in', hustlin' to be noticed, bringing fresh artists to pro-ducers and label executives. These people were probably ripe for the picking.

Next, she googled the agents' names and started a list of phone numbers, e-mail addresses, and physical addresses for possible leads. She managed to collect fifteen names of potential agents before the most rude bunch of teenagers ever, two boys and two barely dressed girls, plopped themselves down at the next table and started rapping, complete with table drums and a low whine from one of the girls.

"I know you think you got swag, you think you got game, but I just rolled through your hood, nobody know your name. They said who that is? He live on our street? He must be a hermit 'cause he and I never meet."

Camille gave them a bit of leeway for at least know-ing the meaning of the term "hermit." But when the next boy spouted off his vulgar lyrics, Camille had to speak up. They owed her a little respect, seeing as she was thirty and all. "Excuse me, could you all hold it down just a little bit? I'm having a hard time concen-trating."

"Aw, miss," one of the girls pleaded, "they already made us move from over there by the computers. Seems like people don't want us anywhere. We just singing." Her innocent appeal was echoed by the group.

Camille smiled. "Sweetheart, what's your name?"

"Diamond."

"Diamond, I can assure you that what you all were singing was *not* music."

"Oh, snap," one of boys said while clapping his hands. "Old-school went off on you."

Before anyone could get seriously offended, Camille continued, "This stuff you call music today is nothing compared to what music used to be. I know. I used to sing with a group called Sweet Treats."

"Sweet Treats? What was that—a group of suckers?" the other girl asked. She was the smaller of the two but obviously had the bigger attitude and much bigger braids swooping across her forehead.

Undaunted, the diva raised an eyebrow. "Come here. I'll show you exactly what Sweet Treats was all about."

The teens gathered over Camille's shoulder as she googled images of her former fame. She clicked to maximize the picture of Sweet Treats sitting next to Destiny's Child at the American Music Awards. "See, right there. That's me."

"Ooh! You was sitting right next to Beyoncé!" Diamond yelled in utter amazement.

"Correction. Beyoncé was sitting right next to *me*," Camille bragged.

"Okay, sing something," a boy challenged.

Instantly, Camille sang her favorite line from the ballad Teddy Riley wrote specifically for their group. "If I leave tonight, you don't have to change the locks on the door. You won't see me anymore."

All doubts about Camille's authority as a singer disappeared as three out of four gave her props. "Dang! You can sang!"

"Can you do it again so I can put it on my cell phone?"

"I want to take a picture with you."

The last, of course, accosted Camille with another stinging question. "Okay, so if you was all sitting next to Destiny's Child and Mariah Carey, how come you ain't in Hollywood or somewhere right now with the rest of the rich people?"

Camille had to submit. "You know what? I've been asking myself that same question. That's why I'm here tonight. Tryin' to get back in the game."

"Well, you can sing," the girl finally admitted, "but don't be actin' like you better than everybody else. That's all I'm sayin'.

"Come on, y'all, let's go."

Diamond grabbed her purse. "Good luck, miss."

CHAPTER 4

Alexis dropped the phone into her backpack and breathed a heavy sigh. "Thank You, Lord." Hearing from Camille after all these years brought both relief and a burden. Not like she didn't have enough stones around her neck already, but—like her parents—Alexis bore them with thanks. This was her season's assignment, and she would gladly endure.

"Who were you singing to, baby?" Momma asked from the couch.

Daddy, who had reclined dangerously beyond the chair's intended range, answered for his daughter. "Ain't none of your business, now, Mattie. 'Lexis got a life of her own."

Momma piped up, "I can ask my daughter whatsoever question I want to ask her!"

"I was talking to Camille, from our old singing group," Alexis ended the argument.

"Oh, yeah," Daddy recalled, "Camille called here

earlier today looking for you. I gave her the number to your car phone."

"*Car* phone," Momma mumbled. "*Cell* phone is what they callin' it now. And mighty fine of you to tell her now. Maybe she didn't want Camille to have her number, you ever thought about that? Act like you the telephone operator or something."

Time for another intervention. "It's okay, Momma. I don't mind Camille having my number."

"See there?" from Daddy.

"What else can she say, Willie? Damage already done now."

Though Momma was never one to let anyone else get the last word in, she wasn't usually so vicious. Alexis hoped that her mother's doctor would soon be able to determine the optimal dosage of blood-pressure medicine, because if not, her parents would have to move to separate corners of the house.

"I never did like that Camille girl," Momma continued with her tirade. "She always tried to steal the show from the rest of the group."

This, of course, was the latest of Mattie's pharmaceutically induced confessions. Not that she was wrong, just that she usually had enough wisdom to keep her mouth shut and pray about such negative observations unless sharing them was absolutely necessary. Rather than listen to her mother rattle off everything she disliked about Camille and the next five people who might come to mind, Alexis stood from the kitchen stool and grabbed her keys from the counter. "I'm out. See you two tomorrow."

She crossed the living room threshold and kissed both parents on their cheeks. The house hadn't changed much in her lifetime except for this converted garage where her parents spent sixteen hours a day eating, watching television, and debating politics. Two lounge chairs, a forty-inch screen, a lamp for each one, and a nightstand between the recliners.

Dutifully, Alexis closed the blinds so that, once the sun sank, passersby wouldn't have a view into the house. She'd asked her older brother to buy solar screens for their parents, but he didn't have the money. Sometimes, Alexis had to remind herself that Thomas was fifty-one, statistically approaching the last quarter of his life with little in retirement, thanks to a failing economy and a son whose drug addiction ate up any and all liquid assets. If Thomas Junior (T. J.) wasn't robbing his parents, Thomas Senior and his wife were still spending funds on lawyers, rehabilitation clinics, T. J.'s restitution, and finally helping raise T. J.'s plenteous offspring.

Alexis had tried to tell Thomas to let T. J. go down his own road—wherever that might lead. But Thomas's heart was too big. She laid off, knowing that if it had been her own child, she probably wouldn't have done anything different. Though her parents fussed and fought more often than not, they were fiercely loyal to family and friends.

As she let herself out the front door, Alexis could hear her parents arguing about which one of them had driven her to leave. All she could do was shake her head. Momma and Daddy were made for each other, really.

Once in her car, Alexis waited for the Bluetooth signal to appear on her dashboard, then she commanded the system. "Call Tonya."

Three rings later, her best friend answered. "Hey."

"You'll never guess who I just talked to," Alexis gushed.

"No time for guessing, girl. Who?"

Alexis announced, "Camille Elizabeth Robertson," in graduation-commencement style.

"Serious?" Tonya quipped.

"Yep."

"What did she want?"

"Nothing, really. Well, she did want to get the group back together, but Kyra already put an end to that," Alexis said.

"Wow," Tonya remarked. "Did she say why?"

"No," Alexis confided, "but sounds like she might not be doing so well. No friends, a job she hates. And apparently she's broke. We need to pray for her."

"I'll add her to my prayer list," Tonya agreed. Then she asked, "Did you tell her?"

"No. I couldn't."

"Mmm," Tonya moaned with concern. "I've gotta go. I'll call you later."

"Okay. Bye."

CHAPTER 5

Sleep eluded Camille most of the night. The excitement of starting over, grabbing what should have been hers all along, pumped a steady stream of adrenaline through her system, causing her to toss and turn. Somewhere in the previous hours, her body had managed to snatch a few moments of peace. Her lively dreams, however, still poked at her ambitions.

In one scenario, she met and fell in love with Kanye West at a barbecue for New York City public schools. The next dream involved a concert with an artist she didn't recognize. She and the artist danced to the edge of the stage, and then, seemingly in slow motion, Camille fell off the edge into a sea of fans who all started kissing her. At first, it was an adorable scene. But then Camille began to feel afraid because some of the fans were groping her. The mob grew increasingly aggressive and, finally, someone in the crowd drew back a hand to slap her.

Camille's eyes popped open, bringing her back to

the real world just before impact. The dream was over, but an unrealistic fear lingered as she took deep breaths in an effort to calm herself. She swiped heavy beads of sweat off her nose. Not since her wild days with Sweet Treats had she experienced such a physical reaction to an imaginary circumstance.

Back then, she had at least been able to blame it on the pills Kyra snuck onto their bus. "Here, try this," Kyra had offered one evening after Camille complained of exhaustion.

"What is it?" Camille asked.

"That new boy who plays drums gave it to me. It gives you energy," she claimed.

"Did you ask Priscilla if it was okay to take them?"

Kyra snarled her nose. "Priscilla ain't my momma. Plus, even if she was, I'm nineteen years old. I do whatever I want, and the law can't stop me, either."

The way Kyra reasoned through things scared Camille enough to stay away from the pills for a while. Four concerts, two days, and seven hundred miles later, Camille changed her mind. "Let me try one."

Giddy, probably from an overload of uppers, Kyra had led Camille down the bus's aisle to her bunk, just beneath Alexis's empty spot. Kyra drew back the curtain and they both ducked to take a seat on the bed. Kyra pulled a black pouch from inside her pillowcase and poured a few of the pills into Camille's hand.

"Just drink it with water. Don't ever mix it with beer or alcohol," she warned.

"You know I don't drink," from Camille.

A smile slithered across Kyra's face. "Not yet."

Whatever mess was in those pills kept Camille on point during the next week's performances, but the side effects—crazy nightmares, sleeplessness, constant itching—convinced Camille to quit. Then, she slept for almost two days straight after the drug's effect wore off.

She was back in a similar position now (minus the itching) since she'd gotten herself high on life's possibilities. This was a good thing, of course. Problem was, there was no way she could make it through the workday without conking out on her desk. Furthermore, she had more important things to do today than set up meetings between sales guys and office managers. She needed to get a few meetings of her *own* arranged.

Camille grabbed a towel, practiced her cough a few times, and called her boss. "Sheryl, I'm not coming in today." *Cough, cough.* "I think I've got some kind of bug. Hopefully, it's just a twenty-four-hour thing." Of course Camille already knew the fake bug virus would only last twenty-four hours because the next day was payday. Even if she *were* sick on a payday, she'd never miss.

"We really need you to come in today. Your team's quota is down this month. They need your numbers," Sheryl admonished.

The whole team concept had never really caught on at Aquapoint Systems, least of all with Camille. The prize for winning the thirty-day challenge was always something silly anyway, like a free lunch coupon or a movie ticket. Nothing anyone would actually work hard to earn.

Cough, cough. She cleared her throat. "I'm sorry. I just can't make it in today."

Sheryl suggested, "You think maybe you could come in early tomorrow? I could set your terminal to East Coast mode and let you work that territory."

Camille coughed again, this time for real. *Is she*

crazy? "I . . . I don't think so. I have to take my . . . cat to . . . my cousin's house so she can take him to . . . dialysis three mornings a week." She had to give it to herself—she could make up a good lie at the drop of a hat.

"Oh, no," Sheryl gasped. "Is she going to make it through?"

"Prognosis is pretty good." *What about my prognosis?*

"Whew! I got goose bumps when you said that! What's your cat's name?"

"Her name is . . . Fluffy."

"Awww," Sheryl sang, "what kind of cat?"

Cats have kinds? "Huh?"

"Is she pedigree or just domestic?"

"She's . . . it's a mutt," Camille said.

Sheryl laughed heartily. "You crack me up. Well, I certainly understand your situation with Fluffy. My little Yorkie, Valectra, had to do chemotherapy for a while, but it didn't do the trick. We had to put him down last summer."

The word "chemotherapy" stabbed Camille's heart. "I'm sorry to hear that."

"He's in a better place now," Sheryl conjectured. "You know what they say—all dogs go to heaven."

A weak laugh escaped Camille.

Sheryl continued, "Why didn't you tell me your morning schedule was so busy?"

"I guess I didn't want anyone to feel sorry for me," Camille said.

"Well, I've walked in your shoes. If you need to come in late and make up for it at lunch, that's fine with me. We have to do what we have to do in order to care for our helpless friends. I'm willing to work with you," Sheryl empathized.

"Thank you."

"Take care. Hope to see you tomorrow."

For the record, she did feel a little guilty about lying. Sheryl's heartfelt offer to be flexible with scheduling, however, opened up yet another door for the lifestyle Camille wanted. Freedom, freedom, freedom. Who knew this sick-cat invention could buy a piece of the pie?

I'm a genius.

After dozing off once more, Camille got to the business at hand. She originally thought cold calling music agents would be a piece of cake compared to pestering people who were more interested in making a little profit from a Coke machine than the water-purification systems her employer tried to sell.

Time to make her own cold calls. She had her elevator speech ready to rip: *Hi, my name is Camille Robertson. I sang with the R&B group Sweet Treats and I'm looking for an agent who can take my solo career to the top.*

The first two agents' secretaries did nothing more than take her name and number and say the agent would get back with her if he was interested. *Yeah, right.*

One assistant advised Camille to send in a demo. "Once you make the investment in presenting yourself well, we're ready to make an investment in you."

Almost sounded like a reprimand. Camille double crossed them off the list.

She refined her approach. "Hi, this is Camille. I just missed Stanley's call. Could you put me through?" The old he-called-me-first trick, a staple in her current profession.

At least she'd gotten past the screen for the next agency and actually spoken to a real live artist representative. But when Stanley figured out that he didn't actually know Camille, he transferred her back to the secretary, who again took her contact information and put her name in file thirteen with the rest of the losers trying to get a break.

Three hours later, she was still at square one. No leads. Nothing. Worse, there was only one agent left to call. Why weren't people listening to her? She had experience. She was still sexy enough to sell at least twenty thousand CDs with just her face alone. And once people heard her voice, the rest would be history.

That's it! This agent needed to sample her singing.

After squeaking past the administrative assistant with another lie, Camille found herself on hold for an agent named John David McKinney. His biggest client to date had been featured in *USA Today* and appeared on one cable television show to speak of. He obviously had some connections but not enough to put him in the top tier. If he had any sense, he would realize that he needed Camille as much as she needed him.

Her stomach twisted with anticipation. What should she sing? What if he hung up on her? What if he had some kind of hearing problem and she messed up his hearing aid?

"John David here."

Camille took a deep breath, closed her eyes, and belted out the same chorus she'd sung to the kids at the recreation center. She added a twist at the end—one of those Mariah Carey high notes, straight from her gut.

Then she waited. Three seconds had never been stretched so wide.

"Quite a range you've got there," John David remarked.

"Thank you." Camille could feel the blood rush to her face. "I need an agent to help me share my voice with the world."

"You got a demo?"

"No."

She heard a sigh on his end and figured she had better say something before she lost this live one. "But I can get one."

"Have you worked in this industry at all? Seriously, a demo is your calling card."

Camille explained her background, exaggerating the group's fifteen minutes of fame into a half hour. She fabricated the CD sales figure, and ended with, "We parted due to artistic differences." She'd read that somewhere online.

"So, basically, you had one hit song, some residual success on a second CD, and then the group split up because its members couldn't get along," John David surmised.

No sense in playing around with this man. "Right."

"Then just say so. I'm a busy man, I don't have time for games, but I do appreciate your boldness and I can't deny your talent. Can you meet tomorrow? One o'clock?"

She smothered a squeal. "Yes."

"Bring some headshots and a copy of your previous CD."

"Okay."

"And another thing," John David added, "don't ever lie to me or anyone on my team again."

"Gotcha."

Camille jumped on her bed like her momma hadn't taught her any better. "Yes! Yes! Yes!" she screamed.

Then, just like in her dream, she slipped off the corner. She landed straight on her butt and yowled in laughter. That hurt. In a good, funny way. Camille cracked up even more now as she rubbed her backside. "Shoot!"

Bang, bang, bang. Her downstairs neighbor communicated his dismay. Camille knocked on the floor and yelled, "Sorry."

She couldn't wait to move out of this apartment complex someday. Someday soon.

CHAPTER 6

No makeup. No brush. No jewelry. Camille's crusty lips threatened to pass along whatever "virus" she'd contracted. When she got to work, her first objective was to saunter by Sheryl's door with a blanket wrapped around her shoulders, Kleenex in hand.

"Hey, Sheryl," she eeked.

"Oh my goodness, you look awful," Sheryl cried. "I mean, in a sick person kind of way."

"I know, I know." Camille sniffed, careful to guard her expression after the near insult. "I just didn't want to let the team down."

Sheryl shook her head. "No. If the office catches what you've got, we'll *all* be down. Take a vacation day. Go home."

The Academy Award nominee put a hand on her forehead. "Are you sure?"

"One hundred percent."

"Okay. If you insist."

Slowly, Camille shuffled down the hallway a few steps. Then she stopped, just like she'd planned, and made a U-turn back to Sheryl's office. "Sheryl, I almost forgot. Can I get my check?"

"Well, you know we're not supposed to give them out before eleven. But in this case, I'll make an exception." Sheryl turned the tiny key and opened the door to the upper-right drawer containing the precious paychecks. "Here you go."

Almost too quickly, Camille grabbed the check. She reduced her speed by a notch as she placed the envelope in her purse.

"How's Fluffy?"

Fluffy? "Who?"

"Your cat."

My cat? My cat! "Oh, she's fine. Dialysis makes her weak, you know."

"How long have you had her?"

Camille shook her head. "Not long. Not long at all."

"Let me know if you need any help with her," Sheryl volunteered. "I'll be glad to cat-sit if you need to get out over the weekend."

Sheryl was taking this too far. "We'll be fine, thank you."

First, she stopped at the check-cashing venue nearest her job. A seedy operation at best. If she ever paid back the money she owed JPMorgan Chase for insufficient fund fees, she wouldn't have to fork over seven dollars every time she got paid. Money orders took up another four bucks. That extra thirty-something dollars a month could have paid for her cell phone. Ridiculous how much she had to pay to participate in the good ole American way. Not to mention the fact that her credit was shot after a defaulted student loan a few years earlier.

Maybe if she'd been a car manufacturer, someone might bail her out?

"One, two, three hundred. Twelve, and seventy-five," the cashier counted the money behind reinforced glass.

Camille scooped the cash from the silver dish between them. "I need three money orders." She'd already figured out whose turn it was to get paid this month. Electricity and cell phone. The others would have to wait until their envelopes turned pink.

Sporting a stone-cold face, Camille finished her business at the window while the line behind her grew. She kept every patron in her peripheral vision. Though Camille had spent several years riding high, she had come of age in the Singing Oaks community of Dallas. Not the roughest neighborhood in the city, but by the same token, not the kind of area to leave your car door unlocked. She knew better than to give the impression she was preoccupied, creating the perfect opportunity for someone to catch her slipping.

The cashier placed the notes in the tray. "Anything else?"

"No, thank you."

The woman looked past Camille. "Next in line, please."

Money orders printed, Camille stuffed everything

deep inside her purse, pulled her strap onto her shoulder, and clamped her arm down on the bag. She marched back to her car and sped out of the parking lot, wise enough to realize it's not a good idea to hang around strangers when they know you've got hundreds of dollars in cash on you—poor neighborhood or not.

Next stop, the post office. Camille mailed her payments to respective creditors. Not exactly on time, but well within the thirty-day window before being reported to credit bureaus.

Final stop, the beauty-supply house for a front lace wig that screamed superstar. She bought her stocking cap and, with an assistant's help, selected an eighteen-inch bone-straight honey blond style that took at least five years off her face.

"Very pretty. I like long for you," the woman, whose own black hair touched her behind, remarked.

"I'll take this one."

Camille returned to her apartment to engage in the most important makeover of her life. Starting with her hair, ending at her feet, she curled and painted, filed and blended until the woman standing in front of the full-length mirror looked almost as good as the girl sitting next to Beyoncé online. Except Camille weighed more. And she was older; one could always tell by the eyes. Still, she looked way better than that Susan lady. Sounded better, too. She *had* this.

John David's office boasted more credits than Camille had been able to dig up on the Web. Replicas of gold albums lined the walls, and pictures of John David with some of top leaders in music gave him credibility that might have excluded him from her list if she'd known better. He was more like an A-minus agent. Sitting in the waiting area, Camille suddenly felt lucky to have landed an appointment with him.

"Miss Robertson, John David will see you now," his assistant, a Hollywood-thin woman with long, old-Cher-like hair, rose to escort Camille through the uptown suite. Even more accolades covered the corridor leading to John David's office.

The secretary rapped on the door, opening the way for Camille to lay her eyes on the man who could change her life forever. He leaned back in his chair and crossed his arms, surveying Camille's overall appearance.

She did the same, taking note of the cowlicks and a long, sloping nose that hinted at Jewish heritage. Slick brown hair and an ample midsection gave him that used-car-salesman feel. Under any other circumstances, Camille might have steered clear of his type, but he was exactly what she needed now because, as far as the music world went, she *was* a used car.

"Timber, this is Camille. She's the one who lied to you."

Camille's mouth dropped.

Timber tilted her head to one side, her eyes scraping up and down Camille. "Humph. Nice move."

"Sorry about that," was all Camille could say.

Timber left without accepting the apology.

Camille returned her attention to John David, wondering why he'd ratted her out like that.

As if he'd read her mind, he said, "Wanted to clear the air. Timber doesn't like being lied to."

Timber better get over it. "I understand."

John David motioned, and Camille sat in the guest's chair. "Oh, here's the material you asked for." She gave him the CD and an envelope containing one of the photos she'd taken five years earlier when Bobby Junior said he could get her booked at a few nightclubs.

Sunlight poured in through opened blinds, which also afforded an enviable view of the city. To her left, a bookcase filled with white binders and books so thick they had to be stuffed with legalese and other reference guides. This all made sense, of course, because online research showed John David had once been an entertainment attorney.

To her right, shelves containing more photographs. Most interestingly, John David was married with a daughter.

John David's desk itself was a work of art. Heavily lacquered wood, gold accents, the stuff old lawyers' offices are made of.

Before Camille could properly savor the moment, John David started. "Let's cut to the chase. I found some of your old videos on YouTube. Was your voice digitally enhanced?"

"No."

"Great. You've got a strong, pure sound, and your face is attractive. You might want to do a little nipping and tucking, file down some rough edges. But overall, your look is hot."

Alrighty, then.

John David detoured to his Apple laptop screen. His fingers danced across the keyboard, then he waited, presumably for a Web page to upload. "So, yesterday, after we talked, I started thinking. Brainstorming."

"Yes?"

"I've got a plan."

Camille sat on the edge of her seat.

"You ever sung gospel?"

"Um, yeah, back when I was little. My mom was the church musician. I didn't have a choice."

"Perfect. That's what we'll do," he stated.

"*What's* what we'll do?"

"Make you a contemporary gospel singer."

Camille stuttered, "But . . . I mean, I *can* . . . it's just not, you know, what I had in mind."

He sat back again, put his hands on top of his head. "You heard of Heather Headley?"

"Of course," she replied.

"Oleta Adams?"

"Yes. She's awesome."

"They were semihot names in R and B, but now they're even bigger in gospel. They've managed to keep a career going by gaining a new audience. Trust me, if you don't hit it big in music by twenty-five, you either give up on being a superstar or go back to the drawing board. Those are your only two choices."

He had a point. Both of them were excellent, unique mainstream singers who had crossed over into Christian music. Still, *gospel*?

"Is there any way I can, you know, do some other type of music. Like light pop, or whatever Bonnie Raitt sings?"

"Camille, you're no spring chicken. The only sector forgiving enough to take you back at this point is Christians. They'll accept anybody at any age and any size, which, by the way, would pose a serious problem for you in the mainstream."

"I can lose weight," she stammered.

"I strongly suggest it, gospel or not," he said matter-of-factly. He laid his eyes on Camille's. "If you're serious about getting back into this business, you're going to have to do what you've gotta do. If you were a man, this would be a totally different conversation."

Camille squinted. "So, men can do whatever they want at whatever age, huh?"

"Pretty much," John David concurred. "Take Jonathan Butler. He does gospel and jazz. Kirk Franklin does gospel, but he's very welcome in the secular crowd. Some might even say he's better received there than in Christian music, just by looking at the charts."

"This is so unfair." Camille crossed her arms. "The arts are supposed to be universal. Transcend race, class, and gender."

"This isn't art, Camille, it's business. It's the way of the world. I didn't make the rules, but I do understand them and I don't break them unless I have to," John David said. "In your case, we need to follow them to get your foot back in the door.

"Trust me, your best bet is gospel. It's good music. Some even say it helps people. Maybe you can do R and B again later, I don't know. But if you're not willing to reinvent yourself as a gospel singer, I suggest you find yourself another agent."

His words bore no hint of compromise. Camille squirmed in her chair. "I wouldn't even know where to start. I haven't been inside a church in, like, three years."

"Then there's your starting point. I suggest you join a church. A *big* one, and we've got plenty of 'em right here in Dallas. Become a member. Get yourself connected with the musicians. Get a demo with a choir or something behind you."

John David handed Camille one of his business cards. "Come back when you've got all that in place, and I'll get busy working on my end."

Camille ran her thumb across the lettering on the card. She felt like her life was slipping away. This one last line had all but shriveled up and left her without a way back to her destiny.

"Have a good day," John David shooed her out.

Camille blinked back tears as she let herself out of John David's office. She breezed past Timber without a word. It probably would have been best to apologize again, but her pride couldn't let the woman get a glimpse of the disappointment brewing in Camille's chest.

The elevator ride down provided a chance to compose herself long enough to make it to the car, where Camille promptly burst into tears. This meeting had not gone the way she'd planned. John David was supposed to ask her to sing again, be blown away by her in-person sound, then whisk her over to someone's studio to record a killer song that he would distribute to a major producer. That major producer would, in turn, sign her, next week, with a huge bonus that would allow her to kiss Aquapoint Systems and the entire Fossil Terrace apartment complex good-bye forever.

But no, no, no. John David would agree to represent her only as a stupid gospel singer, of all things. Not only did he want to make her a gospel singer, he wanted her to *become* a gospel singer before he'd actually do anything to promote her!

And the gospel game was certainly different than R&B. Half the attraction with a worldwide audience

was sex appeal. Booty-shaking, hip-thrusting, cleav-
age-flashing dances sold just as many records and concert tickets as great vocals in her old world. Why
couldn't she just capitalize on her body—after she got it
back in shape, of course?

There was also a teeny tiny part of her that didn't
like the idea of singing gospel just so that she could become a star again. This part, Camille knew, came from
her mother's influence (Bobby Junior would have told
her to jump on the chance). But Jerdine Robertson
would have told Camille point-blank not to play in the
Lord's house.

With a heavy foot on the pedal, Camille screeched
out of the parking lot. She soon discovered that a bad
attitude could be just as distracting as text messaging
on the road. A fellow motorist honked at her when she
stomped on her brake and made a quick right turn without signaling. She honked back. Yes, she was wrong, but
she was not in the mood to be chastised by some guy
driving a wood-paneled station wagon. He was wrong
just for owning that thing.

Just so happened, a police officer witnessed Camille's
rash antics. His siren startled Camille initially. *What did I
do?* All her tags were current. Insurance active. She
slowed to a stop in a restaurant parking lot and waited
for the officer to inform her of why he was stopping
her, adding insult to injury on one of the worst days of
her life.

She leaned forward for a wider angle in her side-
view mirror and soon got an eyeful of tall, dark, chocolate in sunglasses and a uniform. Unfortunately, he was
also sporting a metallic clipboard with a pen. And a
wedding band.

Her driver's window squeaked to the halfway point. "Hello, Officer. Is there something wrong?"

"You," he barked, removing his shades. A dark brother with white teeth was a winning combination in Camille's book. "You were weaving down Commerce, and you cut off another driver at the light. You could have caused an accident. Have you been drinking?"

Such ugly words from such a beautiful man. "No, Officer. I don't drink."

"Could you step out of the vehicle, please?"

She obeyed, taking this moment to offer a reasonable explanation. "Officer, I just got some bad news and lost track of where I was going for a second. I'm not under the influence of any illegal substance."

Despite her justification, she was still subjected to a field sobriety test. She passed, of course, but the policeman still gave her a ticket for failure to maintain a lane of traffic. *What kind of violation is this?*

"Be more careful," he scolded. "Cars are dangerous weapons, Miss Robertson. Don't get behind the wheel if you're psychologically impaired."

Camille accepted the ticket. "I understand."

Upon entering her apartment, Camille dropped her bag and flipped off her shoes. Life was just plain ridiculous. You think you're advancing one square forward when, actually, you've been pushed all the way back to "go."

She plunked onto her couch and fished the ticket from her bag. The back side of the document gave a range for the ticket fine. Two hundred to two hundred twenty-five dollars. She'd have to go to the station to determine the exact amount.

Already, her mind buzzed with thoughts about

what she would have to give up or pull off in order to pay the associated fines without skipping a beat on her bills. Twenty extra leads would cover it. *Dang!* That wouldn't work. Camille had thoroughly convinced Sheryl that her phantom cat needed extra TLC. Trying to come in early or stay later now would bust the tall tale.

Selling twenty CDs in front of the beauty supply might work, if the bootleg DVD man didn't chase her off his turf. Or maybe she could work a week at a retail store. If she hadn't burned her relationship with her Mary Kay director, she might be able to host a few shows.

Ugh! Why don't police officers think about how they're messing with people's lives when they write these tickets?

No matter what, she'd have to add to her forty-hour work week for a while to keep this thing from escalating to a warrant. Yet, even with a payment plan, there was nothing to spare in her budget.

Maybe she should just get pregnant and have a baby so she could get free food, reduced rent, and a small fortune every tax season. She'd always wanted a daughter. A little diva named Madison. Camille snuggled back into her couch at the thought of her mini-me. Would she be a prissy mama or one of those tree-climbing, frog-catching tomboys? Would she inherit her mother's voice and her grandmother's instrumental talent?

Then there was always the possibility little Madison would be a complete horror. Drawing on walls, fighting at school so Camille would have to come off her job to attend parent conferences. And what if Madison grew up to be a serial killer? The world would have one more lunatic on the streets all because Camille Robertson couldn't get one big break. They'd blame Camille, and she'd blame John David.

Snap out of it!

Camille placed a hand on her forehead. The whole kid scheme was crazy, but she had to do something. She couldn't live the rest of her life in a state where two hundred dollars threw her into panic mode. No matter what, she had to work her way out of this. There was no easy path.

And then it hit her. If she was going to put herself to work doing something she didn't really want to do—like give birth—she might as well work for something she *did* want. Seriously, if she was willing to raise a child, she should at least be willing to join a choir and lead a few songs.

John David had said that if she did her part, he'd do his. That probably wouldn't help her in the short term with this ticket, but *something* had to give.

The counsel Jerdine gave her daughter about her first job working at McDonald's came to mind. Camille had been complaining about having to clean the men's restroom. "It's so nasty!"

"Well"—her mother had laughed—"they kick the men out before you go in, right?"

"Yes," Camille conceded while buckling her seat belt.

Jerdine was always on time to pick up her daughter. She never wanted any of Camille's male coworkers offering her shapely daughter a ride home.

"Baby, sometimes you have to do what you have to do first in order to do what you want to do later," Jerdine comforted her only daughter.

Camille sat straight up on her couch now. She

closed her eyes and spoke into the air. "Okay, Momma. I know you didn't mean for me to use your advice in a bad way, but you also said that God lets everything happen for a reason.

"I don't know all the reasons, but I've got to go for it. Singing won't go away, Momma. I have to do this."

CHAPTER 7

Hours at the Medgar Evers center yielded a list of the top-ten churches in the Dallas area, by enrollment. The King's Table, pastored by a man who was probably a household name at that point, ranked number one, with a combined total of twenty-four thousand in attendance at its two Sunday services. Camille scoffed at the idea of attending church twice on a Sunday. If memory served her well, she could barely keep her eyelids apart during the main message every week. And Wednesday night services were even worse with Mother Jackson beating that tambourine all off beat.

Second on her list was Northeast Christian Church. Nineteen thousand. One service. But from what Camille gathered on the Web site, the congregation was mostly Caucasian. She'd send John David a text: **Does the church have to be black?**

His reply: **Yes**

Camille: **Think Kirk Franklin. He crosses over races.**

John David: **HE'S A MAN**

Okay, you don't have to holler. Camille X-ed Northeast off the list.

Next up, Grace Chapel Community Church. They had only fifteen thousand people coming every week. Camille did the math. If fifteen thousand people bought one of her CDs at thirteen ninety-nine each, she'd make only about seventeen thousand dollars after John David took his cut. Barely above full-time minimum wage, annually. Surely, she'd have more than fifteen thousand people buying her music, but the home base needed to be at least twenty thousand to move her into a new tax bracket.

With The King's Table, she could at least hope to bring home close to thirty thousand dollars with each release.

After having performed her calculations, there was no way on earth she could join a church with less than twenty thousand members who actually came to church.

The King's Table it is.

Sunday morning, Camille flicked through the clothes in her closet, looking for something eye-catching to commemorate her walk down the main aisle when she joined the church. No time like the present to start making an impression on the congregation. She selected a black shirt dress with four-inch open-toed, shiny black pumps. Cleaver-ish, yet stylish enough to cause some degree of speculation about her income bracket. The front lace wig would have been over the top, so she decided to sport a sophisticated, black ponytail that bobbed just a little with every step.

Those pumps, however, proved to be a total nightmare. Camille had underestimated how far she'd have to walk from her parking space to a trolley pick-up stop. Even after the driver cleared the vehicle at the front entrance, she still had to walk up another flight of stairs in a swarm of people who obviously had no respect for corns.

Once she passed through the arenalike doors into one of the main seating areas, Camille gasped at the sheer magnitude of the sanctuary. The Web site photographs didn't do this church justice. *Oh my God! This place is crazy!* It might as well have been a rock concert, except rock fans wouldn't assemble themselves at eight o'clock in the morning no matter how famous the singer. *Shoot, I don't even get to work this early!*

Rows and rows, columns and columns of people with Bibles, hats, and notepads found their seats next to fellow members and, presumably, a number of visitors. Though the cushioned seats were covered with bright red cloth, few of them remained visible. The church was nearly packed except for the nosebleed seats, and service hadn't even begun.

An usher escorted Camille's bunch of church-goers to one of the last empty sections in the building. She sat next to a woman who'd been smart enough to bring a jacket. And a Bible, which Camille didn't own, but she'd put that on her list of things to get. She'd have to ask John David if she could write it off as a business expense.

Camille's feet had barely recovered when some old man dressed in African attire approached center stage with a huge horn-looking device the size of a five-year-old child. He raised the instrument to his lips and blew. The all-encompassing sound was followed by a rousing, almost deafening praise from the congregation. These people obviously had supernatural lung capacity.

He blew again, and another round of praise circled through the building. By this time, everyone was standing. Camille refused to stuff her feet into those shoes again. The people sitting on either side of her probably didn't matter one way or another as far as her music was concerned. No worries. She'd let those heels rest until her debut church-joining waltz toward the main platform.

After the call to worship, five people walked out with microphones in hand, and lights hit the band as well as the robed choir behind them. The audience applauded as a man Camille guessed was the worship leader, a heavy, bald-headed guy dressed in a traditional Sunday suit, asked the question, "Are you all ready to go higher in the Lord this morning?"

"Yes!" the crowd roared.

"Are you ready to give the Lord some praise?"

"Yes!"

"Has He been good to you?"

"Yes!"

"I mean real, real good to you?"

Louder, "Yes!"

This was great. Obviously, not much had changed since the days her mother led congregational hymns at their old church. Camille knew all this church jargon like the back of her hand. Leading worship would be a piece of cake.

"Come on, praise team, one, two, three, four!" Pillsbury dough man cued up the band.

Camille took note of this designation. *Praise team.* She listened for the harmony. One soprano, two altos, two tenors. These people must be better singers than the average choir member. This brought things to a whole new level. Being in the choir wasn't good enough. She needed to get on the praise team. They had their own microphones. More camera time, too, evidenced by the five giant monitors strategically placed throughout the edifice. The media team alternated between faces and words, guiding the audience through songs.

The only problem so far was the women wearing dresses. Was it a coincidence or would she have to wear a dress, too?

Two songs later, the male alto took his turn at the center. "Saints of the most high God, take one minute to just glorify Him!"

A whole minute! Camille waited impatiently while the mass of people worked themselves into an emotional frenzy. Again, familiar territory. She had seen people shout, cry, fall out. None of that fazed her. The same people did the same things at the clubs she used to frequent shortly after Sweet Treats's downfall.

Church folk were probably the same everywhere, in her opinion. The only real Christian she'd ever seen was her mother. But she was dead. After all the times Camille had walked into her mother's room to find Jerdine bent over the foot of the bed in prayer, all the gallons of blessed oil Jerdine had slathered on her family's foreheads, and all the forgiveness Jerdine had given Bobby Junior, she'd still died a laborious death at age thirty-nine.

God's motive for taking Jerdine so early hadn't made sense when Camille was a junior in high school, and it didn't make any sense now. So while all this whooping and hollering taking place around her might make people ecstatic, Camille had her own truth. God might be powerful and He might have His mysterious reasons for doing things, but He sure wasn't in the business of making people happy.

The minute passed, and a man erupted in a sweet, soft ballad about God's love. Camille tried to concentrate on his voice, but the words of the song, "More precious than a mother's love," poked at her heart.

She focused, instead, on counting the number of rows in each section and multiplying by the number of seats in each row. It helped that there were a number of peculiar hats to observe as well. Next, she tried spotting white or Hispanic people. There was maybe one per hundred people present who appeared to be of another race. Despite John David's insistence that she join an African American church, he would probably be pleased that there was some representation of other ethnic groups here. The more exposure the better.

The female alto boosted the tempo with an old-time call-and-response song. Camille was glad for the change of pace, but when that woman bleated out a long "Wee-eee-eee-lll, I turned it over to Jesus," Camille had to stop herself from gagging. She sounded like an old billy goat caught in a barbwire fence!

Yet, the people clapped and cheered her on. *Are they not hearing what I'm hearing?* It reminded Camille of those early Mary J. Blige songs, back when her untrained voice was equivalent to the scratchy whine of someone whose half-deaf aunt told them they could really sing. Like Mary, this alto on stage had exceptional music and soulful lyrics to smooth things out. Maybe, with some help, she could get better. Camille would have to pull her aside, give her some tips.

After Goat Woman's song, the praise team shouted and danced for a while. The band was clearly having a good time. Their heads nodded and their bodies swayed awkwardly—a sure sign they'd gotten lost in the music and no longer cared how they appeared to the audience. Camille appreciated seeing a band in "the zone" again. She loved tapping into the musicians' groove, following the song wherever it led.

Finally, the lone soprano gave a breathy speech, as though she'd just finished running a marathon. If Camille was going to keep up with this praise team, she'd need to build up some stamina.

"He is worthy!"

The crowd echoed.

"I said, He is worthy!"

They heard you the first time.

"Our God is an awesome God! He reigns . . ." she sang.

Camille's chest sank. This girl could blow. She'd give any major female artist a run for her money, including the former leader of the Sweet Treats herself.

Supersoprano Girl performed a medley of tunes, showcasing her ability across tempos and ranges. This was *not* good. Camille would either have to convince the man in the black suit that the praise team needed two sopranos or find some kind of way to push this girl back into a choir robe.

Wait! Camille waited for a camera to display a full-body profile of the soprano on the nearest screen. She scrutinized the woman's side view. *Yes!* She was pregnant. Very pregnant, actually. Once this girl had the baby, she'd be holed up for at least six weeks, and that was all the time Camille needed to work her way onto this elite praise team and into the spotlight.

With a plan in place, the rest of the service was insignificant. The pastor's words of encouragement were nice, but the call to fellowship was all Camille cared to hear. When the invitation to accept Christ was given, she pressed her feet back into her shoes. Any minute now, they had to ask for people who wanted to be members to come forward. Camille decided she might as well get up now to start the trek.

"And if anyone would like to join our church," the preacher announced, "meet us in the Mockingbird room, which is directly across from the bookstore, after church."

Camille stopped in her tracks. *Mockingbird room?* What kind of church doesn't give new members the chance to parade before the congregation?

She huffed in disgust and made an about-face and headed toward the exit doors. *Mockingbird room.* Nobody gets the right hand of fellowship in a Mockingbird room.

She found the meeting place and joined about fifty other people waiting for this obscure enrollment to begin. Camille parked herself on the first row and sat to rest her feet again. Some women dressed in white distributed cookies, juice, and warm smiles. "Thanks for being here."

"You're welcome."

Almost immediately following the benediction, which they could all hear through the room's speaker system, several men wearing "Ambassador" badges entered the room and stood behind the front table. The cookie women passed out folders now, and before any ambassador could explain the documents therein, Camille had already flipped to the first page and read something that turned her off right away: *The membership process takes six weeks to complete. Upon completion, you may participate in the ministry God places on your heart.*

Six weeks! She didn't have six weeks! John David was ripe now! Her future was now! And besides all that, pregnant Soprano Girl would be back in action by then!

Camille raised her hand before they even started. "Um, is there any way to expedite the membership process?"

The oldest ambassador, too old to be wearing cornrows, answered, "We'll talk about the requirement in a second. But to answer your question, no."

Requirements? Since when does joining church have requirements? This wasn't a job or the Department of Motor Vehicles. It was *church,* for goodness sake, and she needed to be *in, in, in*!

She swung her foot in little circles throughout the presentation. The month-and-a-half-long process seemed more like a college course. Six classes, ninety minutes each, on Christian living, how to study the Bible, how to honor God with talents, gifts, and treasure. Someone would also come to visit her home and conduct a one-on-one "guidance session," which would give her an opportunity to ask questions about her personal salvation, the church, or any other concerns she might not want to address in front of her group. Then and only then could she join the church on the first Sunday of the month *after* successful completion.

This is for the birds.

Camille shuffled all her papers back into the folder and stomped out of the meeting as soon as the ambassadors dismissed the group. She threw the folder in the trash on her way out the church's main doors and caught the first trolley back to parking lot D, row fifteen.

Who knew joining a mega church would be so complicated?

CHAPTER 8

Medgar Evers to the rescue again. Camille spent Monday afternoon researching churches' membership processes. While none of the churches listed their procedures online, she found plenty of people voicing the good, bad, and ugly about joining area churches in online forums and discussion boards.

Unfortunately, her findings pointed toward Grace Chapel. One could pledge membership immediately there and begin serving in a ministry right away, but they were "encouraged" to attend "Christian Growth" classes. That was the good news.

The bad news, aside from the whole minimum-wage thing, was the church store, which appeared to stock almost exclusively the pastor's books and tapes. Something would have to be done about this nepotism, perhaps by way of response to the church's annual survey, which, according to the head deacon's Web page, weighed heavily in how this "community" church operated. She had already missed her chance for input this year, but it wouldn't happen again.

Ten o'clock service was more Camille's speed. She put on the same dress she'd worn to The King's Table. This time she was smarter about her choice in footwear, however. A wedge sandal did the trick. She arrived in the sanctuary in one comfortable piece, sporting a brand-spankin'-new Bible and a gray knit sweater to take an edge off the cooler temperature inside. She could get the hang of the big-church club.

Grace Chapel had a praise team, too, which opened the morning affair. Seven members. Two sopranos. Just like The King's Table, each one managed a song with the congregation while the words flashed on screens. Both sopranos were, in Camille's estimation, a'ight. They could probably go beast on a song written specifically for them, but they didn't have voices or styles that could adapt to anything set before them. The poor worship team leader probably had to sing their parts for them a few times before they caught on.

And, speaking of the worship leader, he was well within a few years of Camille's age and actually had a cute thing going on. Even from hundreds of feet away, his coffee skin, strong jaw line, and broad shoulders tapering down to a slim waist put him around a five plus on a scale of one to ten. The camera close-up gave him another two points for a full hairline, white teeth, and an ensemble of favorable features. The absence of a wedding band brought him all the way up to an eight. Not to mention his vocals, which bolstered him over the top.

Camille could definitely work with this man, assuming he was straight. Well, even if he wasn't, she could work with him, but it wouldn't be as much flirty fun.

After church, Camille finally got her chance to approach the wide-open platform along with twenty others who wanted to join the church, just like she'd imagined. Pastor Collins led them in the prayer of faith, something Camille had done at least a dozen times while growing up, mostly at her mother's direction.

The congregation clapped for the new additions to the flock. One of the ushers handed Camille a folder. Following the benediction, the elders lined up, walked down the aisle of fresh congregants, and shook their hands. Then, hundreds of Grace Chapel members took the time to greet Camille, and the rest of the audience dissipated.

Pastor Collins and his wife made up the last of the official welcoming committee. Camille took note of the sincerity in his eyes when he articulated, "We're so glad to have you. Is there anything I can pray with you about?"

"Oh, no, thank you . . . Pastor. I'm just glad to be here." She didn't want to get on their radar as one of those needy people who had come to the church only looking for a father figure. She was there to roll up her sleeves and help herself. And maybe help them, if they wanted a rockin' praise team.

With Pastor Collins out of view, Camille and the others stepped out of the greeting line. She glanced back at the band pit and gave an innocent smile to the drummer, who happened to be looking her way. Sooner than later, he'd know her name.

"That's it! I'm in!" Camille screamed after locking her car doors. She'd taken the first step to reclaiming her life, her entire reason for being born: to sing.

*   *   *

First thing Monday morning, Camille hopped out of bed humming an old Faith Evans song. Hearing her own voice scroll up and down the notes precisely warmed her like a cup of hot cocoa in December. This was her element. She needed her voice, needed to know she could do something better than anyone else.

Some kids kept their noses in books growing up. Camille had been tethered to a headset, listening and singing along to whatever blared through the earpieces. Ballads, solos, jazz, pop, neo soul. Across genres, she imitated her favorite artists, rewinding and replaying the toughest notes until she could hit them exactly the way Celine Dion, Whitney Houston, or even Dolly Parton did. She ran through player batteries like water, costing Bobby Junior a small fortune. He didn't mind, though. He always said his baby girl had simply caught the creative bug from himself and dear, rich singing cousin Lenny Williams.

Camille sang morning, noon, and night. When she wasn't singing, she was learning about music. She spent her weekly English class library time researching lyrics on the Internet, following her favorite groups. Momma trained her in the children's and young-adult choirs. Jerdine didn't let her daughter lead every song. Wouldn't be fair. But at almost every Pastor and Wife's anniversary event or women's fifth Sunday program, someone would request that Camille sing their favorite number, usually "His Eye Is on the Sparrow" or "The Safest Place." Like so many other vocalists, she had been tried and tested in church first. She had learned to sing whether she felt like it or not, whether she knew all the words or not. The best singers could skip a whole line and the audience would never know.

Over the thousands of hours she'd spent practicing,

Camille became one with her voice. She could make it do exactly what she wanted it to do. Hop, dip, twist, stretch, climb, whatever.

People at school knew she had pipes. She performed many a recess concert for her friends. Every now and then, some new student would fall under the mistaken impression they could sing better. This, of course, forced Camille to go slamp off on the poor child. She'd pull out an old song most of her classmates hadn't heard, maybe Shirley Murdock's "As We Lay," and demonstrate how a *real* diva blew.

She watched videos and learned the choreography and words of every week's top-ten tracks. In short, she was obsessed with music and singing. After studying *Star Search* and *Showtime at the Apollo*, Camille convinced herself that she had what it took to make it big.

Jerdine insisted that Camille finish high school before she started chasing her dreams. "No matter what happens, no one can take your diploma away from you."

Nowadays, Camille wished her mother had added a college degree to the request, because the value of her high school diploma was shrinking right along with the American dollar.

Nonetheless, Camille had honored her deceased mother's wishes. She completed twelfth grade before she allowed her brother to circulate the cheap demo she'd recorded of a Deborah Cox instrumental. He caught a few tugs on the line and traipsed Camille all over Dallas and Houston until she finally got a meeting with an up-and-coming producer, T-Money, who was trying to start a new record label. He needed a female group to get the ball rolling.

"Cami, this is the most important audition of your life," Courtney had warned her before they got out of the car. "If you get into this group, your whole life will change forever. You understand?"

He didn't have to tell her that. She knew this must be crucial for him to miss work so he could take her to meet these people in Houston. Not exactly the Mecca for R&B talent, but now that Jermaine Dupri was putting Atlanta on the map, and some guys out of St. Louis, Missouri, of all places, were making a name for their town, reputable, well-connected studios were popping up all over the country.

Though only a few years older than his sister, Court-ney had a severity about him that afforded him instant respect with adults. People even called him "little man" growing up because, in some ways, he was never a child. "He's just got an old spirit," Bobby Junior would say.

The day she auditioned was the day she met Alexis and Tonya for the first time, along with twelve other girls they beat out for the top slots. The fourth spot went to a girl named Janiah, who didn't have the good sense to keep the fact that she was pregnant under wraps until she'd signed a contract.

An audition that was supposed to last a day or two turned into a week as the producer called back several of the girls he'd sent home crying. Kyra was one of those girls. Realizing she'd better sing like her life de-pended on it, Kyra nailed the song the second time around. Camille never really thought this was fair to the other girls, but, hey—she was in no position to speak her mind.

Courtney hadn't expected to be in negotiations with T-Money's business associates most of that week, but he was more than ready for the challenge. Camille left all the paperwork and money talk to her big brother while she and the rest of what would later be known as

Sweet Treats sang their throats raw in the adjacent recording room.

When it was all said and done, Courtney's bargaining skills landed him the job as the group's manager and some kind of limited rights that Camille didn't quite understand at the time. She trusted Courtney to handle the legal mumbo-jumbo. He said he'd bet on the group with T-Money, and he hoped that one day, he'd be a rich man. Camille hoped so, too, because staying in Houston had cost Courtney his management trainee job and put him in a rough spot, financially, since he had to pay for a hotel room for the week.

Bobby Junior wired them some money halfway through their stay, which came with thick ropes attached. Though she wasn't actually on the phone, she'd heard her father's words to Courtney, "This is coming from your momma's insurance money. Y'all better make it count, 'cause it's all we have left of her."

Courtney's skinny face never looked so heavy. "Don't worry, Dad. I'm gonna make it happen."

And that's exactly what Courtney did. Up until the day he got replaced.

Camille couldn't think about that now. "Life is too short to look back," she told herself.

CHAPTER 9

Now that Camille believed her days at Aquapoint Systems were numbered, she had a much better attitude about going to work. Bringing her lunch actually morphed into a pleasurable part of her plan to eat healthier and lose weight.

Even Fluffy seemed to benefit from her new attitude. "The doctor says she's never seen such a remarkable recovery," Camille remarked to Sheryl. Actually, she needed to do something to stop this woman after she'd inquired about the feline for two days in a row. The way Sheryl carried on, Camille wondered if her boss had lost sleep behind Fluffy.

"Oh, wow! You've got to give me your vet's name!"

"Okay, I'll have to remember to pick up a card the next time we're there." Camille nodded with a straight face.

Sheryl whipped out her cell phone. "Wait. Before you go back to your desk, let me show you the pictures I took of Lillie last weekend."

Camille oohed and aahed over a shot of Sheryl's purebred cocker spaniel, then quickly darted back to her office before Sheryl could ask to see a photo of the invisible Fluffy.

Good humor translated into a genuinely cheerful tone, which meant mega leads for Camille. Already, she was at twenty-nine appointments, and it was only Wednesday morning. All this, of course, meant she'd bought herself some time to handle church investigation while on the company's clock. The more she accomplished at Aquapoint, the less stuff on her plate after hours. Good thing, too, because after her last two workouts on Medgar's treadmills, Camille was too pooped to do much else.

She figured it would take a few days for the church secretary—or whoever input new members' information—to put her name on the church roll. Since she'd already received a postcard from The King's Table, she hoped Grace Temple wouldn't be too far behind with processing.

Now for the *real* business. Camille skipped on over to her church's homepage and found the link to church staff. She recognized the praise team leader's photo. His name was Ronald Shepherd. According to his biography, he'd earned a bachelor of music degree from the University of North Texas and some kind of theological degree from a Dallas seminary. There were no graduation years posted, but Camille guessed he was probably a few years older than her.

His e-mail address and phone extension popped up when she hovered over his handsome face. She took note, glanced at her watch, and decided she'd better wait until a more casual hour, say ten o'clock, so she wouldn't appear as though her entire existence depended on this call. Besides, she needed some time to get her verbiage together.

She struggled to find an appropriate angle on this one. How could she introduce herself and ask to be on the praise team in the same breath? She needed some history, a real reason for Ronald to thrust her into the limelight. She needed what saints at the old church would have called a "blazing-hot testimony," one where God had picked her up, turned her around, and placed her feet on solid ground. Or did he take her feet out of the "miry clay" first? Was "miry" even a word?

Hmmm. What could she say that was maybe at least partially true. She didn't mind lying about an animal, but she didn't want to jinx herself. *Think! Think!*

Okay, there was one time, during her grade school days, when she got lost in J.C. Penney and a little old lady with almost transparent skin led her to the gift-wrapping department, where a lady paged Jerdine to claim Camille. When she and Jerdine searched for the good Samaritan in order to thank her, she was gone. Momma had remarked, "Must have been an angel in disguise."

That story actually brought goose bumps to Camille's arms every time she recalled the incident, but it had nothing to do with her singing. Other than maybe a song about lost souls, she couldn't find an inroad.

What else?

Her mind blank, she opened up a Word file and brainstormed all the potentially life-threatening events in her life that God might have delivered her from:

1. Cut leg on Slip 'n' Slide
2. Got whole bunch of water in mouth @ Wet 'n' Wild water park
3. Swallowed penny
4. Walking pneumonia

Hold up. Pneumonia was serious. People died from it. She *could* have died from it or maybe lost a lung if her parents hadn't taken her to see a doctor, which they did—but whatever. Point was, it *could* have happened, and that's what mattered.

She thought through her testimony: As a child, she'd suffered from a bronchial problem. Clearly, the devil had been trying to steal her voice. But her mother, a prayer warrior, prayed her through so that God could use this instrument of praise for His glory. And once the Lord healed her from all those breathing-related issues that threatened to swipe her off the earth, she opened her mouth and the most beautiful sound on earth came through loud and clear. She'd been singing ever since!

By midmorning, Camille had rehearsed the narrative so many times she almost believed it. Confident of her ability to garner support, she dialed the church's main number and waited for the prompt to enter Ronald's extension.

2286.

"Hello. You have reached the office of Ronald Shepherd, director of music at Grace Chapel Community Church . . ." Blah, blah, blah.

What on earth could he be doing at ten o'clock? She imagined Ronald behind his desk surfing the Internet, browsing Facebook profiles, basically doing what she did at work. So why couldn't he take her call?

"Hi, Mr. Shepherd, my name is Camille Robertson. I joined church Sunday and I'm anxious to get busy ministering through song. Could you please return my call at your earliest convenience?" She left her number and tacked on, "Have a blessed day," for good measure.

Dang! Now she'd have to write down her story so she could remember it whenever Mr. I'm-too-busy-Web-surfing got back with her.

Camille activated the "vibrate" option on her phone and placed it right next to her keyboard so she wouldn't miss his call. At lunch, she checked again to make sure she hadn't accidentally enabled some feature that might have blocked her phone's reception. She asked Janice to dial her number.

The signal came through, no problems.

By quitting time, Camille was furious. How dare he not return her phone call by the end of the business day? Even if he wasn't in the office, didn't he check voice mail remotely? Even if he wanted to call her today, he couldn't now because of midweek service.

Anger at Ronald's brush-off fueled her workout. She probably burned an extra hundred calories because of him.

Drenched and sore, Camille returned home from the recreation center to find a yellow note taped to her door. *Am I being evicted?* Couldn't be. She'd paid her rent and the late charges. Plus it wasn't pink.

She snatched the note from the door, inadvertently ripping off a smidgen of the underlying paint. *Not my fault.*

The paper read, YOU HAVE A UPS PACKAGE AT LEAS-
ING OFFICE. CLAIM BY 7 OR COME BACK AT 9 TOMORROW.

She checked her phone. Six fifty-four. She could
make it. With gym bag still in hand, Camille cut across
the center courtyard where a cluster of unsupervised
elementary-age kids were flinging empty swings so
high the seats wrapped around the top bar, elevating
the swings to a height that none of them would be able
to reach if they kept it up.

She shook her head. *Kids today are so destructive*.

Up ahead, the main office parking lot was mighty
desolate. Camille glanced at her phone again. Six fifty-
seven. Twenty feet later, it was pretty clear that these
people had vacated the premises. *Are you kidding me?*

Nope. Lights out, doors locked, curtains closed.

"I can't believe this." She grunted. She walked
around the building to a side entrance. A sign listing
the maintenance man's number was her only hope.
Camille called, tried to explain the urgency of her situation, but the complex's answering service informed
her that an unclaimed package from UPS did not fall
under the category of "emergency."

"But I *need* that delivery." Camille added a tearful
twang.

The responder wavered. "Is there medication in the
box?"

"Yes." *Why didn't I think of that?*

"Hold on a second."

Camille waited, happy that her precious parcel,
whatever it was, would soon be in her hands.

"Ma'am, I've talked to the manager. She says she's
willing to page the maintenance man and have him
come to the office, but you have to open the package in

his presence and show him that the content is medically necessary or else she'll charge you for his overtime."

Camille went off. "What? How she gon' charge me for him to do his job?"

"Because, ma'am, the office *is* closed."

"What time you got?" she baited the operator.

"Three minutes after seven."

"Yeah, now that you and I have been talking for five minutes. What time did I call you?"

"My monitor shows seven."

Camille reasoned, "That's what I'm saying! If I called you at seven, they must have been gone *before* then."

"Okay, ma'am, do you want me to call the maintenance man or not?" the operator asked point-blank.

"What about security?"

"For your location, you need to hang up and dial nine-one-one if this is a life-or-death situation."

"Oooh! You wait until I see them tomorrow," Camille hissed as she concluded the conversation improperly through the push of a button. She marched back to her unit and slammed the cheap, hollow door behind her. These people were worse than Ronald Shepherd!

Good old Fluffy's dialysis would have to come through the next morning. Camille couldn't be at her job on time because she had to be at her complex's office at nine o'clock to deal with whoever found it acceptable to discard posted work hours. Though she recognized the irony in her situation, she rationalized that *her* case was different. No one depended on her to be anywhere at any particular time. A leasing agent, however, needed to be in place for a plethora of dire reasons. It all boiled down to customer service.

Eight fifty-eight a.m. Camille took the "future residents" parking spot nearest the door. What could they do—tow her? She sauntered into complex headquarters wearing a dark paisley-print halter dress with a black half cardigan. She had thought about wearing the too tall heels again so she could appear slightly intimidating and overly professional, but patent leather heels wouldn't give her any clout here. Judging from times she'd had to come to the front desk to explain why she needed a few more days to pay rent, tattoos were king with this crew.

Camille immediately recognized LaNetra, the manager who'd actually signed the dotted line on her leasing agreement. For the most part, LaNetra was cordial, which dampened all hopes of a vigorous debate followed by *this* angry tenant's threat to call the home office and a manager's subsequent offer of reduced rent in order to keep Camille quiet.

She approached LaNetra at the circular reception desk. "Hi. I live in A-fifteen. Yesterday, I got a note on my door saying I had a package that I could pick up before seven—"

"Yes!" LaNetra remarked as she stood to shake Camille's hand. "I remember you. Mrs. Robertson, right?"

Attitude still intact. "*Miss* Robertson."

LaNetra shifted her weight to one side as she slipped her hip into classic girlfriend stance. "You know what?

Somebody told me you used to sing with the group that sang that song 'Meet Me in the Hot Tub.' Is that right?"

A smile escaped. "Yes, I was the lead singer."

"Oh my God! I can't believe it's you. My sister used to play that song like it was going out of style! Why didn't you tell me who you were when you first moved in?"

Camille recognized the star-struck look in LaNetra's eyes. People, particularly Americans, were suckers for anyone they had seen on television or heard on the radio.

"I didn't want *everybody* to know." Camille lowered her lashes. "People try to charge you more when they think you have money."

LaNetra rolled her eyes. "Girl, tell me about it. The other week, my baby daddy took me to a car dealership in his Escalade. Next thing you know, they tried to tell me my car note was gonna be seven hundred and sixty-two dollars a month. For a Honda *Accord*!"

Camille tried to register her complaint during the brief lull. "Well, I'm not—"

"That's exactly what I said! I am not going to pay that," LaNetra echoed. "Now, I know my credit is jacked, but it ain't *that* jacked to where I gotta slap almost a thousand dollars a month on the table for a ride that ain't even all that. I mean, they got good trade-in value, but let's be for real.

"Anyway, that was all because we drove up on the lot in his car. The next day, I took my momma's old Chevy Cavalier. Got the exact same Honda Accord car for *way* less, plus I got a warranty, so, I feel you, Miss Robertson. If people try to get over on me because of a Cadillac, I can't imagine what they try to do to you."

Whether through the adoration or the long-winded

chronicle, LaNetra's gabbing had singlehandedly disarmed Camille. "So, you want your package? I love getting packages. Makes me feel like I really done something, even when I know all I did was just order something online."

Fluffy's dialysis wouldn't account for too much more missed time this morning. He might have to die if this girl kept rambling.

LaNetra bent down to retrieve the shoebox-sized parcel. "Here you go."

Camille looked at the return address. *Alexis?* Suddenly, she remembered the impromptu promise of a birthday gift. The last time someone relished her birthday was when her former supervisor had the baker include Camille's name on the monthly employee birthday celebration cake they dumped in the break room.

Just the thought of unwrapping a present that wasn't from the near-mandatory corporate Secret Santa system made Camille tuck both lips between her teeth to keep them from trembling.

"Are you okay?" LaNetra asked.

"I'm fine. Thank you."

Tears trailed down Camille's face as she sat in her car opening the precious cardboard container. Beyond the tape and foam peanuts, she discovered a beautiful scented candle and a book entitled *A Woman's Wisdom from Proverbs*. She read the heart-shaped sticky memo attached to the cover.

> *Now that you're thirty, a proverb for each year.*
> *You probably can't see too good at your age, so I*
> *got you a candle, too. LOL! Happy Birthday!*
> *—Alexis*

The joke sent a wave of laughter through Camille as she leaned back on her headrest. Alexis's sense of humor had always been refreshing. There was always something about her that drew people, made people feel good in her presence. No doubt, Alexis was probably one of the best teachers on campus because she had a way of bringing out the best in people. Even people like Camille.

CHAPTER 10

"Hello, Camille, this is Ronald Shepherd, minister of music at Grace Chapel, returning your phone call."

She turned down the volume on her radio, a futile attempt to hide her mysterious penchant for T.I.'s music. Rap wasn't really her forte, but something about his style pulled her into his world.

"Yes, umm, thank you," Camille prattled through, hoping Ronald hadn't heard too much. "Thanks for returning my call."

"Is this a good time for you to talk? Sounds like you're on the road," he cautioned.

She sidestepped his concern. "Oh, I'm okay. Go ahead."

"Let me first apologize for not getting back to you before now. I was out of town at a funeral."

"I'm sorry to hear that," she stated with a tinge of curiosity.

"Thank you." He welcomed her sympathy but didn't offer additional information. "How can I help you?"

It had been more than forty-eight hours since Camille last practiced her mighty testimony. Frankly, she had given up on Ronald and decided to seek out that friendly drummer instead. Musicians were like a family. Get to know one, and you got to know all of them.

Again, she scuffled through her words. "I joined the church Sunday. And. Your music was amazing. It really moved me." *What am I saying?* "I enjoyed the praise team. And the choir, But the praise team . . . what a team."

"Thank you. To God be the glory. You mentioned something about ministering through song in your voice message?" Ronald kept the conversation moving.

"Mmm-hmm. I used to sing in the choir. Well, actually, believe it or not, I was almost unable to sing because I had asthma as a child." *That's not the segue! That's not even the right story!*

Ronald said, "Praise God you've been delivered."

She hadn't counted on the fact that Ronald wouldn't ask questions about her miraculous healing. His prodding was *supposed* to lay out the red carpet for a staggering account of how God zapped her with abilities that could only be fully appreciated if she were immediately placed on the praise team.

Instead, Ronald's silence pressed her to steer toward a point. Soon.

"So, anyway, I just wanted to know how I can be a part of the music ministry." There it was. He'd yanked it out of her in less than sixty seconds.

"Do you play an instrument? Sing? Write music?"

"I sing. Soprano."

"Great. Well, descriptions of all our choirs and their rehearsal schedules are on the church's Web site, but just to let you know, the church has several choirs, but I'm guessing you wouldn't be interested in the men's choir."

He expelled a slight chuckle. Camille was careful to follow his humor with a breathy snicker of her own.

He continued, "We have the women's choir, the children's choir, youth choir, young-adult choir, adult choir, senior choir, and the unity choir, which is a combination of people in existing choirs who are available to sing on fifth Sundays. The choirs' rehearsals vary because they rotate serving on Sundays and Wednesdays. Really, the only way to keep up is to check the Web site. Sometimes, even I have to consult the Web site to figure out who's doing what."

Again, she trailed his laughter. "Okay. I'll be sure to check the Web site."

"Great. Is there anything else I can help you with?"

Camille wondered if maybe she should wait until she'd attended a few practices before springing the praise-team question on him. But time was of the essence, and he seemed to be a straightforward guy. He could take it. "Is there information about the praise team on the Web site as well?"

"No, not right now. We do hold open auditions twice a year, but we generally end up selecting our most faithful members of the various choirs to serve on the praise team because it requires a higher level of commitment in terms of time and dedication," Ronald explained.

Yada, yada, yada. "I understand. So, when's the next praise-team audition?"

"Let me see," Ronald drawled. "Second Saturday in August."

"This *fall* August?" flew up from Camille's heart and out of her mouth. *I could have stayed my happy behind at The King's Table! This is false advertising!*

Ronald reiterated, "Yes. August, four months from now."

Other words had to be suppressed. "Oh, okay. Thank you."

"I look forward to meeting you at choir rehearsal," Ronald said.

"Definitely. Good-bye."

"Bye."

August! Good thing Camille was already parked between the white lines when he delivered that blow. Stunned, she slowly exited her car and transported herself and her gym bag up the staircase to her apartment, on autopilot.

Would she be able to prove herself "faithful" in four months? Exactly how faithful is faithful? How was she supposed to keep John David waiting a third of a year for this demo CD? And why was everything working against her?

After showering and eating her last ration of rabbit food for the day, Camille consumed three hours of reality talk shows. Though pay day had come again, there was no reason to celebrate. Whatever money she had left over would go toward the citation, which she still hadn't investigated. The ticket showed she had thirty days to contact the clerk. She'd call them at the last minute.

Right now, Camille felt like singing the blues. Liter-

ally. "A lady at the casino," she recited the first line of
Johnnie Taylor's "Last Two Dollars" and instantly sensed
the song's dismal vibes course through her. It was good
to know somebody else understood what it meant to
lose everything by means of gambling.

Though Camille hadn't lost everything in Shreve-
port or Vegas, she wondered if she might have had better odds on a slot machine. Nights like this, when she
realized she was just as broke on Friday as she was on
Thursday, she could just kick herself for betting against
family.

She closed her eyes and pushed the mental "replay"
button on the night before the Sweet Treats's debut
album went on sale. All four of the group members
were bunking in a Comfort Inn just outside Durham,
NC. Stripped of wigs, heavy makeup, and glamorous
stage costumes, they looked as though they could have
been college roommates. By this point, they had all
grown comfortable enough with each other to share a
single bathroom with ease.

Courtney was in the adjacent room, and he'd called
the girls' room more than once, asking them to stop all
the racket, but they couldn't help it. The prerelease
buzz and promotion had positioned them to make a
significant boom in the industry. It wasn't every day
that a group of nineteen-year-olds fell asleep penniless
but woke up the next morning with six figures each to
their names.

Hunkered over a pizza they'd ordered at midnight,
the girls gibbered and made up songs as they ate.

Tonya started off another groove to the tune of the
happy birthday song. "We're gonna be rich."

Alexis added, "Tell your momma 'nem this."

Camille snatched the featured line, "Tomorrow starts our future."

They'd waited for Kyra to round out the melody. Her silence sent them all to the floor, rolling in laughter. That girl was not one for thinking on her feet.

"Wait. Wait, I got it." Kyra cleared her throat and topped off with, "So you betta recognize."

Alexis, Tonya, and Camille had laughed even harder, leaving Kyra confused. "What's wrong?"

The fact that she didn't get it only made things worse.

Kyra grew angry. "What? Y'all don't think I can sing as good as y'all?"

Alexis, the peacemaker, gained her composure long enough to enlighten Kyra. "You need to end with something that rhymes with 'rich' and 'this.'"

Kyra had crossed her arms. "Oh, I *got* a word that rhymes with rich, but I don't think y'all want to hear it."

"Kyra, calm down," Tonya scolded. "Why you always gotta take everything to the streets? Here. Eat some more pizza."

Offended but hungry, Kyra obeyed. The others reclaimed their spots on the bed as they found their wits.

The phone rang again.

"You answer it this time," Camille told Alexis. "I don't want to hear my brother's mouth anymore."

"Hello." Alexis had giggled. Her expression dulled. "Oh, we're sorry. Okay, we'll lower our voices. Good night." Eyes wide, she faced her comrades. "That was the manager. He said one of the guests complained about us. We've got to keep it down for *real* now."

The girls, sobered by the warning, ate in silence for a moment.

Camille was the first to speak again. "I'll be glad when we can stay in *real* hotels. The kinds where we have our own suites, or maybe the whole floor could be ours."

"Not me." Tonya shook her head. "Courtney says that's how artists go broke."

Camille countered, "I know Courtney is my brother and all, but sometimes he acts like he doesn't want us to spend *any* money. He's so cheap. I mean, Sweet Treats is not broke. We deserve to splurge on *some* things. What would our fans think if they saw us in this cheap hotel? We have an image to keep up, you know?"

"That's probably the same thing TLC said before they filed bankruptcy," Alexis took sides.

"And Toni Braxton, and MC Hammer, too" Tonya added.

Camille rolled her eyes. "They were just stupid. I mean, how do you make, like, ten million dollars one year and then you're broke the next year?"

"'Cause if you make ten million dollars, you basically owe five million dollars in taxes," from Alexis, whose parents were both educators. Sometimes that girl was too smart.

"Okay, but still. How do you go in debt in *one year* when you have *five million dollars*?"

"Easy," Alexis chirped, "spend five million and one."

Unconvinced, Camille had smacked her lips. "I don't care what y'all say. All of them should be set for life with that money. They stupider than a mug."

"I know, right?" Kyra jumped in Camille's corner.

The fact that Kyra agreed with her should have been

Camille's first clue that she was off track. Turns out, five million dollars flies away quite easily, especially after all the help gets paid and what's left over has to be split four ways.

When Courtney was the manager, he had done his best to keep the girls grounded, make them realize this money wouldn't last forever. He even tried to get them to invest in different stocks and options. Tonya listened. Alexis listened because her parents agreed with Courtney. Kyra told him to kiss her where the sun didn't shine, she'd do what she pleased with her money.

Camille never felt she had a choice. Courtney and Bobby Junior all but insisted she had to stash some in some fund she couldn't even touch until she'd reached the ripe old age of twenty-five. It was like having your parent be your teacher. Double supervision, double punishment.

Courtney's real-life "big brother" heavy-handed tactics quickly forced Camille to push a Sweet Treats vote. The group was split down the middle about keeping Courtney as a manager. But when Camille proposed a management deal with the smooth-talking, good-looking Aaron Bellamy, who promised them the moon, Alexis and Tonya gave in. Courtney was terminated—with Aaron's help, of course, because none of the girls actually knew how to fire somebody.

Looking back, more than a decade later, Camille realized that severing Courtney's contract was perhaps the most stupid decision she'd ever made. Stupider than spending five million and one dollars in a year. Sweet Treats lost the one person who believed in them enough to take out a title loan on his car to pay for their first costumes.

Worse, Camille lost the one person who shared memories of making Rice Krispies treats and dyeing Easter eggs with their mother. The only one who laughed every time Jerdine had chanted the silly banna-fanna-fo-fanna rhyme.

Melancholy sank deeper into her aching body now. At the gym, she'd done thirty-eight minutes on the elliptical rider, burning two hundred calories according to the machine display. But her temporary soreness paled in comparison to losing the only person she'd ever be able to call brother.

As she hoisted herself off the couch, a saying from the old church suddenly thrust itself into the forefront of her mind. *At least I have my health and strength.*

How many times had she heard *that* one growing up? And every time she heard it, she thought about how silly it was to be thankful for something as intangible as "health and strength" or "a sound mind" and "the activity of my limbs." They should have added twenty dollars to that list, as far as Camille was concerned. Money couldn't buy health, but it probably could have bought some pretty good doctors for Momma.

One painful step after another, Camille plodded back to her bedroom. The creaky mattress begged for a replacement. Her faux down comforter also needed a successor since Camille had experimented with washing it in the gentle cycle rather than spending extra cash to have it dry-cleaned. Actually, the stale scent of her sheets advised Camille she needed to get to the washateria soon. *Hope I have enough coins and washing powder.*

She settled her head into the pillow and took one last look ahead. There, on the night stand, was the book from Alexis, which Camille still hadn't cracked open. Camille was a singer, not a reader. Like most people, Alexis had given the type of gift *she* wanted to receive— not what the recipient desired.

"Well," Camille told herself, "it's the thought that counts."

CHAPTER 11

Willie Nevils used to have A-plus credit. So did Mattie. Never a missed bill, never a lapse in phone service. God had been good to Alexis's parents. Though they were far from rich, Alexis couldn't remember a time when her parents had said they couldn't give her something she wanted or needed because they couldn't afford it. They might have said, "You're not old enough yet," or, "Let's see what your report card looks like," but no hint that money was a deciding factor. In fact, Alexis had been shocked the first time she heard someone at school talk about their lights being turned off.

"What do you mean *off*?" she had asked, wide-eyed.

Michelle Stars, one of the smartest girls in first grade, enlightened Alexis. "Like when you turn on the light switch, the light doesn't come on."

"Oh." Alexis had sighed with relief. "You just have to change the lightbulb."

"No, silly." Michelle laughed and pushed her dirty

blond bangs behind her ears. "There's no electricity in my house. Nothing works. Not even the TV."

Horror ripped through Alexis's tiny frame. "Why not?"

"Because my mom didn't pay the bill."

"Why didn't she pay the bill?"

"'Cause we don't have enough money."

Aside from the fact that she'd never heard of such a predicament, Alexis pondered in awe before asking her next question. "Doesn't your mom have a job?"

"Yes, she works, but when she got her check, she didn't have enough money still."

"What about your dad?"

"I don't have a dad."

Alexis decided she'd better stop asking this girl questions because, in a minute, Michelle might confess to being from outer space. *Everyone* had a daddy, unless they were some kind of alien.

The Nevils' family bubble had been a soft, happy space. At the end of Alexis's private school elementary education, she entered public school and her teen years simultaneously. Only then did she begin to see how cruel people could be. They lied, cheated, and stole. Boys fought, girls got pregnant. Most teachers sat behind their desks reading newspapers while the students did nothing more than copy definitions from a dictionary or answer the questions at the end of a chapter.

Her only saving grace was choir. School choir, church choir, community choir, didn't matter. Alexis seized every opportunity to sing, and her parents supported her efforts. She'd even earned a partial scholarship to Stephen F. Austin State University in Texas.

Of course, the Nevilses hadn't been too happy about sending their baby girl hundreds of miles away, but

Alexis was itching to try her wings. Too bad they didn't work quite as well as she'd wanted them to. Academically, college was no trouble. The social aspect, however, disheartened Alexis. Her roommate, Dionna, robbed her blind and broke every dorm rule possible. Frightened by one of Dionna's boyfriend's advances, Alexis had asked for a new roommate, which, of course, led to what everyone called "snitching."

Dionna's imitation "sorority" sisters had it in for Alexis after that. The Kitty Phi Sleepers, an unauthorized, newly formed social club, wore red and black and couldn't really decide if they were supposed to be little sisters to the Alphas or the Kappas. Just depended on which frat had the most liquor on any given night.

Anyway, their club/gang put Alexis on the hit list. One of them even keyed her car. Campus security acted like their hands were tied without solid proof. Halfway into the second semester, Alexis was ready to drop out, move back home with her parents in St. Louis, and transfer her fifteen hours to a community college. She'd live with Momma and Daddy as long as possible if it meant safety from bullies and irrational people.

Again, the only reason she'd remained at the college for as long as she did was the choir. She couldn't let them down. In their own little geeky way, they had bonded. Not that any of them had her back with Dionna's crew, but at least she had some kind of haven from all the madness.

When her choir director, Mr. Allen, told her about an audition for a female singing group in Houston, Alexis had jumped at the opportunity. She didn't call her parents to seek counsel. Honestly, Alexis didn't think it would amount to much. The world was filled with so many professionally trained singers who had spent their lives connected to microphone stands, Alexis presumed the small-time audition would just be a life experience she could learn from, something to tell the grandkids about.

Mr. Allen must have thought the same thing, too, because he hadn't planned on being at the studio all day. "Alexis, I'm going to have to come back for you. Call me when you're ready. Good luck!"

Turned out, Mr. Allen was nowhere to be found at nine thirty. Alexis ended up hitching a ride back to her dorm with strangers—Camille and her brother, Courtney.

A week later, Camille was more like a cousin, Tonya a sister. And Kyra . . . well, she was the crazy aunt Alexis never had. Kyra got into a huge fracas with one of Dionna's friends at a social event on the college campus Alexis had invited them to. The bad news: Kyra lost four braids and an earring in the scuffle. The good news: Dionna's people now thought Alexis had some kind of backup, especially after Kyra threatened to "come back and bust a cap in everybody up in here wearin' a red and black shirt!" This threat, of course, was followed by a load of expletives only an experienced cusser could skillfully handle. That kind of profanity was not to be tried at home.

Afterward, a security officer had questioned Alexis about the young lady who'd made a terroristic threat.

"I don't know her all that well. She's a girl I sang with a few times," Alexis had bent the truth.

Kyra's hair-trigger attitude might have violated campus and perhaps federal policy, but Alexis wasn't about to mess up the best protection plan she had going. Besides, where was security when *she* needed them?

The decision to take a semester off from school to

establish Sweet Treats didn't go over well with her parents, to say the least. They fussed and stomped, threatened and warned. Alexis was not hearing them.

She realized now that if her parents hadn't been distracted and monetarily stretched in their efforts to underwrite Thomas's issues with T. J., they would have driven to Texas and dragged eighteen-year-old Alexis back, boo-hooing all the way.

The situation with their grandson, however, took precedence. He had managed to get himself all tangled up in a life-or-death court case. Thomas didn't want to leave his son's fate to a free attorney. Wouldn't be able to live with himself if T. J. got the death penalty. The cheapest independent lawyer they could find cost them two hundred twenty-five dollars an hour. And T. J.'s case needed a whole lotta hours.

That was the beginning of change in her parents' financial condition. Daddy stopped buying Domino's Pizza two and three times a week. Momma canceled her long-standing Thursday-evening hair appointment at Miss Olive's salon. Daddy even worked during the summers to help out.

T. J. got a lesser sentence. From what Alexis could tell, he probably wasn't guilty of the charge—at least not the way the prosecution presented it. T. J. had something to do with a man's death, that was for certain, but he didn't pull the trigger and he wasn't actually there when it happened. He probably knew about it ahead of time, though, which always made Alexis uneasy in her nephew's presence.

Right was right, wrong was wrong. If T. J. kept up his crazy lifestyle, it was only a matter of time before he did something stupid again, and the next time, there would be no money left for an expensive lawyer.

In the midst of her family's struggle, Alexis had come through for everyone with her sudden windfall of success. Thank God, she was able to dig her parents out of debt. She refused to give anything directly to T. J., but Momma and Daddy shouldn't have to suffer. They'd raised Thomas right. Thomas had probably raised his child right, too. Everyone had their own mind, though.

Dealing with her parents' finances now was a pretty straightforward matter. They were on a fixed income. Two thousand five hundred twenty-seven dollars a month, combined. The house was paid for and they no longer drove, so there was no car payment or vehicle insurance. The only thing they really owed at this point was the loan to remodel the house. They had the power, gas, water, satellite, and food bills, but those didn't amount to much; maybe four hundred twenty-five dollars. Her father still watched the thermostat like a hawk and put water in half-empty ketchup bottles to make it last longer. Every bit did help, Alexis had to admit.

If Momma and Daddy had been in good health, they'd have been fine. Alas, medications and supplies, doctor visits, Medicare deductibles, and trips to the emergency room because Daddy would not cooperate ate up most of their disposable income. They were lucky to have a hundred dollars left over at the end of the month. And even with that, Momma insisted on giving to somebody she'd heard about who "needed help."

"Momma, *you* need help," Alexis had laughed half-heartedly at her mother's directive to send a donation to a woman on the news who'd lost her home in a fire.

To which Momma replied, "There's always somebody worse off than you, Lexi."

Now that Alexis had gotten into the hang of balancing her parents' budget, she realized that the only reason her parents were in such good financial shape now was because her mother was a giver. She believed in sowing and reaping, and she believed that whatever she gave to the poor would be repaid by God Himself.

Alexis had to admit, He had done a good job of keeping her parents intact, despite the T. J. fiasco. It was no coincidence that she'd been blessed with more than enough when her parents were in need.

She calculated the bottom line in the old-fashioned blue and white checkbook ledger Daddy insisted she use.

"One hundred twenty dollars left," she announced across the kitchen bar.

Her parents barely nodded from their lounge chairs.

"Send some of that over to Sister Paul. She just had hip surgery, and I know that ain't cheap," Momma said.

Obediently, Alexis wrote out a check, then deducted twenty-five dollars from the balance.

A thought skidded through her head suddenly. When she'd finished her own budget calculations for the month, she'd had $357 left over, even after savings. And she knew someone who seemed to be struggling financially. *Camille.*

She could send her a check for a hundred dollars. After all, Camille's Sweet Treats stream of income must have dried up a long time ago. Without some kind of formal training or a degree, she must be really struggling, especially in this economy. And single, too? Yeah, Camille could probably use some help.

But would she be too prideful to take the money? Probably so. Camille wasn't Kyra. *Never mind. Bad idea.*

Besides, sending Camille money wasn't really something she would be doing for Camille's sake. It would probably feel like more of a guilt offering because, fact was, while Camille's stream had dried up, Alexis was still getting paid. So were Kyra and Tonya. And they didn't feel one bit of remorse, because Camille was the one who'd suggested and made sure they got rid of Courtney.

Still, Alexis couldn't keep this from Camille much longer. No matter what the law allowed, this thing wasn't right.

CHAPTER 12

Some people don't try to be sexy. They just are. Ronald Shepherd was one such person and, for the life of her, Camille couldn't figure out why the other single women in the young-adult choir hadn't snatched his behind up already. Had all their church-going holiness blinded them to his obvious hotness? Not to mention a deep, smooth voice that could put a vicious pit bull to sleep.

Whatever. Camille hadn't caught the I'm-too-saved-to-look bug. Unfortunately, Ronald seemed to have the church thing down a little too well. When she arrived at rehearsal fashionably late, he'd looked up from his piano seat and closed his Bible. Annoyance peppered his face, as though she'd interrupted something important.

"You must be . . . is it Cameron?"

"Camille," she politely corrected him.

"Yes, Camille. Nice to meet you." He placed his Bible on the piano stool, stood, and walked toward her, extending his hand for a very professional handshake. Then he escorted her to the front of the room, near the piano where he'd been sitting. "Everyone, this is Camille. Camille, this is everyone."

A soft "Hi, Camille," rose as all eyes settled on her. She tested the female vibe first. Cordial. Yielding. Didn't take women long to figure out who was the alpha female. A few men did double takes, but only what might be appropriate for church. Had she met them somewhere else, things would be different. Church guys were always desperate to get married so they could stop all that fornicating, in Camille's experience.

Ronald continued with his introduction speech. "She joined church last week, and she's thinking about joining the choir. So let's make sure we show her some Grace Chapel hospitality. Sopranos, give her some room."

A smiling woman on the front row wearing a broom skirt and sporting foot-long dreadlocks patted the empty seat next to her. Camille obliged, somewhat thankful to get a seat so near Ronald. He'd be able to hear her voice loud and clear.

"Let's go ahead and close out our study session in a word of prayer," he said.

Study? Prayer? If they were going to have Sunday school and a prayer meeting before every choir rehearsal, she'd come even later.

"Father," Ronald began, "thank You for Your word. Thank You for leaving Your peace, for letting us know that we never have to worry about tomorrow, for You hold all of our tomorrows in Your hands. In Jesus's name we pray. Amen."

"Amen."

Ronald opened the official practice portion of the

meeting by sharing his latest original compilation, en-titled "Use Me, Lord." The young-adult choir, adults age twenty-one to forty, would be singing this coming Sunday. Ronald's song would be their second number, to be performed during the offering.

Not a song Camille wanted to shine on. People would be busy writing out checks and fanning through wallets while the buckets passed through the audience. When she sang, she wanted their undivided attention.

"Sopranos, here's your key." Ronald delved into his teaching. Camille's section caught on quickly. Altos were fine, too. The tenors weren't so easy. Somebody sounded way off, and Ronald was taking the courteous route to correcting the error: having the whole group repeat the line over and over. If a no-nonsense director had been running the show, he'd have had each tenor sing one at a time so he could tackle the guilty party head-on.

This was going to be a long night.

Camille's mind wandered around the choir room. This practice area was bigger than the whole sanctuary at her childhood church. Matter of fact, this choir, which nearly filled up seven rows with seven cush-ioned seats in each row, would have made for a good Wednesday-night crowd back in the day. She had to admit to herself that she preferred this rehearsal space over the wide-open gulf of the church's main gathering room. This was better for blending harmonies, working out the fine musical details.

One wall of the choir room was composed of a row of windows facing the busiest street in the neighbor-hood. Camille craned her neck to watch cars pass. She got caught up in the saga of an old man operating a Hoveround who obviously hadn't gotten the memo that he was supposed to use the sidewalk. Had the nerve to take up a lane of traffic, like he was rolling in a state-registered vehicle complete with bumpers and a license plate.

Just a few weeks ago, Camille nearly ran slamp over an elderly man in a motorized wheelchair while pulling out of the McDonald's drive-through. She shook her head. *We gotta do something about these people.*

"Sopranos, are you ready?" Ronald shouted as he revved up the piano for their line.

Ready for what? She must have missed something.

Everyone in her section seemed to know the words. "Let Your way be known in all the earth," they crooned in unison.

Flabbergasted, all she could do was move her lips softly in hopes of catching the last sound of each word.

"Great. Altos, you're next." Ronald moved on without giving Camille her moment in the sun.

Dang! She'd choked on her chance to make a good first vocal impression. Now every time she sang well, he'd think it was a fluke. *What is wrong with me?*

From then on, Camille paid close attention. She hit every note precisely. Loudly. The woman sitting next to her took notice with an elbow and an "All right now."

All Ronald said was, "Good, sopranos."

Sopranos? I'm carrying this whole section!

An hour later, Camille's cords began to strain. She had to tone it down a notch or she'd be no good Sunday. Some girl on the back row took over the volume lead. Camille decided to let her have it today.

Surprised by this turn of events, Camille began to wonder if she could make it through a full-length concert. If just sitting in a chair and singing intermittently taxed her body, how would she be able to sing and dance at the same time? Did gospel singers dance, anyway?

Maybe John David and the rest of the music industry knew something about turning thirty that she didn't know. Was she slower now? Less apt to recall lyrics? Would the microphone pick up a hint of unwelcomed maturity?

This first rehearsal had been all but useless. She was no closer to the praise team than an usher patrolling the back pew.

After practice, she got the standard, "Nice to meet you, Camille," and, "Hope to see you again," from several of the members.

The only one who seemed to recognize her talent was Miss Smiley-face. She followed Camille to the parking lot, dragging complimentary chitchat with her. "Girl, if I could sing like that, I'd be somewhere with Kirk Franklin's choir right now."

Now that Camille was actually standing face-to-face with her, she could see beyond the old-timey clothes and realize that they were actually about the same age. "What's your name?"

"Mercedes."

"Mercedes, it's not like you *can't* sing," Camille returned the compliment. Mercedes could hold a note, after all. Her pitch wasn't always perfect, but, hey, who needs perfect pitch when you're surrounded by a choir?

"You ever sing professionally?"

"Yeah," Camille admitted as she approached her car.

She watched Mercedes's expression as she must have registered the Lexus emblem. Over the years, Camille had learned that a negative reaction from seeing the luxury icon, even a slight one, signaled a hater.

Camille still remembered the day her boss at her first real-people job called her out about owning the vehicle. She and several other employees were sitting in a conference room that faced their small employee parking lot. Her boss, Martha, fell into category-A hater, the worst kind. Those were the ones who hated because they believed their best days were behind them. They complained about their life *and* yours.

Anyway, Martha had already made a few remarks about how much Camille probably spent to get her hair and nails done every week. The day Martha's true colors came out, the sun had been particularly bright. To warm the freezing-cold meeting room, Martha had opened the blinds. When she spotted Camille's car in the row, she put a hand on her hip and exclaimed, "Who am I paying enough to drive a car better than mine?"

The category-B haters in the room, who still had goals but hadn't reached them yet and didn't appreciate others who had already arrived, offered Camille up to Martha. That next week, Martha saw to it that two insubordination reports made their way into Camille's personnel file. A month later, Camille was fired. She knew now to watch out for how people responded to her car.

When there was no reaction from Mercedes, Camille concluded that Mercedes was just genuine good people.

"I knew you must have sung somewhere else," Mercedes said.

Camille answered the unasked question. "I sang with a group called Sweet Treats. You remember a song called 'Meet Me in the Hot Tub'?"

Mercedes dipped her chin and glanced above the

rim of her glasses. "Girl, yes. My mother didn't want me to listen to it, but I knew every word."

"Well, I was the lead singer."

"Get out!" She punched Camille's shoulder. "For real?"

"Yep."

"Nuh-uh."

Of course, the attention fed a hungry ego. Camille popped her trunk and whisked out a CD. The trunk light provided just enough illumination for Mercedes to verify the face on the cover.

"Oh my goodness! It *is* you!"

Mercedes's outburst caused a few other choir members to approach the car. She quickly explained Camille's background and showed them the CD as proof. Oohs and aahs abounded as each one read the title list and compared the picture to Camille's present-day face.

By this time, Camille's head began to swell. This was the rebirth of her fan club! Plus, she might even be able to make a little money. "Anybody want an autographed CD?"

"Yes!" Mercedes exclaimed as she dug through her purse. "How much?"

"Let's do a Grace Chapel special. Ten dollars."

A few people walked away, saying they didn't have any cash on them. But Camille was able to sell four CDs within ten minutes right there on the church grounds. "Thank you," she remembered to say to each customer.

Yes! Mo' money for my ticket!

The Sweet Treats store stayed open another five minutes as the parking lot cleared. Mercedes said her farewells as Camille lowered the trunk.

She entered the cab of her car and buckled herself into the seatbelt. A knock on the window startled her. Ronald's face and torso appeared on the other side of the glass. Camille braced herself for a conversation.

"Hi."

"Hello. Hope you enjoyed the rehearsal."

"Yes, I did, thank you. You're great with this choir."

"Thanks. Will we see you again?"

She nodded. "Definitely."

"Great." He tapped the hood of her car. "Have a good night."

"You, too."

She watched Ronald walk back toward the building and enter the doors again. *Yes!* He must have come out just to speak to her, to beg her to stay in the choir. Okay, he hadn't exactly *begged*. But the fact that he made a special trip proved the old boy recognized talent when he heard it. He wasn't so aloof after all.

CHAPTER 13

The only method for sitting in Ronald's face every week as well as singing in the choir almost every Sunday was to be in more than one choir. Camille joined every choir for which she was eligible—the young-adult choir, the women's choir, and the unity choir. If that didn't prove her faithfulness, she'd have to bring Mr. Ronald before the elders or something, because it just didn't get any more faithful than being in three choirs.

After a few weeks of practicing (always arriving late to avoid Bible study) and another conversation with Ronald in which she officially signed up for ministry in the music department, she was finally invited to put on a choir robe and sit in the choir stand. This, of course, meant she had to be at church fifteen minutes early. Not part of her plan, but there was no way out of it. The Fluffy excuse wouldn't work in this case.

Her first Sunday in the choir, she performed with the

young-adult choir. They sang contemporary gospel: Hezekiah Walker, Fred Hammond kind of stuff. Most of these songs were seriously group-y. No leader. No way to shine. All she could do was holler "Woooh!" during an instrumental portion. But once she started adding the background sounds, everybody in the choir did the same, turning the "Woooh!" into nothing more than a cheerleading chant.

The first chance she got to blow the audience away didn't come until her second Sunday in the choir stand with the women's choir. A few old heads in the group had asked Ronald to sing a Walter Hawkins song, "Goin' Up Yonder." On her own, Camille practiced for the moment she'd copy the leader. And when the choir reached the encore moment, she was ready.

"One of these old days," the leader screamed.

Camille echoed, "One of these old days." Sounded great. Just like the album.

"One of these old days," the leader sang again.

"One of these old daaays." Camille threw a little twist on the end.

"I said one of these old days."

Camille let 'er rip. "Yaaaa! One of thee-eee-eee-eee-eeese old days." The crowd was loving it. Her voice carried well, the run was perfect. Patti LaBelle would have been proud.

She fully expected somebody to pass her a microphone so she put her foot in this song, but Ronald crossed his fingers, signaling the band to bring it to a close.

"To be with my Lord," came quicker than Camille could think. Ronald sat the choir down and quickly took his place behind the organ as Pastor Collins dove into his sermon.

What the heck just happened?

After service, Camille joined the rest of her choir in the choir room again, where they took off robes and hung them on appropriate racks—one for the closet, one for funky robes that needed a trip to the dry cleaner's.

The good thing about a large church, Camille decided, was that people weren't trying to be all up in her business. They practiced, they sang, they left.

Or so she thought.

"Camille, some of us are going out for lunch. You want to join us?" Mercedes asked.

She wanted to ask if Ronald was going, which would be the only reason to break bread with these folks. Camille wasn't in the market for friends. She was a self-proclaimed loner. Not because she couldn't get along with people, just because people couldn't get along with her.

"No, thank you. Maybe another time."

Mercedes winked. "I'm going to hold you to it."

Oh, great. Now I have choir friends. She didn't want *choir* friends. She wanted only *praise team* friends, if need be. It was important for a singer to bond with backup to some extent.

Camille breezed out of the room and into the flow of traffic exiting the building. She was almost out the doors when she felt a tap on her shoulder. Ronald needed her attention. He signaled for her to step into an empty hallway so they could allow traffic to flow.

"Camille, you have a beautiful voice."

She felt a "but" coming on.

"But without a microphone, the audience can't fully appreciate what you're singing. So, unless the Holy Spirit says otherwise, please don't distract the audience from the leader." His words were genuinely kind, but his face held a stern expression.

Flabbergasted, Camille put a hand on her heart. "What are you trying to say?"

"I already said it." He offered nothing to soften his position. Just stood there, watching her squirm under his hot glare. "And you might want to think about coming to practice in time for Bible study. It's an integral part of our ministry."

All she could do was slant her eyes and huff, "I'll see you later."

Camille stewed all the way home. *How dare he accuse me of trying to steal the show? And who is he to insinuate that I'm missing Bible study on purpose?* Maybe he was correct, but he couldn't prove any of his allegations. For all he knew, she could have been making a mad dash across town after work, making it just in time for rehearsal. Or caring for a dying animal.

Camille held a one-person conversation all the way back to her neighborhood. "He must think he's some kind of mind reader! Oooh! I can't stand him!"

She calmed herself with a Slurpee from 7-Eleven. Feeling the icy liquid slip down her throat took her back to the elementary days. She and Courtney used to get two straws and share this wild-cherry-flavored drink once a week on the route home from school.

Once, though, Camille got the notion that it didn't make sense for them to get just one. They should get two. Courtney didn't think it was a good idea. He told Camille they should ask Momma for more money instead.

"I don't think she'll give it to us," Camille had

whined. "You know she says we gotta be grateful and stuff."

"Then be grateful we get to share one every Friday, all right?" Courtney advised in all his fifth grade wisdom.

"What does it matter to 7-Eleven anyway?" Camille had practiced the fine art of rationalizing crime in her nine-year-old mind. "They already got a lot of money. Plus, one time when I dropped my Slurpee, they gave me another one free."

Determined to have her way, Camille had stood right next to Courtney and poured her own Slurpee. When Courtney went to the counter to pay for the drink in his possession, Camille slithered through the aisles and snuck out while the cashier wasn't looking.

She'd met up with him again down the street, twin slush in hand. "See, I told you I could get it."

Courtney shook his head in disapproval. "You *stole* it, Cami."

Insulted, she cried, "No, I didn't! I only *took* it! We can pay for it next Friday if we want to."

"I'm telling Momma."

Horror snatched her breath away. Why didn't he say this earlier?

Courtney took off running and Camille chased him all the way to their front porch. She didn't have the sense to ditch the evidence, so when Momma met Camille at the door, they strutted right back up to the 7-Eleven. Momma paid for the drink, made Camille apologize for stealing the Slurpee, then poured the remainder in the trash. As though wasting all that good money and wild-cherry flavoring wasn't enough, Camille got a whippin'.

On top of the whippin', a lecture. "Don't you know I pray for you every day, Camille?"

Camille nodded, but wondered what this bit of information had to do with anything. She also wondered if she was going to get hit again with the belt. Momma was sitting awfully close on that bed, still breathing hard. Camille kept her ears open for words, eyes on her mother's hands.

"I can't be everywhere, but God can. And I've asked Him to let me know ahead of time what you're up to so I can step in and stop you myself before the devil has his way with you."

As a child, Camille couldn't imagine the devil doling out anything worse than her momma's whippin'. Except maybe Bobby Junior's.

"You listening to me?"

"Yes, ma'am."

"I want you to hear me and hear me good on this one thing. You might be able to get away with a little bit here and there, but you can't fool God's people too long, least of all your momma."

Camille might have actually heeded this warning were it not for the fact that this time, Momma got all her superspiritual information from none other than Courtney, who was by no stretch of the imagination God.

Still, the part about not being able to fool God's people made Camille leery of lying to bona fide church folk. Momma made it seem like they had some kind of sixth sense that whispered secrets into their hearts. Whether it was woman's intuition or a gift from God, Camille wasn't sure. Whatever it was, all Camille knew was she could hardly get away with anything growing up—especially not where her mother was concerned. Particularly not when Courtney was around. This girl did her fair share of lying and conniving, but when her plans got really outrageous, Momma always found out one way or another.

Well, Courtney was gone from Camille's life now. And so was her mother. Without the two of them watching her like a hawk, life should have been better. She could do what she wanted to do, go where she wanted to go, without dragging along a conscience full of guilt.

Until now. She had big plans, huge plans, but Ronald was throwing obstacles in her path with his unfounded speculations.

"Fine," Camille announced to her empty living area as she entered the apartment. "If he wants me to be on time, I'll be on time." She resolved to play along with Ronald until she got what she wanted out of him.

She cooled off enough to watch a *My Strange Addiction* marathon. *These people are plain old crazy.* She reveled in the fact that she wasn't nearly as bad off as the man who was addicted to licking the backs of gummy bears and sticking them on walls.

Buzz. Buzz. Her cell phone vibrated. "Hi, Daddy."

"Hey. Tell me somethin' good."

"Ummm . . . it's the weekend."

He hinted, "I know somethin' *real* good."

"What?"

"Courtney's wife is pregnant. With twins."

"That's great for them," Camille dampened the news. What good were twins she'd never get to see?

"Look here, this is special. We haven't had twins in the family since, shoot, I don't know when."

Since Lenny? "I'm really happy for them. I hope the babies are healthy."

"Nicest thing you've said about your brother in years."

"I'm not heartless."

"When you and Courtney gonna stop this stupidness? It ain't about y'all anymore. His kids deserve to know their only aunt. You know his wife ain't got no sisters or brothers," Bobby Junior fussed.

"It takes two to get along, Daddy."

"I know that," he harped. "Just so happen *you* the one need to do the most apologizin', if you ask me. And both of you need to stop being so stubborn."

"It was business," Camille attempted to re-explain to her father.

"It was *family* before it was business."

No use in having this argument again. Bobby Junior would always be on Courtney's side. "Can we change the subject, please?"

"How's your Lexus?"

"Fine."

"Time for registration?"

She considered for a second. "Yeah. Actually, it is."

"I'll come by tomorrow and get it done."

"How much will it cost?"

He moaned, "Mmm. You know they go up every year. Probably about sixty, maybe eighty or a hundred dollars."

A hundred dollars my foot. "I'll give you sixty, Daddy, and that's being generous because I'm sure it doesn't even cost that much."

"What about my gas and time and energy?"

"Daddy, this is the only thing you do for me all year."

He crossed her, "I changed your oil twice last year."

She relented. "Yes, you did. At my expense, and then some. But I don't have any extra money to give you for a service most fathers perform for their unmarried daughters out of the kindness of their hearts."

He sighed. "I'll be by tomorrow 'round six."

CHAPTER 14

Fluffy took more turns for the worse than a teenager in driver's ed. Camille kept Sheryl updated on the cat's condition while requesting flex time in the same breath. The charade prompted Camille to download pictures of a brown spotted tabby from the Internet and transfer them to her phone, providing further proof that Fluffy existed.

The charade was going fine and dandy until one of the prerehearsal Bible studies touched on deceitfulness. Ronald recited Luke 16:10, "Whoever can be trusted with very little can also be trusted with much, and whoever is dishonest with very little will also be dishonest with much."

Camille had heard that verse plenty of times in Sunday school. Made perfect sense to her. Dishonesty is bad; honesty is good. *What else is new? Everybody tells a lie every now and then.* She thought about the verse that said whoever said they hadn't sinned was lying. The context escaped her, but just thinking about the fact that she wasn't alone in her little white lies provided some comfort. *We're only human.*

But then Mercedes added a comment to the discussion. "I think the thing we don't understand about lying is that it proves our character before God. I mean, I might lie to my father about something because I don't want to get into a long, drawn-out discussion. But the consequence of that lie might show up on my job when my boss looks over me for a promotion. Not because *my boss* knows about the lie I told my father, but because *God* knows I'm not ready for greater responsibility on my job. He's not going to set me up to fail. He'll allow the promotion only when my character can handle it, not one day too soon."

"So true," Ronald agreed.

One of the tenors piped up, "That's deep, Mercedes."

Camille's thought exactly. She kept her mouth shut, though, for fear of exposing herself. Why hadn't anyone told her this before? She knew that when you cheated on someone in a relationship, it was likely the next man would cheat on you. She'd also seen some really mean people get what they had coming to them by way of freak accidents or extended prison sentences. That was karma. But Mercedes and Ronald were talking about karma on steroids—karma that jumped categories.

Wait a minute. Did the Bible really say that? And even if the Bible said so, was it really *true* even now? Sounded like one of those things her momma warned her about that turned out to be just one of those things parents told kids to keep them out of trouble. Right up there with sex, which, in Camille's experience, seemed like a good thing. With the right person.

By the end of Bible study, Camille had decided she

should at least let Fluffy die so she could end that lie
and maybe buy herself some good luck in her career.
Besides, seeing Sheryl's face go into contortions over
an imaginary cat was starting to get on Camille's nerves.
And researching feline dialysis to come up with new
twists on Fluffy's condition took more energy at the
Medgar Evers center than making the effort to get to
work within a decent time window.

Yep. Fluffy has to die.

Ronald prayed and transitioned to practice mode
seamlessly by rendering musical praise. Camille joined
with the rest of the choir, secretly thanking God that
she could stop this ongoing fiction at her job.

After rehearsal, Mercedes approached Camille again
in the parking lot. "Don't forget about our dinner rain
check."

"Oh," Camille lowered her voice, trying to think of a
reason to postpone further.

Mercedes added, "Another thing. I don't know if
you'd be interested in this or not, but the youth ministry
choir is having their retreat this weekend. They need
more female chaperones. I thought about you, since
most of the young ladies in the Youth Warrior choir
will be going. They usually stay in the same cabin.
You've got some experience singing outside of church.
I think you'd really be able to minister to them about
the music industry. Tell them how to break in, what to
watch out for, you know?"

Flattered, Camille agreed before she realized what
she'd signed up for. A weekend with teenage girls. Hor-
monal, bad-attitude mini-divas. In a cabin, too. *What
have I gotten myself into?*

* * *

She figured the best thing about the trip would be the free meals. After having paid the first installment for her traffic ticket, Camille would take all the handouts she could get.

The bus ride from Dallas to Mount Walloosha Encampment on the outskirts of Oklahoma City took four hours. Though they left the church Thursday morning before the sun rose, the kids talked and laughed the whole way.

Camille sat next to Mercedes, the only person she knew. Mercedes had a tendency to be quite chatty, so Camille packed an MP3 player for the trip. Nothing against the girl. Camille wanted to keep her distance.

That distance, however, faded fast Thursday night after Camille and Mercedes's "team" got their cabin assignment.

"We're a team?" Camille asked.

"Yeah, girl. We'll play games tonight." Mercedes raised an eyebrow. "We're going to wipe the floor with these other teams."

The idea of competition sent a pleasurable spark through Camille. She and Mercedes had something in common after all.

Mercedes moved her backpack to her left side, leaving her right hand to open the cabin door. Six giddy girls trailed them up the winding path of concrete cut through two-foot-tall leafy wilderness. As soon as Mercedes unlocked the door to their weekend living quarters, the teens nearly knocked Camille over as they sped into the main room to claim their beds.

"I got this one!"

"I'm sleeping here!"

Camille sighed. "Okay."

"Oh, we're sorry, miss," one of the girls apologized for their rudeness.

One look around the room raised the question of why anyone would be in a rush to stake a spot anywhere. The main area consisted of hard, gray floors and exactly eight beds. Four on either side of the room with an aisle down the middle. A window over each bed and a back window containing a single air-conditioning unit. That was it. No TV, no mirrors, no bathroom. Just a simple twenty-foot by thirty-foot rectangle.

The last two beds, nearest the entrance, obviously belonged to Camille and Mercedes at this point. *Great. Sacrifice the adults to the bears and coyotes.*

Mercedes dropped her backpack on her bed and promptly called a meeting of the minds. "Okay, everyone. You have three minutes to send your parents a text or call them and let them know you made it safely. After that, I'm collecting all electronic devices. Cell phones, MP3 players, tablets, video games. Anything with an on-off switch.

"Your three minutes starts now."

A frenzy of texting and talking transpired, then Mercedes made good on her promise. "When we leave for lunch, I'll take these devices to the front office for safe-keeping.

"Now, let's make sure we all know each other."

The girls obediently sat on their beds and gave Mercedes their full attention.

"I know you all know me, and you know each other, right?"

"Yes." They all smiled.

Mercedes continued, "Well, this is Camille. She's new at our church."

"Hi, Miss Camille," from them all.

Camille waved slightly.

Mercedes directed the girls, "Go ahead and introduce yourselves."

The tallest one went first. She was model thin with long, straight, black hair and a round face that hinted at an Asian heritage. "My name is Miyoshaki Carter. Everybody calls me Shaki."

"I'm Sierra. Proud, graduating senior at the great James Madison High School," she added with a flick of her sewn-in curly brown locks. Obviously the hairdresser of the group.

"Anyway," from the third girl. Though her innocent face portrayed a shy, reserved church girl, her feisty wardrobe—grungy shorts, a ripped white T-shirt with a hot pink tank top underneath, and a glitzy mountain of necklaces—said otherwise. Her hair, a bushy, unpermed mass of waves, completed her flair. "My name is Brittney and I attend the Arts Magnet High School, where our concert choir has won state for the last three years in a row, thank you very much."

Already, Camille liked this Brittney's style. Smart, sassy, self-defined.

Camille suddenly realized two of the girls were twins. Not identical, but definitely from the same womb. One spoke for both of them. "I'm Mackenzie, this is my sister Michaela. We're freshmen at Grace Chapel Academy."

That was news to Camille. She didn't even know her church had a school.

"Ooh," Sierra inquired, "I heard it's boring. Is it?"

Michaela nodded while Mackenzie shook her head, which brought about laughs.

"Which one is it?" Shaki asked.

Michaela spoke up. "I think it's boring. We have no

sports, no extracurricular organizations. They keep the boys away from the girls mostly. And sometimes I feel like I'm going to church instead of school."

"But I like it because there's not a whole lot of he-said, she-said," Mackenzie explained. "It's a small school. The teachers are kind of strict, too. And if you have a problem with someone, the first thing we have to do is pray."

"Nuh-uh," Sierra contended, "I can't go to school there. I gotta be somewhere where I can bust somebody in the face if I need to."

"And I gotsta have some boys in class," Shaki insisted.

The last teen stood and announced, "I'm Chrisandrea. Before you ask, yes, my daddy's name is Chris and my momma's name is Andrea. I'm a senior at Conrad High School, finishing a year early, attending Texas Christian University in the fall on a full *academic* scholarship." She snapped her fingers and took a bow.

Mercedes and Camille started the congratulatory applause for Chrisandrea, and the other girls followed suit.

"That's exciting," Mercedes said. "College life is amazing. And we're getting a taste of it this weekend."

"It's nice to meet you all," Camille said.

"Tell us something about you," Brittney probed.

"Well." Camille hesitated. "I'm . . . glad to be here?"

Brittney smiled. "No. Important stuff. You married?"

These girls don't waste any time. "No."

"You got a boyfriend?" Shaki asked.

"No."

"Why not? You're pretty," from Chrisandrea.

"Thank you. I've been too busy, I guess," Camille replied.

"You got any kids?" Michaela wanted to know.

"No."

"I'm gonna be like you when I get older," Sierra said. "No kids, no husband, just me and my job and my friends."

"Same here," Brittney echoed. "I'm going to live my life *before* I get married."

"Where do you work?" Mackenzie asked.

"A company called Aquapoint Systems."

Michaela asked, "You go to clubs?"

Camille glanced at Mercedes for guidance. Mercedes shrugged like "I can't answer for you."

"I have," Camille admitted.

"For real? I can't wait to get out of my parents' house and go to college so I can do what I want to do. I'm going to go clubbin' every night," Sierra declared, eyes glowing with veneration.

Camille backpedaled, "I don't go out a lot, though. Clubbing gets old after a while. Keep seeing the same tired people over and over again, just like school."

The girls moaned sadly, as though Camille had let the air out of their pre-clubbing bubble.

Mercedes checked her watch. "We've got about thirty minutes until lunch. Let's make our beds, freshen up."

As they took a moment to get settled in, Camille suddenly felt the weight of the girls' admiration on her shoulders. Clearly, they looked up to her. She understood exactly where they were coming from, too. Having grown up in a church full of holy women who acted like they'd never done anything wrong always made youth events boring and unrealistic. All they ever said was "don't do this," "don't go there," and "stay away from these kinds of people." Easy for them—they dressed so ugly no one would ever invite them anywhere to do anything half fun anyway. Really, how could they talk about how to say no to a boy's advances when they looked like they'd never been *asked* in the first place?

This was her chance to keep it real, to let the girls know that there was life outside of church. Yet, their innocence would require a bit of censorship. The twins were freshmen. Even the older girls had been sheltered enough to believe that clubs were the epitome of adult freedom.

Camille smoothed the blanket in place. She lifted her gym bag up onto the foot of her bed so that she could retrieve a face towel. As she raised the pink handles, a spider stealthily descended from her bag.

"Woop!" Camille scrambled across the room and hopped on Mercedes's bed. The entire cabin erupted in shrieks as the girls leapt on Mercedes's bed as well, huddled together in fear.

"What?" Mercedes, the only one still on the floor, asked.

"Girl, there was a spider on my bag! It crawled under my bed."

Mercedes took off her flip-flop, hoisted up the edge of Camille's comforter, and took a few quick swats. "Dead." She slid the shoe back onto her foot. "Let's go eat."

"Uh-uh," Shaki disagreed. "We will not have bugs in our cabin. Anybody got an extra towel or something they know they're probably not gonna wear?"

Brittney volunteered, "My dad packed an extra blanket for me."

"Okay, we need that blanket so we can stuff it under the door, 'cause if a spider crawls up in my bed tonight, I will *walk* back to Dallas."

Camille couldn't have said it better herself. Despite Mercedes's teasing, the girls managed to secure the blanket under the door from the outside of the cabin when they left for lunch. Just seeing that little inch of fabric plugging up the insect thoroughfare brought some relief.

The camp cafeteria reminded Camille of the original *Parent Trap* movie. Log walls, long tables, lots of open space. She could only hope that none of the kids got the bright idea to have a food fight.

After selecting a cheeseburger and fries in the line, Camille and Mercedes sat at the corner end of a table already filled with loud-talking, boisterous adolescents. They'd lost track of their cabinmates altogether in this mixture of hormones and minimally supervised youth interaction. As much as she still wondered how she'd ended up in this position, Camille had to admit to herself that the sheer electricity of being around adolescents was contagious. Their lives, so full of possibility and potential, brought back fond memories.

When she was their age, she'd experienced one of the worst things that could happen: losing a parent. Only a few years later, she was sitting on top of the world. As she looked around the dining hall now, Camille wondered if the youngsters in the room realized how critical these next few years could be. People make some serious fork-in-the-road decisions that set them on vastly different courses for the rest of their lives at their age. College, marriage, career field. Some of them would even have children before they knew it. Didn't seem fair to push them so quickly so soon, knowing how little information they had to go on.

"What you thinking about?" Mercedes queried loud enough to be heard over the bustle of kids.

Camille swallowed a fry. "Life. I mean, *their* lives. They're so young. Babies."

"I know, right?"

"They have so many options open to them, and they don't even know it." Camille shook her head, looking around the room. Shaki approached by one boy after another, Michaela and Mackenzie laughing with their mouths full. Brittney and Sierra sitting listening to two boys in a rap duel, and Chrisandrea sneaking to send a forbidden text message.

"I think they know they have a lot of opportunities open to them," Mercedes disagreed. "The youth program keeps them pretty active and aware of scholarships, auditions, cultural events."

"Yeah, but . . ." Camille daydreamed aloud, "it just seems like when you're a teenager, you have all this wild optimism. This sense that anything could happen. Hope, you know."

Mercedes tilted her head down as she eyed Camille. "Okay, you're acting like you're ninety years old. You've probably got many more years ahead of you, too."

"Well, I made a lot of mistakes in the past. Mistakes that cost me everything."

"Whatever you did, I'm sure it didn't cost you *everything*. You're still here," Mercedes said.

Spoken like a true middle-class American citizen. Most of them had never walked into a Beverly Hills store and bought something without even looking at the price tag. Never heard a knock in their engine and thought, "Let me go straight to the Lexus dealership," without first thinking about how much money they had in the checking account. Being rich wasn't just about money, it was about living a worry-free lifestyle. No matter what happened, she had it covered. No stress, no second-guessing, no rigging until the next paycheck. Completely liberating.

Only a small percentage of people actually got to a position where what they had to do and what they wanted to do were the same thing, day in and day out. Completely purposeful.

Maybe if she'd never experienced these things, Camille could sit back and live an at-least-I'm-here type existence. But not now. She had to get back on top.

And maybe, while she was here at the camp, she could say something to keep these girls from going up and down that same roller coaster. They needed to know how to get to the top and *stay* there forever, because the ride back down was enough to make anyone throw up.

CHAPTER 15

After lunch, the camp directors gave each cabin a letter. Camille's cabin was Team F, which they unanimously decided stood for "Fly Girls." Thirty minutes later, the Fly team faced off with the Beautifuls in the first round of a volleyball tournament. Turned out, Shaki was nearly an all-American player. Chrisandrea set Shaki up for hit after hit, leading the Fly Girls to hands-down victory over every team except the Divas, who gave them a run for their money. The Divas had a big, strong girl on their team who almost broke Michaela's glasses with a spike so fast Camille heard the wind part. That was okay, though. Brittney came through with five unpredictable serves that no one on their team could return.

The Fly Girls sang "We Are the Champions" as they escorted their small trophy back to the cabin. The girls played a few rounds of Uno and Speed, then later changed into bathing suits and met up with about half of their youth group at the pool. Camille and Mercedes dipped up to their waists to cool off, then covered up in sarongs and joined the other adult chaperones observing from surrounding shaded tables.

Some of the men had gotten caught up in a spirited game of dominoes, talking trash and scoring on each other.

"You'd think they've got money on these games, as serious as they are," Camille commented under her breath.

Mercedes replied, "Knowing Brother Gibbles, they might."

Both women giggled at the thought. Mercedes took Camille up on an offer to buy sodas from the vending machine near the restrooms. Then they sipped and watched the kids frolic in the water, laughing at Sierra, who nearly had a heart attack every time someone came close to getting water on her hair.

Sierra screamed, "Don't make me set it off in here!"

"Why are you in the pool if you don't want to get wet?" Mercedes called her out.

"It don't matter! They see me standing over here!"

Thankfully, the last meal neared before Sierra's do melted. Camp goers showered in the unattached, communal restroom and met up again in the cafeteria for hot dogs and chips.

Truth be told: Camille was pooped. All she wanted to see was her bed when she got back to the cabin, but Mercedes pulled out a folder containing an outline for Bible study.

Bible study? Now?

The girls pushed three other beds up to Mercedes's bed and laid across the large platform, Bibles in hand.

Camille decided she'd better sit upright against the wall if she planned on setting a good example, otherwise, she'd be asleep in no time.

Mercedes led a brief prayer, then began, "Tonight, we're focusing on loyalty."

Instantly, Camille's stomach turned. *Why is everyone harping on stuff like loyalty, integrity, and honesty?* Weren't there other sins, too? Murder. Adultery.

"Our scripture for tonight is Proverbs eleven and three. Shaki, could you please read the verse out loud?"

Shaki flipped through her book, then read, "The integrity of the upright guides them, but the unfaithful are destroyed by their duplicity."

"Thank you. The first thing I want everyone to do is close your eyes and think about a time when someone betrayed you."

That was easy for Camille. Eighth grade. Her best friend, Leah, walked to Tyson Park with Bennie Wright, then lied to Camille about the whole thing. Were it not for Keisha Armstrong, Leah might have gotten away with it. Keisha, however, stayed right across the street from the park. She put out the equivalent to a current-day Emergency Alert that Bennie pushed Leah on the swings, and they disappeared in the big, plastic pipe for anywhere from five to fifteen minutes, depending on whoever retold the story.

Although Bennie didn't know Camille existed, Leah knew that Camille had a huge crush on Bennie.

Camille had cornered Leah in the restroom, a crowd of girls piling in to witness the action. "But you knew I liked him!"

"You never said you liked him," Leah got technical.

"I wrote his name three hundred and twelve times

on my math binder! Haven't you seen this?" Camille
held up the binder. Who could argue against this evidence?

Leah relented, "Okay, but he doesn't like *you*!"

"Oooh," from the instigators.

"Even if he doesn't like me, you're my friend.
You're not supposed to go after him if I like him. Those
are the rules, Leah!"

Several of the girls nodded as the mob continued
to grow. "I'd kick her butt if I was you."

"Uh-uh," someone disagreed. "If he don't like her,
he don't like her. Why shouldn't Leah be happy with
him instead?"

"Shut up. Wasn't nobody even talking to you."

"Come make me shut up."

The crowd shifted its attention. Next thing Camille
knew, the two onlookers were going at it, pulling hair,
swinging wildly. Teachers busted up in the bathroom,
kicked everyone out, and lead the secondary attraction
to the office.

Camille and Leah never spoke again. They rolled
plenty of eyes, spread plenty of rumors about each
other, but that was all. Two years of friendship flushed
down the drain.

For a Bible study, this prompt had certainly gener-
ated some deep thought. Camille could definitely re-
late.

"Okay," Mercedes called them back to the present.
"I'm going to start by sharing my memory. Then, if anyone else would like to share, you're welcome to do so.

"I was betrayed once by my aunt. She was selling
her car for fifteen hundred dollars. I gave her seven
hundred and fifty dollars and told her I would give her
the other half when I got paid at the end of the month.

She agreed, said she would hold the car for me. Well, when I went back with the rest of the money to get the car, she didn't have the car anymore. She said she had sold it to someone else who had all the money up-front."

"That's wrong," Mackenzie remarked.

"The worst part," Mercedes said, "was when she didn't want to give me back the money I *did* give her."

Hostile comments flew across the room.

"Aw, naw. Me and old girl woulda had a serious problem," Shaki joked.

"For real," Chrisandrea concurred. "How she just gon' keep your money?"

"She said she didn't have it anymore. She'd already spent it." Mercedes shrugged.

Camille wasn't sure if it was in line with the goal of Bible study to ask, but she had to know. "So, what did you do?"

"Nothing, really. I mean, I told my mother. My mother told my grandmother. My grandmother paid me back the seven hundred fifty dollars on my aunt's behalf. She said something like my aunt was going through a really rough time or whatever. My grandmother told me to think of it as a lesson not to mix business and family anymore."

"Mmm-mmm," Sierra moaned. "I would have took that seven hundred dollars out of her behind."

Mercedes asked, "Does anyone else have an instance of betrayal to share with the group?"

"I do," Brittney offered. "When my mom died two years ago, everybody came to her funeral and said all these wonderful things about her. But after we buried her, it seemed like people just left me and my dad alone. All those people who said they would check on me and bring meals by sometimes never did what they said they would do. I felt betrayed. Sometimes I still do because people carry on like nothing happened."

"I know exactly how you feel," Camille spoke from the heart. "My mother died when I was seventeen. The week after she passed, I went back to school, went back to church. People just didn't bring up her name anymore."

Mackenzie said, "Maybe they didn't say anything because they didn't want to remind you that your mom was dead."

Camille chuckled. "It's not like I could forget."

"I know, right?" Brittney understood completely. She raised up and sat next to Camille.

"So, how did you get past that sense of betrayal?" Mercedes asked her fellow leader.

"For one thing, I learned how to cook." Camille smiled at Brittney. "Secondly, I got busy doing other things with my life. Concentrated on school, got a boyfriend—which is not the answer to life's problems, mind you. Basically, what I'm saying is that I had to move on. My mother wouldn't have wanted me to stop living because she died. I figured if my own mother wanted me to move on, then I couldn't get mad at the people around me for doing the same."

"That's right," Shaki agreed. "My momma tells me that all the time. If something happens to her, she wants me to keep going."

Mercedes prodded Camille. "What part did your relationship with Christ play in helping you get past the betrayal?"

Camille cocked her head to the left. She felt the girls staring at her, felt Mercedes hoping the "right" answer would come out of Camille's mouth, but since she always told the truth where her mother was concerned, there was no way around her real answer. "Honestly, I can't say I prayed or anything. I was too numb to pray at the time."

Mercedes nodded. "Sounds like one of those times when Christ just took over."

"Yeah," Chrisandrea illustrated, "like that footprints poem. When you look back over, like, the sands of your life and see only one set of footprints, that's not when God left you. That's when God was carrying you through the tough times because you were too weak to walk."

An almost tangible tugging in Camille's chest caught her off guard. Pulled and pulled until she thought her heart might bust wide open. *Why am I acting like this?* She'd read the footprints poem a long time ago. Never thought it meant anything. *But is it true? Can't be true.* It was only literature.

The study continued with a visit to God's promise in Hebrews 13:5 that He would never leave nor forsake His people. "Often, even when we are not loyal to God, He is loyal to us. The Bible says He is not a man that He should lie. If God says He's going to be there, He'll be there."

"That's money in the bank, baby," Sierra preached.

"Exactly," Mercedes concurred. "You can count on Him being there for you no matter what. I know you've heard this all your life, but one day you're going to need help like you've never needed it before. Whether it's comfort, guidance, mercy, love, or just a reason to keep on living. I want you ladies to know where to turn. Amen?"

Automatically, Camille replied, "Amen," with the group. Mercedes asked Mackenzie to end with a prayer.

Again, Camille prayed on autopilot. She hadn't heard anything else since Chrisandrea mentioned the footprints. And though her mind scrambled for ways to quiet the inner Witness, her heart couldn't deny the ringing inside. If God had been there for her like Chrisandrea said, Camille owed Him everything. Everything.

CHAPTER 16

Friday morning looked more like a Friday evening. Cloudy skies and damp air promised a hefty downpour. The campers made it through breakfast unscathed. The midmorning worship service was held inside the gym, so there was no threat of problems there. After lunch, however, the rainstorm put a stop to the day's remaining outdoor events.

Camp leaders tried their best to supplement activities, to no avail. Teams spent the afternoon in their cabins, bummed by the ongoing rain.

"Can we get our MP3 players back?" Shaki whined.

"Or at least tablets," seconded Michaela.

Mercedes stomped. "No, no, no! Don't you people know how to have fun without gadgets or some kind of screen in your face?"

"Uh, no," Brittney said, bearing a benign smile.

Mercedes shook her head. "Y'all ever sit around telling stories?"

Group head-shake no.

"Ever played charades?"

Unanimous verbal no.

Mercedes put a hand on her hip and sighed. "It's a shame what Bill Gates has done to you people."

Camille tried, "How about singing?"

Sierra consented, "Now *that* we can do, seeing as this *is* the girls' choir cabin."

The girls piled onto their leaders' beds. Brittney stole the spot next to Camille.

"What are we gonna sing?" Chrisandrea asked.

Camille laughed. "I don't know. What do y'all wanna sing?"

"Let's do some old-school songs," Mercedes suggested. "Y'all know 'Respect'?"

"Yeah!" they squealed.

Sierra snatched a brush from her backpack to serve as a microphone, and the show was on. Shaki took over Aretha Franklin's role for the first song. Michaela mimicked Diana Ross for a simplified version of the Supremes's "Stop! In the Name of Love." Michaela knew only the chorus, so she had to make up the other words, which caused a wave of laughter to flow around the room.

Their giggling was interrupted by a knock at the door and hysterical demands. "Fly girls! Let us in! It's raining!"

Quickly, Mercedes opened the door and allowed the Beautifuls into the cabin. Their leaders, a short woman with a natural afro that had obviously drawn up with the air's moisture, and a girl barely old enough to be out of the youth group, hugged Mercedes, then Camille.

"Ooh! We were bored to death. We heard y'all singing

and decided to come over, if that's all right with y'all," the woman said, shaking out their umbrellas and setting them on the porch.

"Sure. Come on in," Mercedes welcomed. "Brittney is about to sing us some Stevie Wonder."

The Beautifuls climbed on the empty beds and clapped to get the ball rolling.

Brittney, holding the makeshift microphone, told her audience, "Bear with us. We don't actually know all the words. Y'all got that?"

The small crowd roared. "Go 'head!" "Don't let nobody turn you 'round!" "Swing low, sweet chariot!"

"What in the world?" Mercedes bellowed. She rolled her eyes at Camille. "These girls are too loony."

Brittney and her backup had to compose themselves three times before singing. Despite not knowing the words, she knew the tune. "Something, something, something stayed too long. And something, something, love is gone." Shaki and Sierra knew exactly when to come in. "Here I am. Signed, sealed, delivered, I'm yours."

Impressed that they even knew this song, Camille stood and got the crowd dancing. She and Mercedes led the bump. Next, one of the Beautifuls' leaders broke out with the robot dance, prompting a soul train line. The girls imitated moves from previous generations. The running man, the cabbage patch, the snake, the mashed potato, and stuff no one had even seen or heard of on the planet.

Camille couldn't remember laughing so hard in all her life. Stomach-cramping, tear-jerking amusement.

"Hey! Let's have a singing contest!" one of the Beautifuls exclaimed.

Mercedes chided, "It wouldn't be fair. I mean, this *is* half the youth choir."

"Just 'cause I ain't in the choir don't mean I can't sing," their older leader proclaimed. "I'm down."

The Beautifuls jeered, "Ooh, she told you!" "Fly Girls might not be fly enough!"

"Miss Mercedes and Miss Camille, don't let them roll up in our cabin and try to play us!" Sierra hawked, complete with gangster-style arm movements. "Y'all gotta represent!"

"All right. All right." Mercedes bobbed her head confidently. She grabbed Camille's arm and led her to the back corner of the room.

"What you wanna sing?" she whispered.

Camille's eyes widened. "I don't know. Some kind of duet?"

"Let's bust out with some Michael Jackson," Mercedes suggested.

"*Old* Michael Jackson," Camille said. "'Who's Loving You'?"

"Yes! En Vogue style. You got the lead, Camille?"

She ain't said nothing but a word.

Meanwhile, Shaki and Sierra came up with ground rules. The leaders had exactly one minute to sing a portion of a song, to be timed by Mackenzie's watch. The song also had to be old school. Nothing recorded in this century. These girls had obviously been watching too much *American Idol*.

The Beautifuls cheered for their representatives. The one who claimed she could sing had a few tricks up her sleeves for "Shop Around." Too bad they didn't make it to the chorus in a minute's time. A huge argument broke out about whether or not they should be disqualified since only one member sang.

"Go ahead and let them stay qualified. That way we can beat them fair and square," Mercedes teased.

The Beautifuls booed Mercedes, of course, but that was all fine and dandy. Camille had something for them.

"Now, we're about to sing a song that you all probably think is sung by Mariah Carey. But, in my opinion, the best version of it was recorded by a group called En Vogue in the nineties. Even before that, Michael Jackson and The Jackson Five sang this song," Camille lectured.

An opposing cabin member yelled out, "Sing the song already!"

This was, of course, right up Camille's alley, who busted out, "Whe-eee-eeen I."

Mercedes followed, "When I."

"Had you."

"Had you."

"I treated you ba-aaa-aaa-aaa-aad and wrong, oh my dear."

Simultaneously, the Fly Girls hopped off their beds, cheering and shouting, giving each other high fives. "Snap!" "Miss Camille can sang!" The Beautifuls sat in their pool of defeat, spellbound by Camille's voice, knowing they didn't have a snowball's chance in hell.

When Camille killed the highest note, even the Beautifuls came undone. "That don't make no sense!" "Aw, man! I wish I had my phone!"

Camille and Mercedes ended the introduction to their song in perfect harmony as Mackenzie called, "Time!"

No need for a vote. The Fly Girls' team declared triumph and broke out with a silly impromptu chant: "Fly

Girls in tha house, don't need no swatter. Fly Girls in tha house, go get me some water." Sierra rubbed salt in the wound by hoisting the volleyball trophy, pumping it in the air with each beat.

One by one, the Beautifuls stood. "We're outta here," one of their team yelled over the chanting.

Brittney waved at them.

"We'll see y'all on the basketball court tomorrow," another one said.

The Fly Girls continued their chant while Mercedes and Camille hugged their fellow chaperones and sent them on their way.

"You have a beautiful, powerful voice," the older one complimented Camille. "Too bad you're on the Fly Girls' team."

Camille laughed and thanked her for the kind words.

With the Beautifuls out of hearing distance, team Fly Girls collapsed on their beds in victory.

"Wow! You sing better than Beyoncé and Fantasia put together," Brittney said.

"For real!"

"How come you don't lead every singsong the choir sings?" Sierra asked.

"No offense, Miss Mercedes, but Miss Camille is, like the best singer I have ever heard in person. Ever."

Mercedes sucked in her chin. "None taken. They're right. Camille. God has blessed you with an extraordinary voice."

"You ever thought about being, like, a *real* singer?" Shaki asked.

Camille smirked shyly. "I used to be one, actually."

Mercedes jumped in. "You guys are spoiling the surprise. I specifically asked Camille to be in our cabin because I know you all love to sing, and she has experience in the music business. Hopefully, sometime this weekend, we'll be able to pick her brain."

Sierra jumped the gun. "Ooh, what kind of music did you sing?"

"R and B."

Michaela pressed, "By yourself or with a group?"

"There were four of us. We were called the Sweet Treats."

Face in a scowl, Chrisandrea asked, "Who picked *that* name?"

"My brother made up the name, and it was wonderful, if I don't say so myself," Camille snapped.

Sierra cut to the chase. "Are you rich?"

Shaki smacked Sierra on the knee. "You don't ask people stuff like that."

"I just want to know. Maybe she can hook me up with a new ride," Sierra teased.

Camille confessed, "I was rich at one point. But I was a little hardheaded." She sighed. "If I had listened to the people who actually cared about me, I'd be a lot better off right now."

"You sound just like my daddy," Brittney testified.

"Mine, too," Michaela echoed.

Mercedes glanced at her watch. "This sounds like a very interesting story. Why don't we all go to the dining hall, eat, and then come back, listen and learn from Camille's experiences."

"Yes. I can't wait." Shaki clapped.

Quickly, they donned raincoats, grabbed umbrellas.

"Miss Camille, I'll share my umbrella with you," Brittney offered.

"Love to." Once outside, Camille locked arms with

the young girl so they could lean in closer, avoiding as many raindrops as possible.

Fried chicken with rice hit the spot any day, in Camille's book. She ate a little too much, probably, and waddled back to the cabin under Brittney's cover. Everyone decided they should wait until all showers were complete before Camille told them the story. No one wanted to miss this worldly tale.

Cleaned and full, they settled back into Bible-study formation, beds drawn together. Mercedes got the group to agree that they'd cover the prescribed scriptures in the morning, before worship, then she gave Camille the floor again.

"Like I said, we were the Sweet Treats," Camille began. She told them all about the life-changing audition with Courtney, the tours, the star-studded awards shows, the limos, the money. They all wanted to know what she'd bought with her cash. She listed the Lexus, a condo, Gucci bags, extravagant trips. "The only thing I still have is my car. Everything else is gone."

"What happened?" Shaki asked.

"Had to sell everything."

Chrisandrea dove deeper. "What about drugs? Did you ever try drugs?"

Camille nodded softly. "I did. One of the girls in my group had them. The first time she asked me if I wanted them, I said no. But then, when I saw she had a lot of energy and seemed to be doing fine, I decided to try them."

Wide-eyed, Brittney asked, "What happened?"

"I hated them!" Camille exclaimed. "They made me nervous, I couldn't sleep. It was terrible and I would not recommend them to anyone. Period."

"One time I smoked weed with my boyfriend," Shaki confided. "I felt like everything was moving in slow motion. And everything was . . . stupid. Funny-stupid. I swear, I don't know why people keep getting high. It makes you slow."

"Nuh-uh. My grandmomma said ain't nothin' wrong with smokin' weed," Sierra countered. "She's smoked weed every day of her life. She's fifty-two years old, and nothing's wrong with her."

Except she's the fifty-two-year-old grandmother of an eighteen-year-old girl. Camille kept her mouth shut.

"I heard President Obama smoked weed when he was in college," Michaela added.

"The thing is"—Mercedes steered the discussion back on track—"any mind-altering substance can be detrimental or even deadly. It's not worth the risk. Thank God your grandmother hasn't suffered, as far as you know."

"Well," Sierra acknowledged, "she does kind of act slow sometimes, but I think it's because she's old."

"Fifty-two is *not* old," Camille clarified.

Michaela grinned. "What about parties?"

"Is that all you care about?" Mackenzie accosted her sister.

"Yes!"

Camille shook her head. "There were parties, Michaela. Parties in LA, New York, Miami, Chicago, London. Mostly at clubs or someplace somebody rented out—or owned. We danced, we ate. People got drunk and threw up. People ate too much and threw up. There's a whole lotta vomiting going on amongst celebrities, believe it or not."

The girls eewed and made nasty faces.

"Any one-night stands?" Shaki asked nosily.

"Thank God, no," Camille denied. "But it's almost scary how people sleep around on the road. Some of the guys in our band had different girls every night. I wouldn't be surprised if they had all kinds of diseases and ten kids each.

"Crazy thing was, the girls they had sex with didn't really want a relationship. They just wanted to be able to say they slept with somebody famous, I guess."

"Groupies," Mackenzie snarled.

"When did it all end?" Chrisandrea wondered. "I mean, you did all that. Then what?"

"This is where things get complicated. There was this guy."

"Should have known," Shaki remarked. "There's always a man somewhere in the problem."

"He actually wasn't the problem." Camille took a cleansing breath and admitted, for the first time, "I was the problem. I shouldn't have listened to him. He said he could get us a better record deal, more money, better producers. So . . . we . . . fired my brother."

Mackenzie put a hand on her heart. "Oh my gosh! You fired Courtney!"

"Unfortunately, yes."

"But he was the one who set the whole group up!" Sierra noted.

"I know. I got greedy. We *all* got greedy."

Brittney asked, "So what happened to the other guy you hired in Courtney's place?"

Camille tsked. "He hooked us up with some other major artists, but he charged us so much, Sweet Treats ended up owing *him* when it was all done. He's the reason I had to sell almost everything I owned."

"That's messed up," Michaela whispered.

Shaki yawned. The action grew contagious and spread

around the room. Mercedes took the cue to wrap up the conversation. "So, what lessons did you learn from your experiences?"

She had to think about the question for a moment. She hadn't even told them about Darrion and Tonya. Bad enough what they already knew. "I think the biggest lesson for me was that old saying, everything that glitters isn't gold. People aren't always what they seem to be. In the entertainment business, everyone's in it for themselves."

"That's sad," Chrisandrea slurred. She laid her head on her outstretched arm. "Are you glad to be out of it now? You know, living a regular life?"

"You ask tough questions." Camille paused again.

Mackenzie yawned again. "I don't want to be around fake people. Not for all the money in the world."

"Me, either," Brittney resolved.

"What happened between you and your brother?" Mackenzie carried on despite heavy lids.

"We don't really talk anymore." An understatement.

Michaela wondered aloud, "At all?"

"Nope. He's married now. Has two kids. I haven't even seen my niece and my nephew. I think they're one and three years old. I'm not sure. I'd have to ask my dad."

"Sadder than sad," murmured Chrisandrea.

Mercedes stood and stretched. "All right, ladies. Let's get these beds back in their places."

Groggy and finally descending from their twenty-four-hour adrenaline highs, the girls helped each other arrange the room properly. Shaki double-checked the blanket under the door.

"'Night everybody," Sierra began the roll call.

"'Night," seven times over.

After they were all settled in, Chrisandrea asked, "Anybody in here got basketball skills?"

"Not me."

"Nope."

"Nuh-uh."

"The Beautifuls are going to get real ugly with us on that court tomorrow."

"I know, right?"

Even with her eyes closed, Camille knew exactly which Fly Girl was speaking. They had already etched their individual personalities into her heart. Smart-mouthed Sierra, the mini-Kyra. Mackenzie and Michaela, good twin and wild twin respectively. Shaki, the boy magnet. Chrisandrea, the thinker. And Brittney, with whom she shared a special connection because they had both lost their mothers at an early age.

Somehow, she'd landed herself in a cabin full of impressionable girls who had no idea why she was even a member of their church, that she was the epitome of the type of person they needed to avoid. A user. Someone who was only in it for herself.

They were right about Courtney. They were all too nice to voice what was written on their faces: She deserved whatever she got after ousting her brother from Sweet Treats. That fame was gone forever.

But didn't she also deserve another chance to redeem her career? Even people with bad credit got to start over after seven years.

Still, Camille couldn't help feeling like she was starting over the wrong way. Especially now that she'd given the girls the big moral talk.

I shouldn't have come to this stupid camp. She laid there for a while, listening to the girls' soft snores and crickets' mating calls.

"Camille?" Mercedes whispered.

"Yeah?"

"You all right?"

"Yeah."

"Okay. I'll be praying that God will intervene in your family. Restore the broken relationship between you and your brother."

"Thank you."

Brittney had been right about the Beautifuls. They knocked the Fly Girls out of the basketball tournament in round one, forty to twenty-two. They held their bragging rights high, teasing the Fly Girls throughout the day.

Thankfully, the sun reappeared Saturday, providing several options for entertainment . After taking a turn to lead praise and worship during the morning gathering, Camille and Mercedes hiked the campgrounds. Mercedes's fascination with nature proved too serious at one point as she guided a garden snake off the trail with a tree branch.

"That was gross," Camille stated for the record.

Mercedes said, "He was just a little guy. Needs some help learning the ropes."

The nature walk landed them back at the cabin a little before lunch. Camille could take the stench of wildlife no longer. Her skin screamed for a shower, and her hair said it was time to get back to civilization.

By Saturday night, Shaki and Chrisandrea had somehow gotten into an argument over a towel. Michaela was getting on everyone's nerves whining about the fact she would have over a thousand text messages to check. Mackenzie told her sister to shut up. Sierra had to put an end to their subsequent shouting match. Mercedes led a prayer for good attitudes the remainder of their stay.

Needless to say, the Fly Girls were the first to board the bus back to Dallas Sunday morning. Camille couldn't help but laugh at the attitudes, though. Her experience with Sweet Treats taught her all too well that God never meant for women to stay together for long periods of time. Particularly not when they had to share a bathroom.

Retreat organizers did a good job of planning their arrival to coincide with the dismissal of worship service. The youth traipsed off the bus and into their smaller chapel just in time to wait for parents, who were pouring out of the main building. Camille hugged her cabinmates, thanked Mercedes for inviting her, then flew back home for a much-needed nap.

Those girls had broken her down. In a good way.

CHAPTER 17

Camille didn't know what was worse: lying about Fluffy's ailments, or faking his death. Either way, it was time to let him go. This illustrious falsehood had worn itself out.

She rapped on Sheryl's door.

"Come in."

"Hey." Camille gave a halfhearted smile, her lips intentionally dry. "I just wanted to thank you for all your thoughts and concern. Fluffy is . . . in a better place now."

Her boss wheezed. "What? What are you saying?"

"He . . . sh . . ." Camille couldn't remember if the cat was male or female. "Fluffy died this weekend. Peacefully."

"No!" Sheryl panted, "No, no, no!"

"It's going to be okay." Camille comforted her with a hug.

Sheryl's shoulders shook with grief. "This is awful."

Camille repeated, "It'll be okay." Whose cat was this anyway?

"Look at me, crying all over you." Sheryl wiped her eyes and gazed at Camille. "Oh my gosh, look at you. You . . . you look perfectly normal. You must be in shock."

Camille shrugged. "I guess the loss isn't . . . real to me yet." *Never will be.*

"I understand. We walked around in a daze for weeks after Valectra died."

Enough already. "Thanks, again, for caring. I should be able to get to work on time now." She started toward her little cubicle.

Sheryl asked, "Where will she be buried?"

Hadn't thought of that one. "I . . . donated the body to science. Hopefully they can find a cure for other cats."

"You are sooo selfless."

The adoring look on Sheryl's face dumped a load of guilt on Camille's heart. She couldn't take it. She had to come clean. "I can't do this anymore."

"I know." Sheryl embraced her subordinate.

"No. Fluffy's not dead," Camille tried.

"Yes, she *is*. I know, it's hard to move on."

Camille broke the hug, looked her boss in the eyes. "Fluffy was never alive."

Sheryl spoke as though in a conversation with a kindergartner. "Don't say that. I mean, these last few days might have *seemed* like she didn't have much quality of life, but you mustn't focus on the bad days."

Who says "mustn't" these days?

"Why don't you go ahead and take the day off to think about all the wonderful times you had with Fluffy, okay? I'll let human resources know you're using some personal time." She wrapped her arm around Camille's shoulder and led her toward the office entrance. "Everything will be fine."

Now that she'd accidentally enacted a mini mental breakdown, there was no turning back. "Thank you, Sheryl. I'll be in bright and early tomorrow."

"We'll see you then."

The longer this lie lived, the worse it got. Now this thing had begun eating into her precious reserves. Camille had to pull her story together and get beyond Fluffy. No way could this unreal animal cost her any more anguish or guilt.

Rather than waste a day in phony mourning, Camille decided to drop by John David's office and do a little schmoozing. She didn't want him to forget her face or their agreement, albeit informal.

Timber must have recognized the face despite shorter, slicked-down hair. "Do you have an appointment?" she mocked. "Perhaps returning a visit?"

Payback has jokes. "No, I don't, but I would really appreciate the opportunity to see him."

She flipped her bangs back. "Have a seat."

Camille sat. And sat. Finally, after a forty-five-minute wait, Timber showed some mercy and paved the way to John David's office.

"The pretender is back," Timber announced.

"I was desperate, okay?" Camille retorted. *People get so sensitive about little white lies these days.*

"Thank you, Timber. Have a seat, Camille."

At least someone was calling her by name. "Don't take it personal. It's just that we prefer honesty from our potential clients."

Camille sat across from him, pleased that he acknowledged the possibility of their professional relationship. "I can't be the first person to have used dishonest means toward an end."

"No, you're not," he granted. "But the fact that you're sitting in my office despite your dishonesty doesn't sit well with Timber. I usually don't give such people the time of day, but your voice is golden. I've made an exception in your case."

Was she supposed to be flattered or insulted?

"You got a recording?" he asked before she could decide.

"Not yet. But I'm working on it. I've joined a church, I'm in the choir."

"Good." He bobbed his head. "When can I expect to have the demo?"

"Soon," she promised.

He opened his palms toward the ceiling. "So . . . why are you here?"

Because my fake cat died. Speechless, she smiled.

John David stood and escorted her to the door. "I'm leaving for LA tomorrow. I'll be back in a few weeks. I hope we'll have something to talk about then."

"Gotcha."

She left the office feeling like a complete idiot. John David wasn't interested in small talk. He was all about business. She should have known better than to waste his valuable time.

Blinking back tears, she maneuvered out of the parking lot a little more carefully this go-round and waited until she had a clear view of the road before gunning it to the recreation center for a midday workout.

Her muscles ached fiercely all through young-adult choir practice. Mercedes forked over two Advil after practice and warned, "You better take it easy. You might be a Fly Girl, but you ain't no young warrior."

Camille laughed. "How is the rest of our team anyway?"

"Fine. Asking about you," she said.

"When?"

"I don't usually hear from them until third Saturday at the Mentors and Models sessions, but Brittney sent me a text asking for your e-mail address and Shaki wanted to know if you could sing at her parents' twenty-fifth wedding anniversary party in the fall. I told them I'd talk to you tonight."

They stopped shy of the exit doors to exchange numbers so Mercedes could text the girls' contact information.

"They really enjoyed talking to you, Camille," Mercedes stressed. "They listen to me a little bit, but I've always been a goody-two-shoes, tattletale type, so I can't tell them what it's like to try this or that. When someone who's been there and done that warns them, the advice takes on whole new meaning."

This wasn't news, of course. "Glad I could help."

Mercedes followed Camille to the car. She raised her eyebrows and squinted her eyes. "You think maybe you could help more?"

"Help more how?"

"Come to Mentors and Models. Pretty please?"

"I don't know about all that." Camille unlocked the driver's side. "I'm pretty busy these days."

"It's just one day a month. Plus you'll get to see the

Fly Girls again. Don't need no swatter? Bring me some water?"

Tickled by compassion, Camille signed herself up for yet another item on her plate. This mega-church business was turning out to be darn near a full-time job. And a non-paying job at that. Still, what could it hurt to hang out with the Fly Girls every now and then? And what better role model than someone who was actually living out her dreams? *Someone like me. Kinda.*

A flip of her wall calendar ushered in a somber mood. May. Momma's birthday on the fourth. Mother's Day soon thereafter. The month's corresponding photograph, water lilies, seemed almost planted in this moment. They reminded her of Momma's favorite song. *Sweet Jesus. Lily of the valley, bright and morning star.* Almost automatically, the tune flowed from Camille's mouth and filled her bedroom with its gentle fragrance.

The melody carried her to work, where she signed in a few minutes early, then quietly logged on to her computer. Coffee drinkers hadn't quite downed enough cups for "hellos" yet, which suited Camille just fine. She didn't feel like talking to anyone. Didn't feel like being around people, for that matter.

The first year after her mother passed, Camille could hardly smile on holidays. But, as time went on, she'd managed to limit her funk to these first two weeks in May. If she could make it past the second Sunday, she could exhale and enjoy the rest of her year. She wondered if other people who'd lost loved ones had days, weeks, or months like this.

Though she had come to actually enjoy choir rehearsal, she wished she could forgo tonight's. Mercedes would probably call to check on her, though. For as much as Camille had tried to stay aloof, none of that worked with Mercedes. She was good people. Nothing to fear, nothing to lose. Someone to call on if she ever got a flat tire and couldn't get in touch with Bobby Junior.

Camille noticed fewer cars when she parked and wondered if she'd missed a memo canceling rehearsal. She checked her texts. No messages from Mercedes or Ronald. She entered the choir room cautiously, announced herself to the three people surrounding the piano. She recognized the two men from youth camp. The woman from the alto section.

"Hello! Are we having rehearsal tonight?"

Ronald peeked through the small assembly. "Hi, Camille. No choir practice. Tonight is praise-team practice."

"Oh, sorry to interrupt. I must have misread the schedule online," she said, stepping back into the corridor.

"Wait!" one of the men called to her. He held up his index finger while he addressed Ronald. Then, he faced Camille again. "Felecia usually sings with us, but she had to go out of town suddenly. We need another soprano. Would you mind?"

Would I mind? Hello, praise team! Don't walk too fast. She moseyed on up to the piano, laid her purse down on a chair, leaned her waist against the weathered baby grand like an experienced cocktail lounge main attraction. The men introduced themselves as Nathan and Faison. The woman, Evelina.

"I hear you were quite the hit at youth camp," Ronald teased with an uncharacteristic smile while stroking the ivories. Had he forgotten their last conversation?

"All the girls were talking about you," Nathan commended.

Camille bowed. "We had a fun little singing contest. A good time."

"You know the song 'What a Mighty God We Serve'?" Ronald asked. If he couldn't do anything else, he sure could play that piano. Teeth whiter than the keys.

"Which version?"

He laughed. "I couldn't even tell you. It's old school. Just follow my lead."

And follow she did. The good thing about church songs was every lyric said something about God or Jesus. Exact words were inconsequential, allowing Camille to jump right in and complement Ronald, note for note, line for line, in perfect harmony. She filled her lungs, expressed each iota of air with flawless execution. "What a Mighty God We Serve" never sounded so good this side of heaven.

Faison crossed his big arms and shook his head in awe. Evelina raised her arms as though she'd be caught up into the clouds any second now. Nathan smiled like he'd won the lottery. Twice.

"Hallelujah!" Evelina praised. "Praise be to God! That was glorious!"

Ronald tilted his head respectfully. Camille returned the gesture.

"Oooh-wee!" Faison exploded. "Ron, man, I think you've found your match!"

Awkward.

"I mean, your *singing* match," he clarified. "'Cause she can sing, and you can sing. You know what I'm saying."

"Enough said," Nathan rescued his buddy. "Camille's in for next Sunday."

She questioned, "Mother's Day?"

"Yeah," Rodney verified. "You'll be in town?"

She'd be in town. Hadn't planned on coming to church, though. All those tributes to mothers, all those poems and flowers would tear Camille up. Just looking at the program itself might do her in.

But this was her chance. Her one shot. And John David would return shortly, anticipating a recording.

"I can do it."

"Great," Ronald said.

Camille must have been visibly distracted the rest of the rehearsal because Ronald caught up with her after practice near the main exit door. "Are you all right?"

"Yes. I'm fine."

He took the liberty of walking her outside. "You seemed a little upset after we sang. We could sing something different if need be."

She declined. "It's not that. This is just a . . . really rough couple of weeks for me."

"I thought so."

Suspicion rose. "What do you mean, you thought so?"

"Well, you know, urra," he practiced his best imitation of J. J. from *Good Times*, "I've listened to you sing on that front row a time or two. And you were good." After securing a chuckle from Camille, he continued.

"But in all seriousness, tonight, you sang from another place. Whether that place was pain, compassion, gratitude, experience. Doesn't matter. When you sing from your heart and soul, people connect. That's the difference, Camille, between being talented or gifted and being anointed to minister through music."

Who would have ever put her name and the word "anointed" in the same sentence? The thought was actually kind of spooky. People in her old church who were so-called anointed always spoke in booming voices and wore clothes from the previous generation. Plus they were usually fat, and Camille certainly didn't want to go *there* to be anointed.

"I guess I'm supposed to say thank you?"

He frowned contemplatively. "No, no. Just think about it. Pray about it."

She managed to hoist a smile that would, hopefully, ease any reservations Ronald might have about letting her worship with the praise team. "I suppose I should also tell you that I might be singing from the point of exhaustion. All these rehearsals, you know?"

"Tell me about it. Hey, listen, I want to apologize if it seemed like I came down on you a little hard the other Sunday."

Camille raised one eyebrow. *Seemed like?*

"Okay, I *was* hard on you." He rubbed his head.

"Why are you apologizing now?"

"I heard you really ministered to the female youth choir members at the camp. They were blessed by your transparency. I suppose I misread you."

No, you read me right. Camille couldn't respond.

"But you have to understand," he went on to explain,

"a lot of new members come to a big church so they can be seen or heard. You'd be surprised how many people join right after they write a book or release an album because they think Pastor Collins is going to announce their signings or CD parties.

"Don't even get me started on how many of 'em join to promote their pyramid schemes. Mary Kay. Some kind of body girdle. It's shameful."

Camille puckered her lips in feigned consideration. "I understand."

"Everybody wants to be in the spotlight. The other week, I was helping a family plan their funeral, asking them if they had any special requests for the ceremony. They pulled out this list of eight people who each wanted their names printed on program to sing."

She laughed with him, genuinely now. "So what happened?"

"We cut it down to three songs on program. But during the remarks, one woman who had been uninvited to sing got up there and sang anyway!" Ronald's animated side emerged, hand motions and all. "And the worst part was, she got up there and sang 'Amazing Grace,' which somebody *on program* had just finished singing!"

She had to crack up on that one. "Did you go ahead and play?"

"Had to, for the sake of everyone in the building, because after all the manipulation, the lady could *not* sing! I drowned her voice with the organ."

Camille held herself steady by resting one hand on Ronald's arm as she bent over to laugh. "That's crazy. I didn't know there was so much drama for a minister of music."

"You wouldn't believe half the stuff I encounter on a daily basis. At *church*. But I won't go there. The people of God aren't perfect."

She had to agree. "I'm sure I would believe your stories. My mother was the church musician."

"Oh, really? What—"

"Daddy!"

"Hey, baby girl."

Daddy? Camille traced Ronald's line of sight. *Brittney?*

"Hey, Miss Camille!" She hugged her fellow Fly Girl. "This is my daddy. Ooh, Daddy. This is the lady I was telling you about, from the camp."

"Yes, I know. And you were right." Ronald faced Camille now. "She has a beautiful voice."

Oh, that he were talking about her face. Her body. Anything that might actually lead to a peek at *his* body. *Wait a minute.* This was Brittney's dad. Now that they were standing side by side, the resemblance was undeniable. Same eyebrows, same lips, only his had a slight moustache above them. Okay, so he was Brittney's *sexy* dad.

"Thank you," Camille finally remembered to respond.

"Daddy, I need ten dollars."

"For what?"

"I'm gonna buy some candy for Renatta's cheerleading fund-raiser."

He reached into his back pocket. "Do we really need any more candy at the house?"

"It's only a little bag of gummi worms, gosh."

Camille covered her lips. Watching them was like viewing a rerun of her own teen years; one hand on a hip in defiance, the other extended, begging for money.

Brittney faced Camille. "Ooh! You got any of your CDs?"

"I sure do." She led them to her car. The pop of the trunk officially opened the Sweet Treats store. However, for this customer, Camille decided to give. "Here you go. This one's on the house."

Brittney held out her hand, but her father intercepted the gift. "I'll burn the songs you can hear on a separate CD."

"Aww! Why you gotta be so strict?" Brittney crossed her arms.

Camille felt like doing the same. Been a while since she'd been so insulted. Well, no. Actually, Ronald had done a pretty good job of it when he rightfully insinuated that she was one of the shameful ones. Still. Couldn't he have had this conversation with his daughter at home?

"Bye, Miss Camille. Thanks for the CD. I'll listen to whatever my dad lets me listen to." Brittney gave a sarcastic grin. "See you later." She shuffled back into the building with a single bill in hand.

Ronald spoke again when Brittney was out of hearing distance. "No offense. It's hard enough being the single father of a teenage daughter. She hears enough suggestive material on television and at school. I censor as much as I can."

"What makes you think my music needs to be censored?" Camille rolled her neck to one side.

"I remember the Sweet Treats." He held the case in the evening's last light and read. "'Meet Me in the Hot Tub.' 'Stroke It.' 'Between My Hips.'"

When he read the titles like that, back to back,

there was a certain . . . ring to them. "So, the titles are sexy, but they're nothing compared to what the kids listen to today."

"All I'm saying is, I censor as much as parently possible."

She smacked, "She's gonna go buck wild when she gets to college."

Ronald contested, "Do you have kids?"

"No. I know girls, though. When you keep them sheltered, they don't know how to act when they leave the house."

"Says who?" he challenged.

"Says everybody who knows anything about raising kids!"

"I beg to differ," he half flirted.

Camille crossed her arms and asked, "And what experience do *you* have being the teenage daughter of the church musician?"

He matched her movements. "Try being the bishop's only son."

"Then you ought to understand better than anyone else what it's like to have this see-no-evil lifestyle shoved down your throat," she reasoned.

He paused. Gave in. "I do understand what you and probably two-thirds of the world are saying. But what I know now is that the Word is true. If you train up a child in the way she should go, when she's older, she won't depart from it. That's His promise."

Ronald's eyes darted toward the doors again. Brittney. "The Word worked for this PK. I'm glad to know it works for MKs, too."

Camille cast a questioning glance.

"Musicians' kids," he joked.

She squinted. "That is so corny."

He winked. "'Night."

"'Night."

CHAPTER 18

They say prayer changes things. Alexis knew this to be true, except she never realized it could change her mind so drastically. Make her go back on her word. Perhaps that was because she'd never promised something so sneaky before, never would again.

Her hands shook as she held the cell phone. This conference call, facilitated by Tonya, should have taken place a long time ago.

"You there?" Tonya asked.

"Yeah."

The other line rang once. Twice. "Hello."

Tonya spoke first. "Hi, Courtney, how are you?"

"Good and you?"

"Fine. Alexis is on the line, too."

"Hey, Lexi," he singsonged. "Is everything all right?"

Alexis answered for both women. "Yes and no."

"What's up?"

"We've been thinking about Camille," Tonya ventured.

Tension rose in Courtney's voice. "What about her?"

Tonya continued, "We know what happened in the past wasn't right. She led the conspiracy to fire you as our manager and we all realize that was a big mistake."

"It wasn't simply a mistake," he stated. "It was a matter of greed and betrayal."

Alexis had to acquiesce. "You're right. She was wrong. We were all wrong, to some extent. I'm pretty sure Camille realizes that now, too. I talked to her recently and . . . I think it's time to let bygones be bygones."

Nothing but silence.

"Hello?" Tonya said.

"I'm here," Courtney nipped. "If you all want to rekindle your relationships with her, knock yourselves out. I wouldn't recommend it, but I can't stop you. From what my dad says, she's still the same old Camille, only claiming to be broke now."

"She *is* broke," Alexis said. "She's trying to get Sweet Treats back together."

An all-out guffaw came from Courtney. "She's crazy."

Tonya reasoned, "I really think she's desperate."

"What am I supposed to do? Her problem, not mine."

"We were thinking maybe we could record the songs you have rights to again, release a remix version in the UK and Japan. With Camille singing her part," Tonya suggested.

"No."

"Come on. They love us overseas," Alexis tried.

"Absolutely not."

Alexis sighed. Ran her fingers through her hair in

frustration. "It's not fair, Courtney. We're all still capitalizing on the songs, but Camille's struggling. No, she didn't record those other versions with us, but she's a big part of why the Sweet Treats were even the Sweet Treats in the first place. Some might even say she was the biggest part."

He mocked, "Yeah, *some* like Camille herself. Look, I know my sister. She's always been stingy, always looked out for *numero uno*. Having more money doesn't fix character flaws. Matter of fact, I think we've all learned that money only magnifies the person you were before you got a dime."

"You're correct," Tonya argued, "but I'm having a hard time reconciling the fact that what we've done behind her back is just as conniving as what she did to you. Two wrongs don't make a right."

"I don't feel like we've done anything wrong. Before T-Money's label filed bankruptcy, I secured the rights to songs I wrote and produced. I decided to rerecord them without Camille, which was perfectly within the law."

"But was it the moral thing to do?" Tonya pressed.

"I have to give my sister some credit. One thing she taught me was not to mix business with family or feelings. This is business, not church," Courtney asserted.

Alexis tried another angle. "Have you even talked to your sister lately?"

"No need to. She's got her life, I've got mine. Never the twain shall meet again."

"Stop with the old English," Tonya commanded. "If you've got any sense at all, you'll forgive your sister for your own sake."

"*I* don't have a problem," he snapped.

"Yes, you do," Alexis agreed. "Money and singing

aside, every time we bring up Camille's name, even before today, that little vein in your forehead pops out. I'll bet it's out right now, huh?"

He paused. "And if it is?"

"You need to let it go," Alexis coaxed. "Deep down inside, you know you still love your sister—the good, the bad, and the ugly. If you didn't, you wouldn't get so angry. Yes, she hurt you, but the two of you need to come to terms with what happened. Just like you get upset every time you think about the past, I'm sure she feels ashamed and guilty. It's ridiculous for you two to keep this strife alive when it's only hurting you both."

"I'm not keeping *anything* alive. It's over, all right? I don't bother Camille, she doesn't bother me. I don't wish any harm on her. If she needs a blood transfusion, I'm down. But other than that, we don't deal with each other," Courtney defended himself. "We're not the first family members to come to that agreement, and we won't be the last. Just because you were born under the same roof doesn't automatically mean you get along.

"Furthermore, if my sister's broke, that's *her* fault. My father and I tried to get her to invest. She wouldn't listen. Now she has to suffer the consequences. You reap what you sow."

"Well, since you brought a biblical principle into this," Tonya bargained, "let's go there. We'll leave this whole Camille thing alone on one condition."

"What?"

"As far as the music is concerned, you have the rights. You can pull any four girls off the streets to sing it if you want to. No one can take that away from you unless, of course, you sell those rights. I don't agree with you, but I understand and respect your position."

"True," he stated.

"Here's my condition. If you pray about this and find that you're okay with leaving your sister out of your life and out of future music deals, we won't bring it up again."

Courtney exhaled. "Why do you have to bring God into this?"

"I'm just sayin', if this sits well in your heart and in your spirit, who are we to judge you?"

"I agree," Alexis said.

"What is this—reverse spiritual psychology?"

"It's the truth at work," Tonya clarified. "I only want you to be honest with yourself. If you pray and God gives you peace about your stance, that squiggly line won't pulse on your head every time you hear your sister's name."

Alexis could sense his defenses lowering, which, of course, lined up with their prayer that Courtney's heart be softened.

"Ever since you started singing with that Liza woman, you've always got religious words coming from your mouth. You remind me of my momma, you know that?" He laughed slightly.

"Well, I never met your mom, but from everything you and Camille said about her, she was a wonderful woman of God. So, I'll take that as a compliment," Tonya accepted.

"Good, 'cause that's how I meant it."

"We'll give you some time to think about things with your sister. Depending on the outcome of your prayer, we may or may not need to talk again about rerecording with Camille. Deal?" Alexis asked.

"Deal."

"Good talking to you, Courtney," Tonya said.

"Same here. Bye."

"Bye."

Alexis waited for Tonya to disconnect Courtney.

"Okay, it's just us." Tonya giggled. "God is so good, isn't He?"

"Yes! Did you hear how Courtney's whole attitude changed when you brought up prayer?"

Tonya marveled, "That was wonderful. Let's keep praying. God's gonna work this out for His glory."

CHAPTER 19

Eight o'clock on the money. This concept of getting to work on time was actually a good thing, from what Camille could tell so far. She could get settled in without rushing. No more sneaking through the cubicles, dodging her supervisor. No more paranoia about coworkers reporting her repeated tardiness so they could earn an employee-of-the-month parking spot. They wouldn't have anything to snitch about because she wasn't doing anything wrong.

In fact, she was doing everything right—except sleeping at night. Several times, her eyes had simply popped open, as though something or someone was telling her to wake up. If this restlessness didn't end soon, she'd have to find some kind of over-the-counter meds.

She was tied for top scheduling producer this week, along with a guy named Patrick. He was an old-timer; he had been at Aquapoint Systems since the foundation of the company. It was rumored that the only reason he never got promoted was because he didn't want more responsibility. He'd retired from a school district, and now he worked just to get out of the house, not because he needed a paycheck.

Camille could only dream of such a lifestyle. At the rate she was going, she'd never be able to retire. Not comfortably, anyway. Nothing to look forward to except a fixed income and the occasional bingo prize.

But she couldn't think about that now. She had the choirs. She kind of had John David in her corner. And she had one shot at the praise team this coming Sunday. All distractions aside. There was work to be done.

She got herself situated at the desk, and as soon as she entered the virtual system, she clapped on her headset. Every lead counted.

"Cameee-alll!"

She her heard her name sung before the dialer could put her in contact with the first programmed business owner. The voice was unmistakably Sheryl's. "Yes?"

"I've got something for you."

Seconds later, Sheryl stood directly in front of Camille, bearing a gift-wrapped box with matching lid. She began her speech, "I've noticed how down you've seemed for the past couple of days. I know how devastating it is to lose a pet. So I got you the only thing that can help you get over the loss of a furry friend."

She shoved the fairly large box toward Camille, who swung her chair around to receive this last little remnant of the Fluffy saga. Whatever the animal-shaped trinket, she'd gladly accept it and kindly discard it at some point in the near future.

Camille set the box on her desk and lifted the lid off

the package. *What the heck!* A mass of gray fur all curled up into a tiny ball. *A stuffed kitten.* Then she saw the motion. Swelling and falling, swelling and falling of this mass. Its wide eyes blinked. *Oh, snap! It's alive!* Camille jumped out of her seat, backed up against the unstable wall. One of the things she forgot in all this fiasco was the fact that she didn't like cats. Actually, couldn't stand them. "Sheryl. I don't know what to say."

Her boss flushed with pride and empathy. "I knew you'd love him. I rescued him from an animal shelter. Sure was hard not to adopt his siblings, but I didn't know if you had room for them. I forgot his paperwork at home. I'll bring it tomorrow. Anyway, look at it like this: Through Fluffy's death, he saved a life."

I don't want no stupid life-saving cat! Camille leaned toward the container, using only one outstretched arm to shut the top. "Wow. Wow. Um . . . this is such a kind gesture. I . . . can't keep him, though."

Sheryl coaxed, "Yes you can. He'll fill your empty heart before you know it."

"No, really, I can't. My . . . apartment complex has a no-pets rule."

"Oh. So you snuck Fluffy in?"

"No. It's a no *new* pet rule. Management changed in the middle of my lease. They let me keep Fluffy, but I can't get another pet."

Unfazed, Sheryl wagged an index finger and lectured, "They tried to do that to my friend, too, under these same circumstances. It's against the law. If you paid a pet deposit, you're grandfathered. They have to let you keep a pet until you leave."

"Oh." Camille slumped, tried to think of another lie. *Lies are what got me into this mess in the first place.* Maybe she could come up with something close to the truth. "I don't think I'm ready yet." As in *never* would she be ready to house a cat.

"Trust me. From one animal lover to another. You can't ever *replace* a pet, but taking in a fresh source of love is the best way to move forward. I'll leave you two alone. You might want to take an early lunch so you can take the little guy home and get him settled in."

No need to get this feline settled in. That early lunch might need to come right now. No way was Camille going to sit at her desk through midmorning with a cat in her midst. "Do you mind if I run home now?"

Sheryl shrugged. "Sure. If you take a thirty minute lunch today, that should make up for the lost time."

"You're too kind, Sheryl. Thank you." Camille grabbed Fluffy II's box and rushed to the parking lot. Halfway there, the kitten poked its little head out and meowed at Camille. She nearly dropped the container right there on the concrete.

"Get back in there."

Now that she'd forced its head back into the box, she could see the little air holes Sheryl had poked in the lid.

Meow. Meow. Meow. Sounded like a newborn-baby whining. Ridiculous.

She set the box on the passenger's seat and weighted the lid with her purse. *Meow. Meow.* Camille wondered if it had to pee or something. She couldn't let that thing roam around in her car. Scratch up her leather seats. Bite off her volume knob. *Nuh-uh.* This cat had to go.

She sat in the car thinking about how to get rid of it.

Sheryl had mentioned getting him from a shelter. She didn't say which one, though. Camille wondered whether or not they'd call Sheryl if she returned the kitten. Maybe there was some kind of rule against un-rescuing pets, or they might offer a refund Sheryl didn't even know she was entitled to. *Will this lie ever die?*

Perhaps she could go to a playground and release it near a bunch of children. Surely, they'd find him and somebody's momma would take him in. Or not. Then he'd be back at the shelter, they'd be calling Sheryl; bad news all over again.

Meow. Meow.

She could just let him go. He could be an alley cat. They lead good lives. He'd have to hustle every day, probably, but there's nothing wrong with living on the run. He'd make kitten friends. They'd show him the ropes. Better yet, he might end up finding one of those elderly animal hoarders who'd gladly accept him into their happy brood.

Camille revved up the car and drove a few blocks to the nearest rundown-looking neighborhood, where she was sure the animal would be welcome. She stopped near a house with two cats curled up on the porch. *Perfect.* Those grown-up cats could take over from here.

She parked and opened the passenger's door. Threw her purse on the floor and removed the cover again. Sheryl's unwelcomed gift stretched himself tall, raised up, and set his tiny front paws on the rim of the box. He surveyed his surroundings. Then, his little gray eyes made contact with Camille's. *Meow. Meow.*

Though Camille had never actually spoken to an animal before, this kitten had made it pretty clear to her that he was afraid, and he was depending on Camille for help.

"I can't keep you," she told him. "I don't like cats. At all. You need to find another home."

Meow.

She stepped back so he could have a view of the other cats and the entire world, for that matter. "Go be with your kind," she pleaded. *Am I actually talking to a kitten?*

He relinquished his stance and sat. Looked at Camille again as if to ask, "Are you my momma?"

Okay. Forget Plan A. He was too small and too afraid to fend for himself on the mean streets. A nice-sized rat could take him down. *Great. I've got a scaredy-cat for real.* She closed the box, plopped her purse back in place.

Plan B. The barber shop. Camille figured if barber-shop salesmen could find buyers for everything from car tires to furniture, surely they could unearth some-one in the market for a kitten.

She crossed a major thoroughfare, two sets of tracks, and rolled out on the other side of the freeway to enter her old neighborhood. There were three places where she could probably find Tyree, the same guy who'd sold her the bootleg computer. The first two shop owners said he hadn't been by yet, but they'd let him know she was looking for him.

Cool Cutz, the shop across the street from her old church, proved the lucky stop. She could see Tyree sit-ting in a chair next to two patrons who must have been waiting their turn to receive services.

Camille parked, got out of her car, and cautiously entered the small establishment, its cowbell announc-ing her arrival. The three old men cutting hair, their patrons, and the bench crew looked her up and down, as usual. *Men*.

"Tyree, can I see you for a second? I've got something in the car I need you to look at."

"All right, pretty lady," he agreed, rising from his seat. How he managed to keep his business going despite a bad leg and several teeth missing in action was beyond Camille. Tyree shuffled his old self outside. Camille led him to her car, where she promptly opened the door and revealed the prize with a flip of the lid.

"Voila!"

"No, ma'am." He poked out his bottom lip. "I don't do cats. Only dogs. Pit bulls and Rottweilers, but I don't keep 'em. I'm just the middle man."

Camille groaned. "You can't think of *anyone* who might want a cat?"

He looked at her above the rim of his glasses. "Don't too many black folks mess with cats, in my opinion. They bad luck. You gon' have a hard time givin' it away, let alone sellin' it."

Once again, Camille enclosed the kitten. *Meow*.

"Sorry about that. But let me know if you want a tablet. I got the hookup on iPads and Dells." Tyree wasted no time in pitching his featured items of the week.

Well, if he couldn't help with the cat, maybe he could be of some use in another category. She asked on a whim, "You know anybody who can clear a ticket with the city?"

"Naw, I don't break no laws."

Copying bootleg movies and CDs, fencing stolen property, but he was too good to break the law. "All right. Thanks anyway."

With the hour almost gone, Camille had no choice except to take the cat back to her apartment for the moment. She had no clue about the apartment policy on pets. A few tenants had animals for sure. Whether or not they were *supposed* to have those animals was anyone's guess.

As she entered her unit, the kitten's meows turned into yowling. She set the carton on the couch and opened it to determine this thing's problem. He rose up again, standing on his back legs. Looking at her like she could understand him. *Meow! Meow! Meow!*

Maybe he was hungry. *What do kittens eat?* She had some lunch meat in the refrigerator. Some salad mix that was about to spoil. Unfortunately, she couldn't remember ever having seen cats eat people food on television. Small kittens might not be able to absorb solid food. The last thing she needed was a sick, throwing-up scaredy-cat on her hands.

She thought about every cat she'd ever semiknown and what they might have eaten. Felix didn't eat anything. Garfield ate everything. The cat from the Cat Chow commercials, of course, ate their product, but she was not about to spend good, hard-earned money on cat food.

Meow! Meow! It cried louder.

Suddenly, a picture of a cat drinking milk from a saucer flashed in Camille's mind. She marveled at her memory, as this mental image was probably something she'd seen in one of her first grade readers.

In haste, she forgot to close the lid as she scampered toward the kitchen and prepared the serving of milk. When she returned to the box, the cat was nowhere in sight. *What!* She looked left. Right. No gray fur ball.

"Here, kitty, kitty. Here."

Meow!

The sound had come from floor level. Camille set the milk on the coffee table and peeked below her couch. Sure enough, there it was, scrunched in the tiny space underneath.

"Come out, kitty," she coaxed. "I got you some milk."

But no amount of kitty-calling seemed to do the trick. If this were a puppy, she could just reach under and pull him out. Cats, however, had scratchy claws. People with cats always sported those tiny marks on their arms, laughing about the scars like they were funny. *About as funny as letting a two-year-old slap you,* Camille always thought to herself.

She didn't play when it came to cats.

"Cat, get your butt out here," she demanded. This only caused him to retreat farther.

She took off her shoe and swiped the tip at him. Immediately, he forced himself deeper beneath the couch in fear. Only, this time, she heard a screeching yelp from the animal. He tried to move around but seemed stuck.

This is just great. She hoisted herself to a standing position and proceeded to lift the couch off the ground. To her horror, the kitten cried even louder. She set the furniture back down and examined the situation from behind. That's when the awful truth revealed itself. The cat had gotten his tail caught between metal springs on the couch's underside. Movement only made matters worse.

Why me?

It took the next ten minutes to get the cat unhooked,

get a good grip on him, put him back in the box, and give him enough hints about the nutritional value of cow's milk before he finally figured out that Camille was trying to help him for the moment. Nearly sweating from this debacle, Camille stopped to reclaim her breath while the kitten gracefully lapped from a tea saucer she'd have to trash once this crazy mini-episode of her life concluded.

CHAPTER 20

Having Cat in the apartment proved a welcomed distraction on Mother's Day morning. He gave her something to feed, something to talk to while getting ready for church. "Cat, you've been decent so far. I'm gonna find you a really good home this week, 'cause I don't like your kind."

Meow.

"Nope. I'm sorry, but you're not my type, Cat."

He didn't have a name. Didn't need one, actually, because soon and very soon, he'd be gone and someone else would give him a real handle. In the meantime, turned out Cat wasn't so bad after all. Camille had gone online and figured out how to make a litter box using newspaper so he'd have somewhere to do his business. And when Sheryl brought the paperwork, she also brought a starter kit, which, hopefully, contained enough food to hold Cat together until he got to his permanent residence. So long as she gave him food and a place to "go," Cat didn't bother her.

He wasn't as destructive as she thought he'd be. He tore paper towels to shreds when he got the chance, but that was about it. Maybe Cat was one of those calm kittens. She'd be sure to put that information in his adoption papers.

Growing up, Camille and Courtney had a dog. Butch. He was a classic German shepherd, black with brown spots. Camille remembered how he used to jump all over them when they were younger. As the years passed, he was content with a pat on the head. Finally, in his last years, he would raise only an eyebrow when they came outside to play. Butch died when Camille was in seventh grade.

Though the dog was more Courtney's than hers, she had missed Butch's presence. It seemed almost foreign to walk in the backyard and not see the big blob of fur somewhere on the landscape, even if he was only laying down.

Bobby Junior had said that God probably let Butch die to prepare them for Momma's death. That was a nice thought, but Camille realized nothing can adequately prepare someone for the loss of their mother. And nothing could permanently subdue the painful flares that burned in her chest when she sat down and thought too long about Momma.

Yes, Cat was good for something that morning.

Camille drove to church on autopilot, thinking about the song she would sing with Ronald and the rest of the praise team. She knew all the words. More importantly, where she'd throw in the runs and special notes. She'd been practicing since the impromptu rehearsal. Ronald's talent and intuition would undoubtedly add to the performance. This was going to be great. And it would all be memorialized with the help of her little friend: the digital recorder with lapel microphone she'd rented from the library.

Ronald requested that the praise team members not wear flashy clothes so the audience wouldn't be distracted by their costume. If she'd had a few rhinestones in her closet, Camille might have been offended. As it turns out, all the black in her closet was perfect for this morning. She was perfect praise-team material. Ronald needed to get with it.

Just before joining her cohorts, Camille stuffed the recorder inside her bra and attached the microphone to the knit shirt underneath her button-down blouse. Just yesterday, she'd experimented with this equipment wearing the same outfit, making sure her voice could be heard clearly while the microphone remained invisible.

She met up with Ronald, Evelina, Faison, and Nathan in Ronald's office, adjacent to the choir room, for prayer. Glancing around the room, she noted his degrees posted on the wall and several pictures chronicling his daughter's life. There was one picture, barely visible at the end of a row of books, featuring a much younger Brittney standing between Ronald and the woman who was obviously Brittney's mother. Same wavy hair, button nose. Quickly, Camille scanned the parents' hands. They had been married. It hit her: Ronald was a widower. She knew Brittney's mother had died, but somehow none of it clicked until this morning. Ronald, too, knew what it was like to lose the one person who had vowed to love you unconditionally.

Maybe they did have more in common than not.

Ronald reviewed the order of the songs. "'Precious Jesus' first for the older mothers. Nathan, you'll take the lead there. Then Faison goes into 'I Give Myself Away.' Evelina, you've got 'Change.' Camille and I will end with 'What a Mighty God.' That's our plan, but we all know to yield to the Holy Spirit's plan. This is God's house. Amen?"

"Amen," from the team.

"We'll meet back in here after service." Ronald led them in prayer, and they filed out of the room toward the sanctuary. Camille lagged behind, giving herself just enough time and space to manipulate the recorder's "on" switch.

Within the next minute, Camille felt a flood of memories overtake her as she took the stage. This was the life! Hundreds of people on their feet, clapping, awaiting the sound of her music and voice.

Everything went as planned, with Camille singing background through the first two songs. Nathan and Faison led their songs, no problem. Camille peeked down a few times at the huge, red digital timer facing the stage. Fourteen minutes had passed. She was still perfectly within the alleged three hours' battery life.

Then Evelina ministered before she sang. "Today is Mother's Day. Can I get all the mothers to raise their hands?"

Thousands of hands waved back at Evelina. "Amen. Happy Mother's Day to you."

Annoyed slightly, Camille still kept a smile on her face. This whole Mother's Day speech was *not* on their official agenda. Actually, the dance ministry was doing the official tribute, not the praise team.

"I know we've got a lot of people here this morning that we don't get to see very often," she said.

A slight laughter rose from the audience as they recognized the truth. After today, a good third of the people probably wouldn't be back until Christmas.

"Let me tell you something, it's every godly mother's wish to see her child grow up to love the Lord. To serve Him with all their heart. I know you came here today for Momma, but I'm here to tell you Momma's prayers won't go unanswered!"

"Yeah!" the congregants roared. Several women let out desperate shrieks as Evelina continued, "Mommas, some of us may not be here when the Word of God is fulfilled in our children's lives, but how many of you know the prayers of the righteous availeth much! A mother's prayer never dies!"

With that quote from the Bible, Camille sensed a change in the atmosphere. A reverential, earnest mood that stole attention from time itself and slammed Camille square in the midsection. What if Evelina's words were true?

"I'm a living witness. Some of you came here because you wanted to make Momma happy, but let me tell you something, Jesus wants to make *you* happy. He wants to make you into the person that God and your momma's prayers, grandmomma's prayers, and Jesus's prayers have already proclaimed over you. He wants to change you."

Cued by her last sentence, Ronald and the band lowered the volume to a whisper as Evelina stroked each note precisely. By the time she got to "He changed my life complete," her voice had pierced a tiny opening in Camille's stomach.

"And now I sit at my savior's feet," she sang simply, sweetly, with her eyes closed, palms toward the sky as though God Himself might come down and lift her into the sky at any moment.

The hole in Camille's stomach spread now, causing a bubbling sensation to spread through her insides. She wondered if the audience could perceive what was happening inside her body.

As Evelina approached the encore, an all-encompassing intensity swept over Camille's body and forced her hands up in praise.

"I'm not the same!" Evelina declared.

Camille was supposed to follow with the word "changed" along with the other singers, but she was afraid of what might come out of her lips if she moved them. A cry? A scream? Words she didn't even recognize?

Instead, she simply stood in place, arms extended, while tears rolled down her cheeks. The bubbling swelled up to her throat, where she fought to keep it contained. She swallowed twice. That seemed to help, but her body was still shaking.

Evelina parlayed into another praise composition Camille didn't recognize. Ronald shadowed on the piano. Nathan and Faison chimed in. Again, Camille could only be silent because, unlike all the other 99 percent of church songs, this wasn't one of those get-in-where-you-fit-in numbers. She might as well be sitting in the audience right now because, since Evelina stepped forward, Camille had barely mumbled a word into the microphone.

Confusion about exactly how she could contribute to the praise team's praises brought her back to reality a bit, but the bubbling refused to cease.

I have to pull myself together for my song with Ronald!

Camille took a deep breath when Ronald played the

opening chords for their duet. *Calm down. Calm down.* Calm down from what? Why was she suddenly so emotional? She reminded herself of the people at her church who got up to sing, got "touched" by the Spirit, then couldn't finish what they'd started. The crowd would first try to help the person with, "Let the Lord use you," and, "Sing for Jesus." If the vocalist still couldn't produce another coherent note, the audience would falter, "That's all right, God understands."

Usually, Momma would steer the congregation to the good old standby, one-word hymn, "Yeees," and a minister would take the pulpit, now that everyone had seen the power of God move.

Camille had felt the move of God's Spirit inside her before. In all those years of going to church, she'd learned to respect His presence and power, even if she wasn't willing to surrender to it when everyone else around her seemed to succumb. She never wanted to be the type to get so overcome with emotion that she couldn't sing. But this morning, that's exactly who she was. In fact, she was probably the very person she never wanted to be but Momma always wanted to see: Camille in the Lord's house singing His praises.

Her moment of truth came with the second verse. *Her* part. She was supposed to sing "He's the Alpha and Omega," but the crackly sounds emanating from her diaphragm barely qualified as words. She turned her head slightly, managed to see Ronald's eyes through a blur of tears, and knew he would take it from there.

CHAPTER 21

The only thing Camille had managed to acquire during her big praise team debut was a honking headache. Once she stepped off the stage, her head seemed ready to explode from the thirty-seven minutes and forty-nine seconds of bright lights followed by the relentless rush between her stomach and her brain. She was very near exhaustion. Partly hungry, too. She needed some chicken, two Advil, and a good nap. And after she came to her senses, she would probably need a brown paper sack to cover her face, seeing as the spectators were surely wondering why Ronald had brought this crying girl on stage during praise and worship rather than the drama ministry's presentation.

She made a pit stop in the restroom after the benediction to remove the recorder from its hiding place. She might as well erase the file. There was probably nothing to hear except the sound of her sniffing up snot as she cried.

A quick text from Mercedes lightened her spirits. **So nice 2 see God move N U today. TTYL -M**

Later, she joined the rest of the team in Ronald's office for their mandatory closing group prayer. Only a few hours ago, she had envisioned herself walking back into Ronald's office with a small crowd of groupies following her to say what a wonderful job she had done this morning. Maybe even Pastor Collins himself would appoint Camille to the praise team.

Not.

Ronald closed the door behind Camille, since she was the last to enter his office. "Wow. Thank God for a powerful praise service."

"Amen," Faison agreed. "Evelina, you tore it up."

She pointed upward. "Bless God."

"Really, we could have stopped after you sang," Ronald said, "'cause there wasn't anything else left to do but praise Him."

What's he trying to say? I didn't need to sing my song?

"Thank you all for letting the Lord use you this morning. And thank you, especially, Camille, for standing in for Felecia."

"Glad I could help." She wondered if he meant "standing in" like she had been a replacement, or "standing in" as though she had literally just stood there. Which she had, mind you. He didn't have to bring it up, though, if that's what he was doing. Camille couldn't be sure.

"Let's pray." Again, Ronald led them, asking God to restore their strength and keep the Word on their hearts.

Camille couldn't remember the Word. She'd been too preoccupied with regaining her composure. Well, that and trying to turn off the microphone without causing alarm, since it had slipped out of place when she raised her hands. She hadn't practiced recording while fully engaged in worship. Not part of the plan, either.

"Camille, can I see you for a second?" Ronald asked as she sought to bow out of his office with her self-esteem still intact.

She could only imagine what he wanted to say to her. The phrase "Why didn't you sing?" came to mind. Without a word, she stopped shy of his door, turned back to face him.

"Your presence on stage this morning was a blessing to the congregation," he said.

You ain't gotta lie and make things worse. "I really didn't do much."

"This is the praise team, not the singing team. I know what it's like to have the Spirit come in and arrest your voice. Sometimes all you can do is weep before Him. He accepts all forms of sincere worship."

"That's nice to know." She grinned slightly at his attempt to give her some kind of credit before assigning her a permanent seat to the sopranos section of the choir. No way would he let her perform with the elite if she came unglued every time she got front and center.

She stood there a moment longer, wondering if she was dismissed.

"I also wanted to ask you," he hesitated, "if you would go to lunch with me. Brittney's spending time with her mother's family this weekend, so I'd like the company. If you don't already have plans with your family, and you'd like to."

Truth was, she could use the company, too. Camille was glad Brittney had the opportunity to be around those she loved, because the only thing worse than a motherless Mother's Day was spending Mother's Day alone.

"That would be great," Camille answered as a nervous flicker settled in. First bubbling, now fluttering. What next?

"Cool. I'll drive."

She wouldn't dare turn down the offer. Gas was almost four dollars a gallon, and she still had two more payments to go on her ticket.

Ronald drove a country man's truck: a Ford F-150. Double cab. Camille was taken aback when he opened the passenger's door for her. She couldn't remember any man undertaking this gesture for her, and she wasn't sure if she should be flattered or insulted. Her great-grandfather used to perform this task for his wife, but he was a mean, controlling old thing. Wouldn't even let Great-grandmother learn to drive.

Again, Camille checked out Ronald's turf as they both buckled seat belts. Clean, dustless dashboard. Vacuumed floorboards. If she didn't know any better, she'd think he'd been planning to take someone out to dinner after church today.

He started the engine, and a gospel song brushed through the vehicle. Camille wondered if Ronald listened to only church music. She surveyed the CD cases stacked beneath the dashboard and read their titles as best as she could. Suspicion confirmed. All Christian music.

"What do you like?" he asked.

"Anything and everything. I'm starving," she admitted.

He laughed. "You need a buffet?"

"That'll work."

"Chinese?"

"Okay."

So this is it. A date at a Chinese buffet. *Is this a date?* She wanted to ask, but she'd already made a fool of herself on stage. Besides, the more she got to know Ronald, the more she realized he really wasn't her type. He was too . . . churchified. He was like old-school saved, only he was her age. She'd hate to see him when he got sixty years old. He'd probably look like Moses.

He busted out with, "Camille, I've been thinking about what you said. Our conversation really ministered to me." He looked both ways, entered traffic.

She racked her brain for a clue about their last words. "What did I say?"

"When we talked about being musicians' kids. Sometimes, Brittney does and says things that make me doubt whether or not she'll grow up to be the woman God has called her to be. She's entering this little rebellious time, but I'm going to stand on the Word. I want to see her come full circle, like you and me," he explained.

Suddenly, Ronald slammed on his brakes. They jerked forward. Brakes screeched. Tires skidded, a horn blew. Camille glimpsed the Dodge emblem within feet of her door.

Ronald cried, "Jesus!"

Camille cried a four-letter word.

Instinctively, she grabbed the door's handle and braced herself for the crash.

Everything froze, including her heart.

Finally, she breathed. No impact. Somehow, both cars had stopped within inches of what could have been disastrous. The other driver backed up and sped around them, continuing along her illegal, light-running path.

"You all right?" Ronald asked, reaching for her trembling hand.

Camille squeezed his strong hand in return. "Yes."

He looked up and exhaled. "Thank You, Lord, for protecting us from that fool."

Camille had some other words she would like to use instead of "fool," but she figured she'd already done enough cussing in front of Ronald for the day.

Taking turns going to get their food gave Camille a chance to regain her wits. Still shaking from the incident, she couldn't remember anything Ronald had said on the way to the restaurant. She hoped a little sweet and sour chicken with rice would advise her body that the danger had passed and the adrenaline pumps could be switched to stop now.

"You want to lead the prayer?" Ronald asked after they had both fixed their plates.

"No. You go ahead."

He obliged, then dove into his food as though he hadn't just almost lost his life to someone who was drunk and/or didn't have a driver's license in the first place. She wondered how he could be so calm. If she died, no one would suffer. Bobby Junior might cry a little, but he'd be the first to go through her drawers looking for a life-insurance policy.

Ronald, on the other hand, had a child to raise. Alone. He should be more upset!

In the middle of his chat about the record-breaking temperatures, Camille interrupted him. "Dude, we almost lost our lives a minute ago. Doesn't that faze you in some way?"

He stopped. Raised his eyebrows. "Yeah, that was close. But it didn't happen. Besides, dying isn't the worst thing that can happen to you, you know?" He added a chuckle, took another bite of beef with broccoli.

Easy for him to say! He probably still had his mother. "I disagree. Totally. And I don't see anything funny about dying."

Dropping his fork onto the plate, he apologized. "I didn't mean to upset you. Are you okay?"

Camille slammed her spoon and wrapped her fingers around her forehead. "No. I'm not. It's Mother's Day and my mother is dead, all right?" *Great. I just ruined our nondate.*

"I'm so sorry, Camille. I had no idea." He shook his head. "I thought you said she was a musician."

"She *was*. Past tense."

He repeated sincerely, "I'm so sorry."

"Why do people say that?" She looked at him now. "It's *not* your fault."

He sat silently. Probably unsure of what to say next. She resumed eating. Ronald followed her lead.

"Do you mind me asking what happened to your mother?"

"She had cancer."

"How old were you when she passed?"

"Seventeen."

"Mmm. You were not much older than Brittney was when my wife died. I don't know what it's like to lose a mother, but I've watched what it's done to my daughter. I know, for her, it's a tough time of year. I admire your strength, Camille. To get up there and sing this morning—"

"I didn't really sing, all right?" She had to correct him. "I choked, all right? Evelina started talking about people's mommas praying, and that was the end of me."

"No, it wasn't," Ronald stopped her. "You continued to praise God through the—"

"Stop with all this church talk, okay?" She was sick of him being so holy all the time. Church folk and all their pacifying clichés irked her. If they were going to do this buffet-date thing, he needed to at least be real with her.

"What do you mean, 'church talk'?"

"You're always praying, always putting God in everything. And who calls out 'Jesus' when you're about to get pulverized by a car?"

"You think what *you* called out helped?"

"No," she admitted. "I don't cuss. I was just scared. I didn't even think. It was just the first thing that came out of my mouth."

"Same here." He nodded. "I didn't have time to think, either. The name of Jesus is the first thing to automatically come out of my mouth when I'm in trouble."

Camille stopped chewing on the food in order to digest Ronald's statement. The blank expression on his face spoke the truth. He wasn't kidding. This *was* the real him.

She rolled her eyes. "I see. Well, I'm sorry about using profanity. I see your truck is all holy. Probably never even heard a cussword in it before."

He smiled at Camille. Not fair. He had one of those contagious Magic Johnson smiles that warmed each recipient's heart. Made Camille relax a bit now. The adrenaline pumps halted, swapped places with the flirty-nerves machinery factory.

"Why are you smiling at me?"

"Because you crack me up," he said. "And for your information, my truck has heard a cussword before."

Camille smacked her lips. "I bet you know exactly who cussed in your truck and when, where, why, and how, don't you?"

Again, his grin crossed the line, opening Camille up in his presence.

He nodded dramatically. "As a matter of fact, I do. It was Brittney. She got mad at me because I wouldn't let her go to driver's ed. I believe she said the word 'hell' and that was the end of our conversation about her getting behind the wheel anytime soon."

Camille always knew there was something she liked about Brittney. Somebody had to give Ronald a taste of reality.

"So," he asked, "who cusses in your car?"

She entertained the question, tried to remember the last time someone was in the car with her. Bobby Junior wasn't really into cussing. He made up his swear words, like Esther on *Sanford and Son*. Pig-eyed bunion-face was the closest he'd come to cussing in her car.

Kyra was probably the last one to use profane language in Camille's car. Matter of fact, Kyra had told Camille off in a very systematic fashion before slamming the door as she exited the vehicle. Camille wouldn't even try to recall the twisted blend of choice words Kyra had concocted that day.

"No one cusses in my car these days."

"No one except you?"

"I don't cuss, I told you."

"Just today."

She half rolled her eyes. "Only under extreme circumstances like almost getting killed."

He smirked.

"Okay, look, I can't be going out to eat with you if

you're going to give me the third degree about everything," Camille warned.

He laughed again. "I'm not giving you the third degree. Do you see a third degree in my hands?" He held them up for inspection.

"No. But you really need to lay off me *and* Brittney. Leave some room for growth. Nobody's perfect, you know?"

Ronald wiped his chin with a napkin. "I like how you said that. Leave room for *growth*. Not necessarily mistakes or rebellion, but *growth*."

"Why you gotta be so deep all the time?"

"I'm not!" he exclaimed. Then he added, "But I like the way you say things. You speak the truth, even when you're not trying to sound philosophical. You make me think, and I appreciate that. I really do."

Ronald's accolades fell on Camille's guilty heart. How he heard truth from the very lips that had attempted at first to deceive him was beyond her. She wondered if he'd be sitting across from her if he knew why she'd joined Grace Chapel. Probably not. *Definitely* not.

Like Mercedes, Ronald was good people. He didn't deserve to be lied to. And he certainly didn't deserved to share his buffet with someone whose natural instincts leaned toward profanity in the face of danger.

He deserved better.

CHAPTER 22

Camille's first meeting with the Mentors and Models went very well. She introduced herself, told the girls about her former life as a "star" at Brittney's request. The sponsors thanked Camille for "keeping it real" with the young ladies.

There was something about this whole "being real" concept that seemed almost foreign to these people. Yet, this was the very quality that caused the teen girls to direct most of their questions toward Camille during the question-and-answer session about boyfriends and dating.

"I want to ask Miss Camille if she ever dated someone who didn't believe in God," a girl who barely looked old enough to shop in the juniors' section asked. A boyfriend should have been the last thing on her mind.

Always, Camille answered truthfully but responsibly. "When I was your age, I didn't even care if they believed in God or not. All I cared about was how good they looked. Once their looks got old and I found somebody cuter, that was the end of the relationship."

Another one delved further, "Do you ask guys *now* about their relationship with God?"

Ronald came to mind. Even if she didn't know him from church, who he was and what he stood for probably wouldn't have been hard to determine. "No. I don't ask because people can lie and say whatever they think you want to hear. The way you really know what a guy believes is by how he acts."

Miss Abernathy, one of the older sponsors, quickly stood and initiated a round of applause after Camille's answer. "Young lady, you ain't tellin' nothin' but the truth!"

Before they dismissed, Camille made yet another plea in front of a crowd, as she'd done at the end of almost every choir rehearsal for weeks now. "Does anybody want a free kitten?"

A collective "awww" encouraged her to describe Cat in depth. "He's gray with blue eyes, for now. He doesn't tear up stuff. All he does is eat and sleep."

But after the initial cooing, no one stepped forward to relieve her of Cat. He was still on the market, which wasn't a loss entirely because she'd hoped he would eat up all the food she had had to buy him before he left. Wasting money was not an option.

Mercedes, Camille, and the rest of the Fly Girls held a spontaneous minireunion after the meeting. Mercedes invited them all to her cousin's movie theater to watch some movie about escaped lab rats. It sounded corny, but Camille joined them anyway. Broke people don't turn down free stuff.

Afterward, she took Brittney home and switched partners, heading back out again with Ronald for an outing he wouldn't explain ahead of time. Since their first unofficial official buffet date two weeks earlier, Camille and Ronald had seen each other only once more outside of church. They texted here and there. Talked casually. Whether he was trying to keep things quiet with the church folk or still hadn't made up his mind about Camille, she wasn't sure. Either way, she liked the pleasant distance between them. Close enough to suggest opportunity, far enough to preclude disappointment should one person suddenly decide to stop returning calls.

Brittney, however, had given Camille plenty to ponder about the relationship on the way back from Mercedes's place. "Miss Camille, I'm not tryin' to get in grown folks' business, as my daddy would say, but I think he likes you."

Awkward!

"Hmm. That's nice to know. I think your father is a likeable person, too."

"No, I mean *likes* you likes you. And I like you, too."

Camille had made light of Brittney's remarks. "Well, I like that you like me and you like that your daddy likes me, too. Sounds like there's a whole lotta likin' goin' on, right?"

Now, as she secured herself in Ronald's truck for the second time, Camille wondered if she should say something about Brittney's comment. Knowing Ronald, however, he would scold his daughter for interfering. He probably fussed at Brittney for everything already, as parents of teens tended to do. No need adding another reason to the list.

She decided to tackle another issue. "When do you plan on telling me where we're going?"

Ronald winked. "When we get there."

She crossed her arms. "You're enjoying this, aren't you?"

"Immensely."

"I don't like surprises."

"Neither do I," he said, "unless I'm the one doing the surprising. Just sit back and relax. You're acting like I'm some kind of axe murderer you met on the Internet who's about to make you his next victim."

"You might be," Camille shrieked.

"A bishop's son who's an axe murderer and a widower, heavily involved in ministry, with a fifteen-year-old daughter?"

Camille answered, "Axe murderers pride themselves on blending into society."

Ronald laughed fully. "Aw, Camille, you crack me up. I always know I'm going to laugh when I'm with you."

"I never know what's going to happen when I'm with you," she teased. "I might get a sermon, might get a lecture. Might not even know where I'm going."

Ronald's refusal to let Camille in on their destination proved a wise move. "Nuh-uh," Camille fussed when he parked in a spot outside what appeared to be a small art gallery labeled Paintings by U. "I know we did not drive clear across town to go look at art by somebody with a one-letter name."

"We're not *looking* at art. We're *making* art," he clarified as he helped her out of the truck. "*U* stands for *y-o-u*."

She objected, "I can't draw anything except stick figures."

"We're in the same boat, but you don't have to be able to draw. They'll teach you," Ronald said. He unlatched the back cabin door and produced a grocery sack.

"What's in there?"

"Our food. Hope you like my specialty, grilled ham and cheese."

"Sandwiches?"

"Don't worry," he taunted, "I cut yours up into triangles."

He closed and locked the doors. "Ladies first."

Camille looked him upside his head. She'd been real with him so far. Why stop now? "Ronald, this really isn't my speed."

"Hey, I've never done this, either." He shrugged. "One of my friends told me about it, said it was fun, said I should try it some time. I've never had anyone to try it with until now."

Softened only by his vulnerability, she took the first step toward the building and into a new experience. Turned out, Paintings by U was a make-and-take art studio. The instructor, a young man named Wess with a mess of brown hair on his head, explained the concept to the first-timers. He would give them precise direction on how to create the night's painting: a fruit bowl on a pedestal. The canvas, paint, and aprons had already been provided. All they had to do was listen and paint. And, of course, they were welcome to enjoy food, wine, and whatever else they'd brought to snack on.

Camille took one look at the picture and whispered to Ronald, "I can't."

"Yes, you can. Stop being such a wimp."

She slapped his arm. "No, you didn't. You know what? Since you called me a wimp, my painting is going to be better than yours."

"Bet?" he challenged.

"Bet."

For the next two hours, Camille and Ronald, along with twelve other amateur artists, created their own versions of the master illustration.

"Keep your arm steady, now," Ronald said as he attempted to sabotage Camille's masterpiece by jiggling her elbow slightly.

"Stop." She laughed. The distraction had actually reminded her to swallow. She'd been paying such close attention to Wess's direction, she'd almost forgotten she was on an afternoon date with Ronald.

She took a brief recess in order wash her hands and eat her sandwich. Ham and cheese wasn't exactly her favorite main entrée, but Ronald had been right about his special skills. High-quality, deli-sliced ham, just enough mayonnaise, bread buttered slightly and toasted to perfection.

"This is good," she had to admit. "You could open a ham-and-cheese sandwich store and be set for life."

"Thank you. Secret family recipe."

"And thank you for my triangles."

"My pleasure."

Camille snacked on a few chips, took a swig of apple juice, and got back to work on her painting, which was shaping up quite nicely. She could tell by Wess's directives that he had coached plenty of art-challenged subjects toward success.

As she added the finishing touches, Camille began to declare victory. "My brother, I do believe I've outdone myself today."

Ronald leaned over, got a look at the canvas perched on her easel. She snuck a glance at his work. Not too shabby, but his pedestal was a tad bit squatty. Could have easily been mistaken for a stool. Ronald must not have been watching closely when Wess showed them all how to measure from the bottom with their paint brushes.

"I do believe I've won the bet," he declared.

"How you gon' win the bet with that tiny pedestal? Look at Wess's, look at mine, and look at yours. Please!"

"That's why mine is better. Yours is a cookie-cutter image. Where's your sense of style, Camille? Your flair?" he flirted. "This here, what you've done, is almost an exact replica."

"Isn't that the idea?" A smile wiggled free from her grasp.

"No." He couldn't hold a straight face, either.

"Let's ask somebody to be the judge," Camille suggested.

"No way." Ronald removed his smock. "I'm not showing this thing to anybody."

Camille squealed in victory but quickly recanted when she saw Ronald slide his work into the ventilated box. "Ronald, it's not that bad."

"It's hideous."

"No, it's not."

"So . . . you're saying it's better than yours?"

She backed up, suddenly aware of his psychological scheme. "I ain't said all that."

They drove home with the smell of fresh paint filling the car. Ronald rolled down the windows so they wouldn't suffer adverse reactions, in accordance with Wess's caution. The breeze swishing through the truck thwarted any real conversation. Camille simply caught on to what she could hear coming from the speakers. Another gospel song. She recognized Yolanda Adams's voice, hummed along with a few bars.

As soon as the front wheels of Ronald's truck rolled onto the driveway, a boy hoisted his sagging pants, dashed off the front porch, and ran across the lawn while the front door simultaneously slammed shut.

"What's going . . ." Ronald's voice trailed off before he could finish the phrase.

Ronald had barely parked before his foot hit the pavement. "Stay in the car. Call nine-one-one." Then he bounded toward the door, hollering, "Brittney! You okay!"

Camille sat dumbfounded. Ronald was clueless. Here he was thinking Brittney was under attack. Camille, on the other hand, was certain about what she'd just witnessed. Brittney was either saying good-bye or hello to a male friend, and her father had returned home just in time to see it all go down. No need to get the police involved. Not yet, anyway.

Next thing she knew, Ronald tore out of the house, tracing the boy's escape route.

Unsure of what to do next, Camille let herself out of the truck and grabbed her painting. She sat the box in her trunk, threw her purse in the front seat, and locked the door again. She stood in the driveway. What else could she do? She didn't want to just take off like, "I'm outta here," but this really wasn't her business.

Ronald appeared at the edge of the yard, huffing and puffing, anger etched in every nook of his sweaty face. Camille thanked God he hadn't caught the boy, because Ronald's mind was obviously far from Jesus right now.

"I've got to deal with Brittney."

"Okay."

She watched him enter the house again and slam the door almost as hard as Brittney had earlier. She heard

Ronald yell his daughter's name and knew there was nothing she could do to save her young friend. Sweet little Brittney had been exposed. Camille could only hope their arrival had interrupted a bad decision, prevented Brittney from doing something stupid—assuming this was her first time contemplating company in her father's absence.

Probably not, though. In Camille's experience, you never got busted the first time you did something stupid because, initially, you were careful. It wasn't until the fourth or fifth time you'd gotten away with something that you stopped watching your back.

She ought to know. She'd snuck her fair share of friends into the house back in the day. Courtney was usually at work, Bobby Junior at some other undisclosed location when Camille returned from school. The only person she had to dodge was Miss Gracie from across the street.

Brittney, however, had a different situation altogether. She had a father who hadn't lost his mind when her mother died. She had her mother's family. There was no reason for her to get involved with this whoever-he-was boy. No reason except infatuation and teen stupidity itself, which didn't need a reason at all.

Camille carefully transported the painting from her trunk to her living room when she arrived home. Cat was meowing like crazy, so she let him out of his living quarters and allowed him to roam. He squeezed into his usual spot beneath the couch to watch television. He'd stay there until Camille went to her bedroom. Then he'd follow her and curl up under the bed. Cat didn't want her attention so much as her presence to ward off his massive fear of being alone outside of the bathroom.

After watching a few YouTube videos and reading up on blogs about cats, Camille had figured out that Cat wasn't your usual feline. He was more like a lapdog than a cat. Or maybe he was just slow. Slow to get himself another owner, that was for sure.

True to his pattern, Cat found his place in her room as Camille settled in for a nap. A ding on her phone registered a text from Ronald. **Had a nice time painting with you. Sorry I didn't get to say good-bye.**

Camille responded. **No worries. Is Brittney still alive?**

Moments later, he replied. **Y**

She ventured. **Are u ok?**

N. Can't believe this is happening. She says he was just a friend. Nothing happened. Not sure what 2 believe.

One could never be sure when talking to a panicked teenager. If she were having this conversation with anyone else, she might suggest a stiff drink. Ronald, however, needed a little encouragement in his own language. Camille texted: **I will b praying 4 u & Brittney.**

Thx. We both need it. Don't know when Britt will see light of day again.

Camille laughed. **This 2 will pass. Room 4 growth?**

She imagined Ronald shaking his head as he replied. **Room 4 a beat down. Had to count 10 to calm down. Still breathing hard. Thx 4 understanding. Ttyl.**

Ttyl.

CHAPTER 23

Cute gray kitten. Answers to "Cat." Sweet disposition. Docile. So far, all he does is eat, pee, poop, crawl under furniture. Not destructive at all.

Perfect for an older person who just wants a companion.

214-555-8766

The first two calls she got were actually from guys who chatted briefly about Cat, then got to the point where they "wanted to get to know her." She promptly declined their advances. By the third call, Camille had figured out how to cut to the chase. One real contender wanted a pet for her two-year-old. *Didn't she read my ad?* Cat wasn't for kids. He wasn't playful or outgoing. He'd be terrified of a two-year-old; back at the shelter in a hot minute for scratching the toddler's face in fear.

The second person claimed he didn't have other pets, but Camille could hear dogs barking in the background. When she viewed the person's profile, she noted he owned several rough-looking pit bulls. Cat would probably be ripped to shreds by the time his dogs finished practicing their aggression on him. A quick chat in a cat-lovers' room confirmed Camille's suspicions. 4Cats4Me commented, There are a lot of mean people out there. Be careful giving your kitten away. Why don't you just keep him?

Camille thought about writing the truth—she didn't like cats. But the people in this forum would go coo-coo. Instead, she wrote part of the truth, Someone gave him thinking I wanted another cat, but I don't.

FelineFemale posted, Sounds like you care nuff 2 want a good home 4 him. I say he's yours ;0)

Not likely. Camille figured you were either born a cat person or not. She was a *not*. Furthermore, she learned via the Web that the pet deposit for her complex was two hundred fifty dollars. *Certainly* not going to happen. Even if she wanted to keep Cat, which she didn't, she couldn't afford to. According to the paperwork Sheryl gave her, he'd need shots soon, too. More money.

Still, the thought that she might turn Cat over to a torturer wasn't something Camille could live with. She immediately removed the ad for fear of coming in contact with a sadistic animal-killer. *After all,* she told herself, *they start with animals and graduate to people. I'm not gonna be somebody's first human victim on account of Cat.*

Sheryl, of course, basked in her good deed. "How's the kitten?" she'd ask every morning.

"He's fine," Camille would reply truthfully. For as much as she didn't appreciate Sheryl's unwelcome gift, she had to admit it was nice to talk to her boss without all the guilt for once.

"We'll have to get our cats together sometime for a playdate," Sheryl suggested.

"I'm sorry. I can't. I'm very busy on the weekend with church and all."

"Oh"—Sheryl seemed shocked—"you go to church? I didn't know you were . . . I'm guessing . . . like, a Christian, right?"

Camille cleared her throat. "Yes. It's a Christian church."

"What do you do there?"

"I sing in several choirs," Camille shared. "I'm always at rehearsal or mentoring young ladies. The church keeps me *very* busy." She'd hoped to see Sheryl give up on her quest for cat fellowship. Yet, she wondered why Sheryl's eyes had suddenly taken on a new shine. She never got this excited about anything except animals.

"Oh my goodness! That's wonderful." Then she dipped her head, stepped fully into Camille's cubicle. "Lately, my husband and I have been talking about going to church or something. Gotta figure out the whole life purpose, you know? I don't know if we need to start going to church or volunteering, but we've been so fortunate, we gotta do something."

"You're such a sweet person. You'd be great."

She smiled. "You think?"

"Yeah."

"Okay. Here." She pointed at the sticky notepad on

Camille's desk. "Write down the address to your church. Maybe one of these Sundays, my husband and I will get to visit. No cats allowed, right?" She tilted her head, jeering.

"No cats allowed." Camille hoped Sheryl was joking.

Since the boy-on-the-porch incident, Camille found herself on the receiving end of dozens of questions from Ronald about what might be going on in Brittney's head. He seemed lost about how to handle his baby girl now that he realized she wasn't a baby anymore. In his mind, Brittney had morphed into a foreign creature capable of all manner of evil, never to be trusted again.

"I just don't see how she could do this," Ronald anguished for the millionth time in a week. He glanced at Brittney, who was sitting alone at her own table in Panera while he and Camille occupied a different table in the restaurant. He didn't trust his daughter to stay home alone anymore, so she had to tag along like an . . . irresponsible teenager who couldn't be trusted to stay home alone.

Camille, too, snuck a peek at her mini-me. Poor Brittney's clothing expressed a complete lack of interest in her appearance. Aside from the fact she was on punishment, Camille realized that Brittney was ashamed and embarrassed about the whole situation. She couldn't look her father in the eyes. She barely whispered when speaking to Camille.

"Ronald, stop taking this personally. It's not about you," Camille tried to explain over baked-potato soup.

"She didn't ask herself, 'What can I do to break my father's heart?'"

He winced. "What *did* she say to herself? What *did* go down in her mind?"

Camille blinked once. "What went down in *your* mind when you were fifteen years old and falling in love, sneaking behind *your* parents' back to talk on the phone or spend unsupervised time alone with *your* girlfriend?"

He admitted, "My problem exactly. Wasn't but one thing on my mind when I thought about being alone with my fifteen-year-old girlfriend. Same thing that was on *that* boy's mind."

"True, true," Camille agreed, "but from what I can tell about Brittney, that's not what was on *her* mind. She didn't set out to disappoint you. She probably just . . . really likes the kid. I'm sure he makes her laugh, he tells her she's pretty. He probably does things Brittney would never do, tells her about all his thuggish adventures. It's pretty enticing, actually."

"I'm gonna be sick." Ronald fake gagged. "You make it sound like a good thing."

"It's not, but you have to understand where she's coming from. The boy talked her into doing something she knew she shouldn't have done. I'm sure he told her it wouldn't be that big a deal. He really wanted to see her, he can't stop thinking about her—"

"Lies," Ronald fumed.

"We know that, but Brittney doesn't."

He defended himself, "But I've taught my daughter *better*."

"Look, anybody can be tricked into doing the wrong thing. If it happened to Eve and her daddy was *God*, it could happen to Brittney, all right? This is not about you, Ronald. And the last thing Brittney needs is for you to make her feel like a complete idiot who can't do anything right. An *unloved* complete idiot, to make matters worse."

Ronald inhaled deeply, covered his face with his hands. "You're right, but whose side are you on anyway?"

"I'm not on anybody's side," she assured him, pulling down his physical barrier to expose his eyes again.

"What am I supposed to do? She can't *not* get punished."

Camille nodded. "She should have consequences, of course, but you need to talk to her. She might have lost her phone, her computer, her freedom, and whatever else you want to take away from her, but she shouldn't have to lose you, too. Don't ever forget, you're the only parent she has left."

He lowered his hands in submission. "Okay, okay. I'll talk to her. Will you talk to her, too? She really looks up to you. Sometimes I feel like what I tell her goes in one ear and out the other."

"I'll talk to her, *after* you."

"Thanks. Have I told you lately that I like the way you explain this mixed-up woman's world to me?"

They locked fingers. A brief flush emanated from his touch. "Yes, you have. I'm glad to help."

"I could kiss you right now."

Go 'head then! Camille helped a brother out. She leaned across their tiny table, kicked off their first peck. Delicious little smack. And that's all it was, too, since Brittney's position at her table could change at any moment.

"You've done more than help, Camille. You've

opened my eyes to reality. Sometimes, I think I'm so caught up in the church and all the ministries, I forget there's life outside of the sanctuary."

"No arguments here," she had to concur. Though their relationship hadn't been formalized, Camille had come to the conclusion that the real reason Ronald didn't have much of a social life was because he'd already married Grace Chapel. And now that he'd added babysitting Brittney every moment she wasn't in school to his list of obligations, he'd have even less free time.

Back at home, she was reminded of their first planned date every time she walked by her unique painting. Sometimes, she found herself wishing she could do that date all over. Not to change anything, just to experience it again. She remembered how close they'd been when he tied her apron from behind. Remembered his gentle nudge when he'd tried to interfere with her drawing. Those thoughtful sandwiches and chips. Even the hug and second kiss tonight when he dropped her off would be memories worth holding on to. She wanted more times like these with Ronald, but it wasn't looking too good.

If this were a *real* relationship, she would voice her concerns. Unfortunately, the *real* truth presented itself every time Camille got an e-mail or a text from John David. He must have had a live one on the line, because all week he'd been questioning Camille, wanting to know when she'd have the demo available. Couldn't she get a DVD of the church's ceremony and lift the audio? Was there any way she could ask some people from the choir to back her up on a simple song? Did she really want this, or was she wasting his time?

Of course she wanted it! That was the whole reason she'd joined church and the choir. Not too many people would be willing to give up their good Sunday morning rest and several week nights to rehearsal unless they were serious about singing.

Still—no demo, no deal.

Hanging out with Ronald, getting involved with the youth had gotten her off track. Messed up her priorities. Maybe his preoccupation with Brittney's love life would give her an opportunity to refocus. All she needed was one taping. After that, she could just go on with things as usual until John David got her a gig. Then, of course, she'd have to relinquish some of her commitments at Grace Chapel. Everyone would understand. Who in their right mind *wouldn't* hop on the next bus to LA for a recording contract and a tour?

She'd keep in touch with Mercedes and Ronald. Maybe come back and make a special appearance at Mentors and Models. Send Brittney souvenirs from the tour cities. And maybe, once Camille had stacked up some bills in the bank, added some zeroes to her checking account, she'd settle back at Grace Chapel. Check back in with Ronald, if he was still on the market. She hoped liked crazy he'd still be available, because she desperately desired to start over with him. No lies, no schemes. Just regular old boy meets girl. Or, girl comes back to boy after she gets rich.

This all sounded like a fine and dandy plan when she put it in those words. Easy in, easy out. No harm done to anyone, least of all her reputation.

Now, if only she could figure out a master plan to help her sleep through a full night without fidgety twists and turns.

CHAPTER 24

"Camille, it's now or never," John David barked through the phone. "I've given you months to get me the demo. I told you I had an interested client. If you can't give me the demo this week, I'll pass the opportunity on to my next prospect."

No! "I'm trying. It's not as easy as I—"

"It's not that difficult! Don't you have, what, five or six friends you could ask to sing?

"You could *hire* a choir, for cryin' out loud."

Yeah, if I had some money. Nevertheless, she promised, "Okay. I'll get it to you by Friday."

"Friday at *noon*."

"Okay." She disconnected the call. John David was trippin'. Up until now, he'd been pretty casual about this recording. Camille wasn't stupid. He'd probably lost a prospect, and now he was trying to fulfill a promise with Camille. No matter, she needed to come through for him.

She made a second trip to the library and checked out the digital microphone again. After her last experience with this thing, she'd almost wondered if God Himself wasn't trying to stop her from making the demo.

She couldn't think about that now. As she walked through the apartment, dressing and warming up her vocal chords, she blocked out all thoughts of impropriety and questionable motive. "La-la-la-la-la-la-la-la-la." Up an octave. Repeat.

Cat followed, meowing as though she were talking to him. He tried to match her, syllable for syllable. Camille looked down at him, leaned over, and sang in his face. "La-la-la-la-la-la-la-la-la."

Myyaaa! Myyaaa!

She cracked up laughing. "Cat, you really think you can sing, don't you?" Maybe she should have added his vocal abilities in the description she'd posted at the recreation center. Sadly, Tyree's observation about black folks and cats had proven true. No takers there, either. Now that she'd actually purchased a kitty litter box, Camille almost hated to give all that good money away. But if someone called, she'd have to let Cat go. For as much as she disliked anything on four legs with whiskers, Cat might be the exception. For somebody else.

No time for pondering Cat's future. Choir rehearsal and her own future awaited. Camille slid guilty second thoughts to the furthest recess of her heart and positioned her digital equipment for action. She walked into choir practice with one thing on her mind: get this stupid recording over with so she could satisfy John David and her conscience once and for all.

I gotta do what I gotta do.

Practice flowed as usual, with Ronald guiding the young-adult choir through its separate parts, then having them sing altogether.

Camille marveled at his ability to stay in choir director mode despite their personal connection. No one could have guessed that he was closer to Camille than any of the other choir members. Come to think of it, his dual personality could be a problem. *What if he's dating several women in the choir? Probably that skinny new alto!* He might have had a different woman in every choir, for all Camille knew.

Wait. We're talking about Ronald here. He didn't have time for her, let alone a bunch of other women. That wasn't how he rolled, anyway. *I'm trippin'.* Her ill motives had obviously sparked suspicions about everyone else's MO.

Mercedes hugged most of the sopranos after practice and chatted with Camille for a while. This was good news for Camille. She needed the people to kind of clear out a little before approaching Ronald.

"Well, I'll catch up with you later. I see you're hanging around to talk to your . . . *friend.*" She winked, smirked slightly.

"What are you talking about?" Camille whispered.

"You. Ronald. Stevie Wonder can see what's happening between you two."

"How? We don't even say anything to each other."

"First of all, there are people all over the city who belong to Grace Chapel. Second, don't forget the Brittney factor."

"Should have known."

"But don't worry about it. We're happy for Ronald.

We're glad to see him getting back in the swing of things. I, personally, can't think of a better person for him."

Camille smiled uneasily, told Mercedes she'd talk to her later.

When there were only a few tenors left, stacking up chairs so the custodial staff could vacuum, Camille made her moves. First: activate the recorder. Second: approach Ronald before he could close the top on the piano.

"You remember that song by BeBe and CeCe Winans? 'Heaven'?"

"Yeah," he said, tinkering with the ivories a bit.

"I was thinking the choir could sing a modified version next month, during the church anniversary. It's right in line with Pastor Collins's series theme, live with heaven in mind."

Ronald struck up the chorus for "Heaven" on the piano. He definitely knew the song.

Camille didn't waste any time. She jumped on the first line. Ronald fell in place right behind her, giving her all the space she needed to showcase her vocal capabilities.

They both sang the chorus. "That's what I live for."

Yes! This is perfect! Okay, maybe Ronald wasn't a choir, but he was definitely great backup. John David would have to get over himself.

"Willing to die for."

Faison hopped his happy behind in the song and took Ronald's part for the next refrain. Though he sang the correct words in key, his voice wasn't nearly as rich as Ronald's. Another tenor, whom Camille didn't really know, added his two cents and almost ruined the song.

Camille turned from him so his mouth wouldn't be so close to the microphone. Thank goodness this wasn't a group audition.

Ronald changed up the ending a bit, choir-ized the melody so it could be sung in three-part harmony. Camille ad-libbed the soloist's part so she'd shine through.

When it was all sung and done, Camille had a good five or six minutes of herself singing and singing well! *John David is going to love this!*

"Wow! That song is perfect for the anniversary," Ronald complimented. "Good lookin' out."

"Why, thank you." She was so excited, she almost grabbed him in front of everyone.

Calm down.

"I'll put 'Heaven' on the agenda for our next unity choir rehearsal."

Still high on her overwhelmingly successful accomplishment, Camille floated out the building and to her car alongside Ronald.

"Hey, you want to go get some coffee?"

"Mmm, I don't know. I was trying to get to the gym tonight."

"You look fine to me," he flirted.

"Thank you, but that's only because I've been working out lately."

"It's definitely paying off. But I was really hoping we could grab a bite since Brittney's still in practice."

How could she resist. "Cool."

Finally, some time alone with her "friend," as Mercedes had referenced him.

She hopped in Ronald's truck. As she secured herself, she realized the recorder was still in place. She switched the lever off but knew she couldn't remove it right then without putting herself in a questionable position. No problem, though. She'd been super-smart this time, taping it directly to her chest so it wouldn't slide around.

Starbucks coffee, cookies, tea, whatever. Sitting in Ronald's presence was a treat all by itself. The strawberries and crème frappuccino added little to the moment.

They unwound—she talked about work, he spoke of the upcoming youth summer musical workshop, which he'd actually delegated to another musician on staff. He wasn't sure if his designee could pull of the task, but he had to give the younger man a chance.

"If I ever expect to have a life outside of church, I'm gonna have to learn how to trust other people," he acquiesced.

"Have some faith in him," Camille cheered. "He has to learn, just like you did. Room for growth?"

"Room for growth. You know, you always got something constructive to say. What's up with *you*? What problems can I help you solve?"

"I'm straight. No issues here."

"Hmm. A woman with no issues? I don't think so. I'll be right back."

If only he knew he'd just solved her biggest problem about thirty minutes ago when he sang with her. *Hmmm . . . maybe I should tell him*. Really, he wouldn't be mad. He probably would have done it if she'd asked. Problem was: She didn't ask. The worst-case scenario played out as Ronald gabbed about the upcoming basketball season. If she told him, he'd want to know why she didn't ask, which could lead to questions about why she needed it so badly in the first place. She'd tell him the truth, that John David wanted the demo. He'd probably ask why she couldn't just go home, get in the shower, and record herself singing. She'd have to say she needed a choir. Before you know it, he'd put two and two together and discover her original purpose for joining Grace Chapel.

Naaa. I ain't sayin' nothin'. It wasn't absolutely essential for Ronald to know about this. No harm, no foul.

With Ronald gone to refill his drink, Camille attempted to reach into her shirt. A little blond-haired boy at the next table looked up and studied her movements, almost in awe that a woman had put a hand down her blouse. His big, blue eyes studied her every move, as though she might expose herself at any moment.

Owww! Some kinds of tape weren't made to be stuck on skin. No use.

Between the adhesive and the child's gawking, the recorder couldn't be removed.

Wonder if his momma will let him have Cat.

She'd never seen anyone look so good carrying a cup of java. Seriously, Ronald could have been a spokesmodel for Starbucks. He was fit, masculine, looked smart.

"Hey. We gotta run. Brittney just sent me a message."

"Okay."

Camille grabbed her purse and slid out of her chair.

He stopped shy of the passenger's door. "We might as well say our good-byes now, before we get back on church grounds."

She laughed. "Oh my goodness, I haven't heard any-one use the term 'church grounds' in a minute. Re-member when people used to turn down their radios if they were listening to FM radio when they passed the church?"

"Yep. Back in the day, even if people weren't living right, they used to have respect for the house of God. No cussin', no smoking. Our neighborhood wino used to take off his hat when he passed the church," Ronald recalled, a hint of nostalgia crossing his complexion as he pulled her into a hug.

Instantly, she felt the bulky metal against her chest and realized Ronald had probably felt it, too. She backed up, but it was too late.

"What's that?" Ronald asked, trying to maintain re-spectable eye level.

"Oh." *Dang!* "It's. I didn't want to say anything about it, but . . . I have"—*I can't tell him!*—"a pacemaker."

"A pacemaker? Wow! I mean, wow. I didn't know they could be so . . . big. I mean, I'm sorry. Did I mess it up? Are you okay?"

"Yes, yes."

Ronald redirected his gaze as she settled the device. *Oh my gosh! A pacemaker! Anything but a pacemaker.*

"I'm really sorry. I'll be more careful, now that I know."

"It's okay. I need to get it . . . tightened up." *Tight-ened up? This ain't no weave!* "They can dislodge slightly, I mean. But don't worry. You didn't cause the problem, and it's really a simple procedure for them to fix it."

Relieved, he opened the door for her and held out an arm so she could steady herself on the step rail and be seated.

"You in?" he asked. Already, he treated her with kid gloves.

"Yes. Thanks." Camille slapped her hand against her forehead as her unsuspecting date trotted to his side of the vehicle.

What have I done?

CHAPTER 25

Three weeks earlier, they'd buried her father's life-long best friend, Mr. Otis. His death had reminded Alexis that she wouldn't have her parents forever. Her mother's sassiness and her father's stubbornness on top of their medical issues was a handful to deal with, but she'd rather have a handful than none at all.

Mr. Otis's son, Jackson, had been submerged in grief throughout most of the service. Alexis used to wonder why people cried so hard at elderly people's funerals. After all, they had lived good lives. One look at Jackson's distraught face gave the answer. The longer someone lived, the more memories you shared. The more you'd miss them.

Jackson's older sister, Jetta, seemed to handle their father's death much better. She outright comforted her brother, laying his head on her shoulder. For as long as Alexis had known Jackson and Jetta, they had been a close pair. Alexis imagined that, as children, Jetta must have pumped him on her bicycle, beat up bullies for him, tied his shoes until he was able. With so many years between Alexis and Thomas, she'd never really experienced the kind of sibling camaraderie that people laughed about, where they fought like cats and dogs but wouldn't let anyone else mess with their brother or sister.

She was jealous. She'd been jealous of Camille and Courtney when she first met them, too. Courtney's faith in his little sister's singing ability, Camille's confidence in her big brother's business know-how. When Alexis really thought about it, neither Camille nor Courtney really needed the Sweet Treats ensemble. Those two could have made it all by themselves.

Too bad they didn't recognize.

"That's not true. They *will* recognize and be reconciled," Alexis spoke to the doubts creeping into her mind.

"Who betta recognize?" her father asked.

"Oh, I'm sorry, Daddy. I was talking to my negative thoughts." She grabbed a magazine from the stack resting on the coffee table in the doctor's waiting room.

Her father rolled his eyes. "You young folks and your positive-thinking craziness. Never seen so many broke, can't-stick-to-a-job, can't-stick-to-a-marriage folk always talkin' about self-esteem and stuff. What y'all need is to get a job! When you work hard, you won't have time to go around talking to yourself all day."

"There are a lot of people without jobs right now. It's not their fault," Alexis whispered, trying to model an appropriate indoor voice for her father. He was worse than her students, sometimes.

"Yes, it is," he squawked. He'd missed her hint to lower his voice. "If y'all had some kind of loyalty,

America wouldn't be in this mess. Ain't loyal to the job, shole ain't loyal to the country, all these foreign cars on the road.

"And you ought to be shame. Public school teacher driving a Honder. Teachin' your kids math and science, then turn around and give the Japanese kids more jobs to make more Honders. Might as well shoot yourself in the foot."

Daddy's ranting reminded Alexis to ask Dr. Ewell about the side effects of the medication her father had recently been prescribed. Alexis had taken advantage of Mr. Otis's death to convince her father he needed to schedule a full physical. Now, with another drug on the list, she wondered if Daddy's medications might be interacting negatively, yielding the crabby old man who'd fuss about the color of the sky if somebody would listen.

A nurse poked her head out of the door leading to the main portion of the office. "Nevils?"

"Here." Alexis laughed at herself. School habits die hard.

She stood to accompany her father, but he insisted he could handle this appointment on his own. "I don't need you standin' behind me while I got my hospital gown on."

The sitting area fluttered with snickering.

"Okay, Daddy." Alexis flopped back down into her seat, almost embarrassed at herself. Her father was right. She could only sit and wait now.

Times like this, she wished Thomas was with her. She also wished he'd take a more active role in caring for their parents. At one point, she had even grown resentful, but her coworkers convinced her that it was normal for daughters to bear the brunt of the responsibility when it came to parents. Not *right*, but normal as it happened in many families.

If only she had a sister.

A text broke her train of thought. Tonya. **Courtney called. Call me.**

Immediately, Alexis responded. "What did he say?"

"He's open!" Tonya hollered.

"Yes!"

"He didn't promise anything," she warned, "but he's already got some foreign labels interested."

"Great!" Alexis could barely contain herself. "Praise God. I'm so happy I'll be able to cash my checks without feeling guilty."

"Me, too. And I'm glad to get this whole thing with Camille behind us, you know? I didn't lose any sleep over it, but it's not about me, you know?"

"True that," Alexis cosigned. "So when do we call her?"

"Not yet. He wants to work out the business details first."

"Okay. I won't say anything. Thanks for the great news, girl."

"Bless God.

"Did you talk to him about the other thing?"

"Yes," Tonya said. "Since he owns the lyrics, he can revise them, or we can do kind of a dance remix to reduce the number of suggestive phrases. Courtney was like, 'Y'all serious about the Lord, huh?'"

"He got that right." Alexis laughed. "I can't be singing stuff I don't want my future kids to hear. I still haven't played every song on our CD for my parents. They'd have a cow and have our old managers up against a wall somewhere."

"I know, right?"

Alexis reiterated, "Thanks again. I'll keep quiet until I hear from you again. Love you, girl."

"Love you, too."

As she hung up the phone, she smiled to herself. She did, after all, have a sister in Christ.

CHAPTER 26

Timber showed no signs of releasing the grudge. She was obviously one of those one-strike-and-you're-out types. "John David will see you in a moment."

"Thank you." Hopefully, Camille wouldn't have to kiss up to Timber much longer. The woman might have a better attitude once she realized Camille's talent paid part of her paycheck.

This time, John David emerged from his office, arm extended, wearing a tell-all grin. "He *loved* the demo. Absolutely loved it."

"Great!" she shrieked.

Timber huffed to indicate we were interrupting her telephone conversation.

"Sorry," Camille spoke softly, but she couldn't stop the squeal from leaking out of her throat. "What do we do next?"

"Timber, draw up a representation contract."

Yeah, Timber! Draw us up a contract! Camille could

say whatever she wanted in her mind; she'd never have the nerve to talk crazy to Timber.

"Come on back to my office. Let's make some calls."

John David punched the conference button, dialed ten digits, then a male voice with a thick Spanish accent thundered through the speakers.

"*Hola,* John Daveeed!"

"Hey, Ignacio. I've got the magic voice here. Say hello to Camille Robertson."

"Oh, my Carmelita! Where have you been all my life?"

Camille leaned closer to the phone perched on John David's desk. "In Texas."

Ignacio laughed. John David echoed with a snicker of his own. This Ignacio must really be somebody, so Camille giggled right along with them.

"We're ready to make a move, my friend. What do you have in mind for her?"

"It's just as we discussed. The film needs a hot, hot song for the scene. Perfect for someone whose voice can go high, low, and everywhere in between."

John David nodded at Camille, that money-sign beam in his eye. "Camille is definitely your singer. She's got a wide range. And I'm sitting here looking at her. She's hot, Ignacio."

Where was all this hotness coming from? Last she checked, gospel music wasn't about steamy songs.

"And tell me, Carmelita, who was that man singing with you?"

"Oh"—she shrugged, as though Ignacio could see her—"he was just a guy from my church."

"You two"—Ignacio's voice lowered—"not the first time you have made beautiful music together, I see?"

For the sake of the contract Timber was supposed to be typing that very moment, Camille hid her disgust. "Like I said, we're in the same choir. He's a friend."

"Aha. Johnny boy, can you get *him*, too?"

The agent shot Camille an anxious stare.

"I could ask," she said.

"Fabulous, Carmelita. You are perfect! Johnny, Angelica will send details. *Gracias!*" Ignacio didn't give them an opportunity to respond.

John David picked up his receiver, then laid it back in its cradle. He turned to Camille and asked, "Ignacio works quickly. How soon can you get in touch with your church partner?"

She shook her head in confusion. "Wait a minute. Is this a gospel song Ignacio has in mind?"

"No. It's more like pop. Slated for a spot on the soundtrack for a blockbuster movie, however. You'll get lots of exposure with this song. Lots!"

"What happened to gospel?"

"Forget gospel. This is a once-in-a-lifetime chance for you to get back on the charts that matter. Don't freak out on me because it's not gospel," John David scoffed. "Now that we've got some money behind us, I'll set up some time in a studio for you and . . . what's his name?"

"Ronald Shepherd."

"Hmmm . . . might have to change it to Ronnie. Anyway, I'll have Timber call you and set up an appointment."

"Ignacio said the song was hot. How hot is hot?"

"Remember that ballad from the sex scene in *Top Gun?*"

She guessed, "'Take My Breath Away'?"

"Yeah."

"Multiply it by ten. It's sizzling, seductive—wait! I think I actually have the lyrics in an e-mail." He focused his attention on his laptop, clicked a few buttons. The rollers on the printer warmed for a moment, then a piece of paper ejected from the top slot. John David handed her the document.

One look at the title ruined all chances of getting Ronald involved. "On Top of Me." Her heart sank into her stomach. The first verse was the female's recount of how it feels to have the man on top of her body. Vice versa for the second verse. The chorus line mentioned body part eruptions. This was almost too hot for even Camille to handle.

"Are they glued to these lyrics?" she asked John David.

"When Ignacio Mendes asks you to record a song, you don't question the lyrics. What's the problem?"

She exhaled. *I've come too close to my dreams to quit now.* "No problem."

None of this second-party nonsense sat well with Camille. John David was supposed to be representing *her*, not her and some other guy he'd never met. Why couldn't that loony Ignacio just pair her up with Musiq Soulchild or Anthony Hamilton and get this ball rolling?

Wouldn't be such a problem if Ronald wasn't so holier than everyone she knew. He needed to lighten up, but she didn't have the time to talk him out of his rigid beliefs before the studio date. Timber had set it for Wednesday at twelve thirty PM and she wouldn't reschedule it no matter how much Camille tried to explain that she couldn't take off any more time from work.

"This is a state-of-the-art facility. We were fortunate to get a slot," Timber claimed. "Take it or leave it."

"Fine." How could Camille not pursue her destiny because of a day job? She didn't want to be ninety years old, rocking in a nursing home, recounting the day she chose a measly old job over worldwide fame. Sad enough she'd already blown her first chance at stardom.

Camille completed yet another request for Wednesday afternoon off and placed it in the plastic wall file holder outside Sheryl's door.

One more logistic left to handle: the missing duet partner. Ronald was out of the picture. The only other men she knew with decent voices were Faison and Nathan, and Nathan was right up there next to Ronald on the holiness ladder, from what she could tell. Plus, he and Ronald seemed to communicate regularly.

Faison, however, told an occasional off-color joke or two in practice. She'd also seen quite a few fresh tattoos ascending his arms. No old-school Christian would have body art let alone expose it freely, in Camille's opinion. For a few dollars, she could probably get him to do anything. His voice wasn't nearly as strong as Ronald's, but a little less perfection on the male end might actually work in Camille's favor. Maybe Ignacio would X the whole man thing and pick her alone for the song. If he didn't "Ronald" would become "Ronnie Faison."

She didn't have Faison's number. Didn't know how to reach him outside of church. And he had no clue that he was part of phase two of her scheme, but he was about to become one of her closest confidantes. Thanks to a message Ronald had e-mailed to members of the young-adult choir, Camille obtained Faison's e-mail address and sent him a generic note, asking him to give her a call.

He responded to her request quickly. She answered at work, spoke in hushed tones because Sheryl wasn't too happy about the request for time off, probably because it wasn't animal related.

"Hello?"

"Hi, Camille. It's Faison. I got your message. What's up?"

"Thanks for calling me back." Okay, how was she supposed to say, "I need you to sing a nasty song with me because I know you're not all that saved?" She advanced cautiously. "Well, I've got a little proposition for you."

"Uh-huh."

"I don't know if you know this or not, but I used to sing in an R and B group. Sweet Treats?"

"Yeah, yeah. I'd heard. Y'all had some good songs back in the day. 'Specially 'Meet Me in the Hot Tub,' you know what I'm sayin'?"

She thought she picked up on a slightly suggestive twang in his pitch. Maybe it was just her imagination. "Anyway, I've got an agent who's interested in me. He wants me to go to the studio and record a song, with a male vocalist in the background. I was wondering if you'd be willing to accompany me."

"I'd love to. But if you don't mind me asking, why not Ronald instead of me?"

Why he gotta go there with a question?

"Well . . . it's not a gospel song, and I don't want him to put his position at the church in jeopardy, you know what I'm sayin'?"

"Pastor wouldn't fire him for singing a secular song, I wouldn't think."

Ugh! "This particular song is . . . let's just say it's . . . a love song he probably wouldn't want Brittney to hear."

"Oh"—Faison finally caught on—"it's one of *those* type of songs, huh?"

"Yeah. It is," she had to admit.

"I'm cool. To me, music is music. As long as God knows your heart, people can't judge you."

Funny. Before she started going to Grace Chapel, listening to Pastor Collins, and observing the living truth in Ronald, she might have agreed. But when Faison spoke those words, something within her knew he wasn't exactly right. Good thing, too, because he probably wouldn't have agreed to sing with her otherwise.

She gave him the when and where, and breathed a sigh of relief when Faison said there was no schedule conflict for him because he was off on Wednesdays and Thursdays.

"Great. I'll e-mail you the lyrics so you can look over them. Thank you so much, Faison. I can't pay you any money for doing this, but since you won't have to speed back to work, I'll treat you to lunch."

Camille understood well: People like food. Especially free food. She'd be sure to watch the mail for a two-for-one restaurant coupon.

CHAPTER 27

For the first time she could remember, Camille saw a smile on Timber's face as she and Faison checked in at the studio.

"Hello, Camille. Good to see you again."

I guess. "Good to see you, too. This is my friend, Faison. He's going to sing with me today."

"Hello, Faison. Pleased to make your acquaintance." Timber's eyes fanned up and down his body twice.

Obviously aware of her interest, Faison opened up a borrowed can of chivalry. Without a word, he kissed Timber's hand and Camille thought the woman was going to unzip the back of her pencil skirt on the spot.

"Ooh, Faison. The pleasure is all mine."

"It *can* be," he intimated, pulling up his sagging pants.

Can y'all wait until we finish taping? Why is she here anyway? This ain't her office.

"Follow me," Timber said as she switched her nonexistent behind down a short corridor leading to the sound room. There, Timber handed them off to a man who introduced himself as Stevie.

"Thanks, Timber. I'll take it from here. Tell John David I said hello."

"Certainly."

While Faison busied himself exchanging numbers with Timber in the hallway, Camille made sure Stevie had things in order for the recording. She took in the control room, noting obvious changes in equipment over the past ten years. Six-foot sound engineering boards lit up like Christmas trees, computer monitors contained images that floated from one screen to the next.

The actual recording booth, however, hadn't changed. Just a headset and a microphone. Even with all this new technology, there was no substitute for the human voice.

From his seat behind one of the boards, Stevie assured Camille that he'd been in touch with both John David and Ignacio. "They're a great team to work with.

"And I look forward to working with you two. I heard the demo. Awesome."

Then he switched into music producer mode. "Let me have you in the booth first. Then, we'll bring Ronald in—"

"Oh, he doesn't go by Ronald, professionally. Call him Faison," Camille interjected, thankful that Faison was still outside the room flirting. That Timber was good for something after all.

Stevie made notes on a sheet of paper. "Faison what?"

"Just Faison."

"Okaaay. Since you're in the spotlight, per John David, we'll start by recording separate tracks. We'll

probably end up laying Faison's track on top of yours."
Stevie chuckled slightly. "Goes with the song, wouldn't
you say?"

"Yeah. I guess so."

"Afterward, we'll run the duet."

When her singing buddy finally made his way into
the studio, he stood there hollering like a straight-up
country fool who'd never been off the farm. "Daaang!
This is off tha chain! You didn't tell me we were going
to a *real* music studio!"

Stevie glanced at Camille curiously.

She, in turn, pulled Faison's balled fist from his lips.
"Alrighty, then. Let's get started."

After listening to the general beat, Camille delivered a sultry, strong performance in a relatively short
period of time.

"You hit the spot, Miss Robertson," Stevie complimented her.

Next came Faison's turn. Maybe it was the computers,
or blame it on his lingering infatuation with Timber—
Faison butchered "On Top of Me." He hadn't any more
studied those lyrics than a man on the moon. And his
dreadful voice surprised both Stevie and Camille.
Without the padding of other tenors, Faison sounded
like Keith Sweat *without* LeVert covering him up, all
that off-key, off-beat begging and whining.

After several hours' worth of stopping, restarting,
redoing Faison's track, Camille was fit to be tied. And
one of poor Stevie's clients had been waiting for his appointment in the studio almost forty-five minutes. Stevie obviously hadn't dreamed he'd be in the studio this
long with someone who'd already been handpicked by
John David and *the* Ignacio Mendes.

"Well," Stevie finally exhaled after yet another rerun. "I think I've got enough to play with. I'm thinking we don't need to attem—I mean, *record* the duet. I'll mix the two tracks and get the master over to John David in the next few days. Might take me a little longer."

Good old cut and paste, along with some audio *voice* brushing.

Faison nearly danced on his tiptoes. "Ooh, can I get a copy?"

Stevie sat back in his chair. "Ummm, no."

"Why not?"

"Don't be *silly*," Camille cooed, slapping Faison's shoulder. He had no understanding of the fact that he'd never own the raw tracks—he'd *never* own the rights to the song, for that matter. All that belonged to the producer and writer. "Let's wait and let Stevie work his magic."

"And magic it will be," Stevie commented under his breath.

He stood and escorted Camille and Faison out the door while simultaneously motioning for his next appointment to come forth.

"Nice meeting you," Camille said to Stevie as Faison bounded toward the reception area.

"You have a beautiful voice," Stevie reiterated.

"Thank you."

"But your partner . . . sounds like he was having an off day. Waaay off."

"I see. Thank you."

She walked out of there like a dog with its tail stuck between its legs. Faison, on the other hand, was wagging his tail in the parking lot. "That was sweet!"

"No. It wasn't. Faison, did you even read the words ahead of time?"

"Naw," he admitted unashamedly. "Why? I don't read the words before choir rehearsal."

Camille decided to save her breath. Faison had done her a favor. Horribly, but still, he'd done it. She reached into her zipper bag and brought forth a twenty-dollar bill. She gave it to Faison, saying, "Here. This is for lunch. I'm not feeling too good. You'll have to go without me."

Sheryl was back to her pre-Fluffy, pre-Cat self. Bossy and demanding, cracking the whip in a never-ending attempt to increase the number of appointments. Camille found herself working through lunch to keep pace with her coworkers' achievements. For the life of her, she couldn't imagine why the computer kept putting her in touch with the meanest, rudest office managers in the entire central time zone.

"No! Someone from your company called last month. I already told them we do *not* need a stupid water machine!" a lady from an educational publishing house yelled.

"I'm sorry," Camille apologized. "I'll take you out of our system."

"Thank you!"

Another ex-potential client fussed, "Don't you people get the hint? Call here again and I'll report you to the FCC."

By the end of the day Friday, Camille had heard enough people tell her that they'd already been called by Aquapoint Systems that she figured she'd better say something to Sheryl. Just before clocking out (lest she dare work one minute past five o'clock), Camille cautiously let herself into Sheryl's office.

Sheryl looked up, glanced at her visitor's face, focused back on the papers before her.

"Uh, Sheryl, I just wanted to let you know that several of the companies I called on today had already been contacted by Aquapoint Systems in the past few weeks. I'm guessing maybe the system isn't deleting previous contacts."

Her boss laid the papers flat, looked Camille squarely in the eyes. "You're programmed for callbacks."

"Callbacks?"

"Yes, callbacks. Sometimes, the second time is the charm."

"I've been working here for months, and I've never done callbacks before."

"Well, Camille, there's a first time for everything."

Which begged her next question, "Is *everyone* doing callbacks?"

"No."

Baffled, she asked, "So when can I stop doing callbacks and get back to regular, first-time office managers who haven't already decided they don't want Aquapoint Systems."

"That will probably be when you start taking this job seriously," Sheryl quipped.

Politely, she asked, "Who said I didn't take this job seriously?"

"No one has to say anything, Camille. You just took off work Wednesday to . . . what was it, audition?"

Camille joked, "So, it's okay to take off for *cats*, but not *careers*?"

"This *is* your career," Sheryl fumed.

Camille intentionally resisted the urge to put her hands on her hips. No need in going all the way there with Sheryl just yet. She planned to keep a day job until she got at least six figures saved up from CD royalties.

Worst-case scenario, Camille hoped, would be John David deciding to pair her with someone on his dormant male roster who could actually sing, have them rerecord with Stevie, then submit the finished product to Ignacio. Since her track was near perfect, all of the studio time hadn't been lost.

Too embarrassed to call John David but almost sick from waiting for him to respond, Camille sat on the couch, tucked her feet underneath her behind, and braced herself to call John David's office. It had been four days already since the session. Granted, only two of those were business days, but surely, by now, Stevie must have finished the mixing. All he really had to do was nix most of Faison's recording and duplicate the hook a few times. How long could that take?

Cat curled up next to Camille, hiding himself in the tiny cranny between Camille's waist and the couch's arm. He purred lightly and pressed his nose against her body, a gesture she had come to recognize as "hello." He always seemed to know when Camille was on edge. Last week, when she'd forked over the money for the last payment on her ticket, Cat had laid his head on her lap as if to say, "It's okay. I know you're broke. I won't eat that much this week."

Chalking up her actions to nervousness, Camille

stroked Cat's back and tail in long waves as she pressed John David's ten digits on her phone's screen.

"Hi, Timber, it's Camille Robertson. Is John David in?"

She sighed. "Yes, he is. But he doesn't want to talk to you now or ever again."

Panic slit a gash in Camille's chest. This was worse than she'd imagined. "Bu . . . but . . . did he say why?"

"You *know* why." She chuckled. "You nearly made a fool out of him. Faison is *not* Ronald, thankfully, and—"

"Wait!" Camille slithered through a cracked window of opportunity. "Timber, you know how serious I am about my singing career. I jumped through all John David's hoops before he'd even officially agreed to represent me. I . . . I have to fix this. I have to talk to him. Isn't there anything you can do to help me? I mean, I *did* introduce you to Faison."

Timber sighed again. Camille held her breath.

"Well . . . only because of my boo. I'm going to step out of the office for a second. I won't forward the phone to our other office or to voice mail, so John David *may* decide to answer it if you let it ring long enough. That's *all* I can do, and I'm only doing it once.

"I'm getting up to leave now. You've got five minutes to make it happen."

"Thanks, Timber."

"Don't show your gratitude just yet. You'd better hope this works or you're on your own."

Click.

Camille counted to ten, then she redialed. The phone rang seven times, no answer. She ended, redialed again. Nine times. Repeat. This time, on the twelfth ring, John David answered in an exasperated tone, "Yeah?"

Too bad she hadn't thought about what she'd actually say when he answered the phone. Timber's plan didn't allow time for concocting a good lie. The truth would have to suffice. "John David, I am *so* sorry about the recording."

"Is this Camille?"

"Yes."

"You must think Stevie and I are total idiots."

"That's no . . . no."

"I'm hanging up the phone now."

"No! Wait! I can explain everything!" She rambled through a truthful explanation, told him that Ronald was too religious to sing "On Top of Me," and she'd tried to cover up with Faison. "I knew I had to come through with something or someone. I didn't want to let you down." Before she knew it, Camille's eyes had begun to water and emotion slipped through her speech, splitting each of her words in two.

"And why on earth didn't you tell me this *before* we wasted my money and Stevie's time and expertise?"

"Because when we were talking to Ignacio, you practically promised him Ronald."

John David clicked his cheek. "Aren't they teaching you anything at that church you're going to? It's better not to agree to do something than to agree to do something and then not follow through."

"I tried to—"

"Do you have any idea how many people would love to be in your shoes right now? Not just *people*, actual *singers*. *Wonderful* singers with way more integrity than you." He laughed. "I should have known you'd stoop pretty low when you agreed to join a church so you could start singing again."

Since when did he get so religious? Wasn't this his bright idea in the first place?

"You're the worst kind of client, Camille. You're beyond daring or desperate. You're dangerous. You'd sell me out to the next agent who offers you a bigger lollipop."

Suddenly, this whole scenario seemed liked déjà vu, only ten years ago, she'd faced similar accusations from Courtney. She'd eventually lost everything after she lost Courtney. She couldn't go through the same loss twice.

"I am sooo sorry, John David. I've learned my lesson. And this is my *passion*," she begged for life. "Please don't throw it away."

"Don't put this on me. *You* threw it away by lying."

"Wait!" Camille shrieked. Then she proceeded to explain her revelation to John David. She told him about how she'd sold out her brother, how she thought she'd learned her lesson with him, but now she'd *really* learned it twice. "I promise, John David, I'll never lie to you again. Please give me one more chance or else . . . I don't know what I'll do with the rest of my time here on the planet, I'm serious." Maybe that was a little dramatic, but she'd just poured out her entire heart to him. He had to believe her. He just *had* to.

John David spoke softly. "I'll put your replacement on hold. You. Me. The *real* Ronald. Stevie. Tomorrow. Six AM at the studio. Not one minute late, or I'll call in my backup, have her record it, and sell Ignacio on a much younger vocalist with a whole lot more character than the one I'm talking to right now."

"Thank you, John David."

"Don't thank me. I'm only doing this because Ignacio loves your voice, otherwise, I'd have hung up on you ten minutes ago."

John David didn't trouble himself with a proper dismissal.

Six am? Worried, Camille briskly swiped her hand along Cat's spine again. John David had had it up to his neck with her. If she didn't produce Ronald Shepherd in the flesh in less than twelve hours, prepared to sing "On Top of Me," her professional career was dead. Forever.

CHAPTER 28

It seemed a bit odd to pray and ask God to touch Ronald's heart so he would agree to sing "On Top of Me," but she figured it was worth a shot anyway. She slid down onto the carpeted floor, sank her elbows into the couch cushions, and laced her fingers. "God, I'm sorry about all the lies and joining the church for all the wrong reasons. I just didn't know what else to do. I don't know what to do now, either, but I know You know Ronald. Can You talk to him for me? This means everything to me, God. You created me to sing. My momma said so herself. I know this isn't exactly the kind of song You want me to sing, but God, I know You work in mysterious ways. I'm hoping that this will get my foot back in the door. And maybe You will bless me with better opportunities later. All these blessings I ask in Your son Jesus's name. Amen."

Next, she rushed to the restroom to wash her face. Get her thoughts together. How, exactly, was she going to explain this to Ronald? What if John David mentioned Faison?

The logistics puzzled her as well. Studio at six in the morning. With Ronald present, Stevie would probably want to record several parts with both of them in the sound booth, which meant there was no way she'd make it across town and back to work by eight. Sheryl would not be happy. Camille had to face facts: This time tomorrow, she might not have a job.

How long will it take for them to legally evict me? Probably a good three weeks. Less than that if they found out about Cat. She could find another job. Temporary services were always hiring. She wasn't sure how she'd answer the question, "Reason for leaving last job?" No way could she write, "Fired for going to the studio to record a demo."

In the restroom, she prayed again and asked God to keep her from getting fired. In the past, she wouldn't have had any problems with writing, "Moved away to care for a sick relative," and then explaining in the interview that the relative had passed, so there was no need to worry about her having to take off again so abruptly. Sickness was a last resort, but Camille always rationalized that after losing her mother at such a young age, she'd lived through one of the worst things that could happen. She'd earned the right to play the dying-relative (or, most recently, ailing-pet) card every once in a while.

But now, things were different. Camille was tired of lying. Tired of pretending. Tired of waiting for the shoe to fall. Worshipping at Grace Chapel, singing with the choir, spending time with Ronald—this stuff was taking a toll on her conscience. Not to mention every time one of the girls from camp or Mentors and Models saw her in the sanctuary, they hugged her like a long-lost big sister, looking up to her in love and adoration. Their naïve respect for her weighed most heavily on her heart. Kept her awake at night. She'd been driven to depend on a cat for solace, for goodness sake, how much worse could it get?

Maybe, if she stopped lying now, everything from this stage forward would be okay.

Since it was almost seven, Camille figured she'd better get on with calling Ronald. He'd probably have to make special arrangements to get Brittney off to school since she didn't ride the bus. Plus, he'd probably be late to work himself.

She tried his cell phone. No answer. Sent him a text. Thirty minutes passed. No answer. Called again. Same game. *What's going on?* What if Faison said something to Ronald about the recording? What if Ronald knew somebody who knew somebody who knew Stevie, and they told him about the whole fiasco?

Quickly, she dialed Mercedes's number. "Hey, Mercedes. How are ya?"

"I'm good, girl. Trying to nab me a machine at the gym. What's up?"

Camille suppressed her anxiety. "I know this is weird, but do you have Brittney Shepherd's number? I really need to get hold of her."

"No, but I can get in touch with the lady who's over at Mentors and Models. She has all the girls' numbers. I'm sure I can get it from her.

"Is everything okay?" That Mercedes didn't miss a beat.

"Oh, yeah, yeah. Everything's fine. I just really need

to catch up with Ronald, and he's not answering. I'm hoping everything's okay with *him*."

"Hmmm," Mercedes pondered aloud. "He's usually pretty quick to get back. Let me make the call. I'll text you Brittney's number."

Two minutes later, Mercedes came through. Camille wasted no time in calling her young friend. "Hi, Brittney."

"Hey, Miss Camille! Oh my gosh, I'm so glad you called me!"

Taken aback by Brittney's enthusiasm, Camille temporarily shelved her reason for the call. "It's good to talk to you. How have you been?"

"Not too good."

"What's up?" Camille asked.

Brittney gave a drama queen sigh, then blubbered in a teary confession, "My dad. He hardly even talks to me anymore since . . . you know."

Putting her own life on hold, Camille paused for a moment to consider Brittney's dilemma. Camille knew all too well the pain of losing the trust of a family member. "You have to give him some time to heal from this. Play by his rules, do everything you can to reassure him that this won't happen again. This *can't* happen again, you know that, right?"

"I know, I know. I've learned my lesson, Miss Camille. Why won't he believe me?"

Did somebody put a recorder in my apartment?

"Trust me on this, Brittney. The way you earn trust back is by telling the truth. Admit what you've done wrong. Apologize. Have you apologized, by the way?"

"No! He won't let me!" she cried. "Every time I try to talk to him, he just gets mad all over again, so I stopped trying. At church, when we're around other people, he acts like everything is okay. But at home, we just walk around the house like strangers. I can't do it anymore." Brittney's sniffles reached an alarming rate.

"Take a deep breath. Have you talked to anyone about this? Your grandmother, maybe?"

"No!" she wailed again. "I don't want my grandmother or anyone else to know what happened. The only people who know are me, you, and my dad. If other people found out, I would, like, die of embarrassment."

A loud meow came from the bathroom. Camille asked Brittney to hold for a moment while she checked on Cat. He'd gotten himself entangled in a mountain of toilet paper. Charmin was one of Cat's crazy, inexplicable fetishes. "Ooh, this cat is crazy," she told her young friend.

"You have a cat?"

"Yes," Camille said, realizing this was the first time she'd actually acknowledged permanent ownership of the animal to anyone other than Sheryl. "I tried to give him away, but no one wanted him."

"*I* want him."

"For real?" Camille perked up.

"Yeah, but I can't have him. My dad says I can't have any pet until I master the art of keeping my room clean first," Brittney lamented.

"Well, he's got a valid point. Pets are a big responsibility." She finished pulling the paper off Cat and shooed him out of the restroom, closing the door behind her. It was time she moved Cat's litter box someplace else, away from this weird temptation.

Camille jumped back into their mentor-mentee talk. She had to ask, "What about the boy?"

"Who, DeShawn?"

"Was that his name?"

Brittney admitted, "Yeah."

"Well, did DeShawn tell anyone?"

"There was nothing to tell. He didn't actually come into the house."

"But you were *about* to let DeShawn in, right?"

"Right. Well, maybe. I don't know," she vacillated. "Either way, nothing happened, so why is my dad making such a big deal out of this?"

Camille tried to explain, "He's afraid of what *could* have happened."

She huffed one of those teenage know-it-all huffs. "But I'm not *stupid*. I mean, if I *did* let him in, it was only gonna be for, like, ten minutes. Can't my dad trust me for ten minutes alone with a boy? Nothing's gonna happen in *ten* minutes?"

Camille tsked. "A whole lot can happen in ten minutes. *It* can happen in ten minutes, Brittney."

"Oh," she gasped. "Well . . . I mean . . . on TV . . . I thought it takes longer, doesn't it?"

"Uh, no. Especially not at your age, but that's TMI. Let's get back to you and your dad."

"Hold up," Brittney said. "I just want to ask this one question."

Now that the can of worms was open, Camille had to oblige. "What?"

"What's it like?"

"What's *what* like?"

"Sex."

Alrighty, then. "Brittney, I don't really think I'm the one you should be asking that question."

"Who else am I gonna ask? I can't ask my dad. And my mom's gone."

Ask the school nurse; shoot, I don't know!

Brittney pressed, "I mean . . . some people say it's fun, some people say it hurts."

Camille remembered asking a similar question when she was around Brittney's age. It was after choir rehearsal. She and some of the other members of the youth choir were sitting on the front steps of the old church talking while the adults remained inside handling fund-raising business. Tammy Henderson, one of the oldest members of the youth choir, schooled Camille and four other younger girls on sex. Tammy said it felt so good it made you want to slap the judge, said the only reason grown-ups didn't want them to do it was because no one who does it ever wants to stop. She also said it made your boyfriend love you more, kept him from other girls.

Brittney framed her questions better. "I know they did it before they got married because I saw their marriage certificate, and I was born, like, five months later. But every time I try to talk to my dad just about boyfriends—not even sex—all he does is start talking about the Bible, like him and my mom never broke the rules."

"So why don't you start by talking to him about the marriage certificate? Not in an accusatory way, but just let him know you want to keep the conversation real."

She piped down a bit. "Because I don't want to, like, make it seem like my mom was a bad person. But then I think, if they did it and he married her and they loved each other, what would be so wrong if me and DeShawn did it? He already said he loves me and he wants to marry me."

"But he ran away and left you to face your father's anger alone, right?" Camille asked.

"Yeah," she said.

"Brittney, when people love you, they stand beside you when you get in trouble—especially if they're part of the reason you got in trouble. If DeShawn runs at the sight of your father, what do you think he'd do if you got pregnant with his baby?"

"I don't know."

"Well, if you don't know, you sure don't have any business having sex with him. DeShawn ran like a little boy, which is exactly what he is right now. Maybe when he's older, he'll be a good husband to someone, but not right now."

"So, you think I'm too young to have sex?"

"Definitely. And it's not a matter of how *young* you are. It's a matter of whether or not you're—"

"I know," Brittney butted in, "*married*. My daddy and my church people have told me that a million times."

Camille was glad Brittney interrupted because that wasn't exactly the word she was going to say. She was about to say something like "committed" or "in love," which was pretty much the general public agreement. Hearing the word "marriage" tied to sex took Camille way back. But for the sake of consensus with Ronald, she concurred, "Right. Married."

"Ugh!" Brittney fussed. "I'm so tired of everyone saying that when they didn't wait!"

"How do you know everyone didn't wait?" Camille countered. "Some people did. And, yes, sex can feel great to your body, but it also hurts—in more ways than one. I don't recommend it to anyone who's not married because, well, for one thing, we all know you could get pregnant. No matter what anybody says, boys always get off way easier when that happens.

"Second, no matter how much he loves you or you love him, when it's over between you two, your heart will be completely broken. Smashed to smithereens, seriously, and it could take a long, long time to get over that. Don't commit your heart and your body to someone who hasn't committed himself to you in front of the whole world."

How 'bout that? Nice, neat, and not too much. Camille was proud of herself. She'd spoken the truth to Brittney and, somehow, she knew Brittney would listen to her if not anyone else. At least for a little while.

"Huh. Okay," Brittney said. "I hear you. You're the first grown-up to actually admit that it feels good."

Is that all she heard?

"I said it *can* feel good. But I can tell you from experience, it's hard for *anything* to feel good when you're sneaking around behind your parent's back to do it. You're a church kid. You know better. You'll never feel good about doing stuff you know you shouldn't be doing. Other people might, but not *you*."

Brittney laughed, then shared a story about how she'd once tried to steal a pack of bubble gum from the store but returned it to the cashier in tears. Camille relayed her stolen Slurpee story, and the two laughed again at the ridiculousness of it all.

"I gotta go. My daddy's home," Brittney whispered.

"Hey, can I talk to him?"

"Um"—she lowered her voice even more—"can you call him on the house phone? I'm not . . . um . . . really supposed to be on my cell phone . . . that much."

Camille rolled her eyes as though Brittney could see them. "Bye, Brittney. Stop all this sneakin' around, you hear?"

"Yes, ma'am. Bye."

After a few minutes, Camille decided to try the house line. She picked up her phone again, but Ronald's incoming call beat her to the punch. *Thank goodness!* She didn't want him to think she'd morphed into a stalker.

"Hey, I saw you called. Got your text, too. Sorry I couldn't get back to you right away."

Her immediate thoughts were to ask him why he hadn't made an effort to at least text a line or two earlier. Again, she reminded herself that she wasn't exactly his woman. He owed her no explanations. She was a friend. A friend who liked his kisses, adored his daughter, needed him to sing a song with her before the sun came up.

She decided on a subtle approach. "How was your day?"

"Busy, that's why I couldn't call. Two funerals, a meeting with the musicians, another meeting with pastor. He saves his most lengthy sermons for meetings." Ronald snickered.

"I see," Camille said. "You got a lot on your schedule tomorrow?"

"Um, not too much. What's up?"

Might as well get this over with. "Would you sing with me tomorrow morning?"

"Uhh . . . yeah, I guess. Where?"

"At a studio. I'm recording a song for my agent to pass along to a producer."

"Cool. I didn't know you had an agent."

"Yes. I'm trying to get back in the saddle. Here's the bad news. We'd need to be there around six."

"Six *am*?"

"Yes. I can pick you up if you'd like. You're closer to the studio than me."

Ronald thought out loud, "Brittney needs to be at school by seven thirty . . . can't get there before seven . . . I could ask my neighbor, Alicia, to take her."

Who's Alicia? Down, jealous non-girlfriend.

"Okay," Camille agreed. "Can I pick you up at five thirty?"

"Hmmm," he hesitated, "that would leave Brittney home alone for almost an hour and a half."

"Ronald, you're going to have to give her the opportunity to earn your trust again. Besides, there aren't many teenage boys up at five thirty in the morning. I think she'll be all right."

He exhaled in surrender. "Okay. See you at five thirty, but you'd better have some kind of latte or tea with you, 'cause that's earlier than a mug!"

"I know, right? But thank you. I really appreciate your willingness."

"You're welcome. I'm always glad to help you, you know that, right? I was thinking about you today."

"Pray tell," she urged.

"Thinking about what a blessing you are to me. And to Brittney."

"Awww, that's so sweet."

"It's more than sweet. It's something else. It's what I've missed since Brittney's mom died. Since I stopped thinking about companionship because I really didn't think I was up to it. Camille, I'm glad God brought you into my life, and I hope you're willing to stay in and see what else God has planned for us."

Wow. She hadn't been expecting these words from Ronald. She realized now that, deep down, she'd been *hoping* for them, but not anticipating them. It was as though Ronald had turned on a switch inside her. Everything appeared different in light of his revelation. He liked having her in his life. She felt the same. And whatever God had planned for them was perfectly fine with her, too, since most of His stuff seemed to work out pretty good anyway. Pastor Collins had preached on following God's plan just the other week and, in her heart, Camille had whispered a prayer to God that she wanted His plan more than anything else. Now, it seemed, Ronald might be a part of that vision.

"By the way, what are we singing?" Ronald stuck a pin in her bliss bubble.

Camille had already practiced her answer, should this question arise. "It's an original compilation. You haven't heard it before."

"Did you write it?"

Her lips tightened. "No. Someone else did."

"Okay, if you wanna be all hush-hush about it." Yet, he persisted with the guessing game. "Anyone I would know?"

"No." Camille closed her eyes and blurted out the truth before her common sense overrode her decision to be upfront with Ronald. "It's a secular song. For a movie sound track." All true.

"Oh." His voice had fallen an octave. "Well, you know me. You know what I stand for. I trust you wouldn't be asking me to sing the song if it violated who I am. I'll see you in the morning. 'Night, love."

"'Night."

He just called me "love."

CHAPTER 29

Camille could barely close her eyes without hearing Ronald's words. *I trust you wouldn't be asking me to sing the song if it violated who I am.* More than the whole song issue, the idea that he trusted her, period, haunted Camille so much that she nearly rubbed Cat's fur off. He escaped under the bed to get his own sleep and avoid getting patted to death.

Throughout the night, Camille ran through several scenarios of what might happen tomorrow with Stevie, John David, Ronald, and herself. The best-case scenario would be if Ronald read the lyrics, looked in Camille's eyes, and decided to sing the song anyway because he (according to his own confession) was on the road to loving her. That would be great. Not likely, but great.

Scenario number two, Ronald and Camille would sit down with Stevie and John David and come up with a plan to use Ronald's voice without him actually saying perverse words. Or maybe they could ad lib a line about a wedding ring or a veil—something symbolizing mar-

riage. Then it would maybe be like Roberta Flack and
Peabo Bryson's classic honeymoon song, "Tonight, I
Celebrate My Love." Granted, "On Top of Me" was a
bit raunchier. But, hey, some newlyweds are bound to
be kinkier than others, Camille could reason. With a
little creative compromise, technical genius, and artistic liberty, setup number two could work well for
everyone.

Or number three. Next-to-the-worst development.
Ronald could take one look at the words and say no.
John David would explode, Stevie would shut down
the system, Ronald would walk out, and Camille would
bust out in tears. She could either chase Ronald out of
the studio or get down on her knees and beg John
David not to end their contract because, after all, he
would have seen with his own eyes that Ronald's refusal to sing was not her fault.

Finally, the most horrible script would be if Ronald
walked out and John David told Camille to follow him
no matter how much she begged and pleaded. She
could hear him already, "I'm tired of dealing with you,
Camille. It's over." In this case, she wasn't sure she'd
chase after Ronald. Could she forgive him for nailing
the coffin on her dreams?

The very thought that her singing career might
come to a complete end tomorrow nearly choked the
breath out of Camille. Some people say that before a
person dies, her life flashes before her eyes. For
Camille, a series of songs rang in her ears. She thought
of all the hours she'd spent singing, remembered times
she'd actually cried because a note was outside of her
natural range. She had to grab every note, *had* to.

She thought of how her legs used to ache from
standing next to her mother so long while she played

the piano and Camille sang along. She'd used Camille to flesh out the different parts of the song, the harmonies. Now, Camille realized her mother had been preparing her to do and be the professional singer she had been, and hoped to be again.

The last time she was at a make-or-break moment, she'd been able to call Courtney. He always reassured her, told her she was the best in the business. "Camille, your voice is exclusive," he had said once. "No one else has it except you. No one can even *imitate* you well, so don't worry. If they don't want you, they're deaf." One thing was for sure, if Courtney had been her agent instead of John David, he'd have been able to work something out with Ignacio and this stupid song.

She had the strange desire to call Courtney and listen to his encouragement again. Fat chance. She didn't even have his number. Bobby Junior had it, of course, but it was far too late to call him. And even if it weren't three twenty-four in the morning, she was triple certain that Courtney wouldn't have any nice words to say.

To get her mind off the studio problem, Camille cranked out another script. What would she say to Courtney if she talked to him? She'd apologize for throwing him out of her career. Her life. He probably wouldn't accept it, though. Camille knew her brother. Courtney was black-and-white. Once he made up his mind about somebody, that was all he wrote.

Maybe she could use Bobby Junior as a go-between. He could set up one of those classic television episodes where both parties come to a meeting on the premise that the other wants to apologize. Then, when they get there, they argue for a minute, then decide to get over themselves. Problem was, in those episodes, the people had fallen victim to some type of misunderstanding. That wasn't the case with her and Courtney. She'd been wrong. Totally wrong. Yet, so much time had passed, it almost seemed futile to even think of apologizing now. Might only add insult to injury. Really, is an apology still valid after so many years? And would he think she was sorry the new manager didn't work out as opposed to being genuinely sorry she'd asked Courtney to leave Sweet Treats? This, of course, made her second-guess herself all the more. Would she be apologizing if she was a multimillion-dollar artist right now?

Maybe. Maybe not. Courtney probably would have sued her by now.

Frustrated with all these scenarios, Camille tried to shut her lids again. If nothing else, she could at least give her eyeballs a rest.

An hour later, her orbits stung from lack of real sleep, but the adrenaline pumping through her veins fueled her through the morning routine despite the darkness outside. Even Cat knew it was too early to get out of bed. He remained in place, looking up at her once as if to ask why she was messing with the natural order of things.

She roused her voice, climbing up and down scales softly so as not to wake her neighbors. No one deserved to be up at this hour. After showering, dressing, and grooming, Camille sent a text to Ronald. He quickly replied, letting her know that he'd be ready by the time she got to his house.

As a peace offering, she made a quick pit stop and picked up a cup of coffee and a bagel for him at the gas station near the entrance to his suburb. None of the really good coffee places had opened yet, so this would have to do.

Inside her stomach, the jitterbugs danced crazily.

Not only was she nervous, she was delirious from lack of sleep.

When Ronald hopped into the car, he picked up on her disconcerted aura right away. "You all right, babe?"

Babe? I'm "babe"? "I'm okay. I bought you some breakfast."

"Thank you," he purred, leaning over the console for a smack on the lips.

Okay. We're a couple for real. She wished she could break up, do the recording, and get back together. Ronald was too good for this. She didn't deserve him.

To make matters worse, a pre–rush hour side-road accident clogged the major arteries on the way to the studio. *Is everyone and everything against me this morning?* Her nerves frazzled even more, Camille couldn't concentrate on Ronald's small talk.

"I take it you're not a morning person," he commented after the second time he'd had to jar Camille from her own thoughts.

"No. Not really," she agreed, thankful that he'd attributed her diminishing attitude to the time of day. She wanted to confess: *I'm not just a no-morning person, I'm a no-good person, too.*

At least, then, the sinking feeling would stop. She'd get the chance to take a deep, cleansing breath. Cleansing confession.

Two intersections and ten minutes from the studio, Camille got a text from John David. **Where are you?**

The crawling pace of traffic allowed time for a reply. **Almost there.**

"So, tell me about this demo," Ronald asked.

Camille could have sworn he'd already asked her this question. "It's for a sound track," she snapped.

"But it won't be for anything if this traffic doesn't clear. John David's already texting me."

"Oh"—Ronald perked up—"I've heard his name tossed around. He's got some big-time connections."

"Yeah. We're almost there," she cut him off with her no-nonsense tone.

Without a minute to spare, Camille swerved into the studio parking lot and nabbed the closest parking spot. She put her car in park and grabbed her purse simultaneously, almost leaving Ronald behind in the effort to place her foot inside the building at exactly 5:59 AM so John David couldn't accuse her of being late. She'd already given him enough reasons to drop her like a clingy girlfriend.

Ronald caught up with her halfway down the studio building's hallway, doing double-time to keep up with Camille's near running. "Where's the fire?" he joked.

"Right here," she said, pausing momentarily to knock on the door to Stevie's studios.

Almost instantly, John David opened. He looked at his watch, raised an eyebrow at Camille.

Nervously, she chirped, "Six o'clock on the dot."

"To be on time is to be late," he scorned. Then, his countenance switched gears as he focused his attention on Camille's guest. "You must be the man with the voice that melts perfectly with Camille's. Ronald?"

"Yes."

They shook hands.

"I'm John David. Mind if I call you Ronnie?"

"Yes, I do," Ronald said. "Ronald will suffice."

John David dipped his forehead in submission. "Ronald it is, then."

Camille bristled inside. Why wouldn't John David

listen to her like he listened to Ronald? *James Brown wasn't ever lyin' when he said this is a man's world, rest his soul, wherever they decided to bury him finally.*

John David introduced Ronald to Stevie, and the three men talked like old friends for a second. John David sucked up to Ronald like he owned a straw factory. Camille stood near her . . . babe, she guessed . . . and nodded as the men talked music mumbo-jumbo. They seemed pleased that Ronald knew much of their jargon.

Stevie remarked to Camille, "*This* Ronald knows what he's talking about."

His obvious reference to Faison sparked Camille into action. "We'd better get started. I've got to get to work as soon as we're finished." Assuming she'd still be employed.

"Sure thing," Stevie said. He sat down, fiddled with the switches, plucked a pair of headphones from a stand, and handed a pair to Ronald.

"I'll let you listen to Camille's track first. Have you read the lyrics?"

"No," Ronald said as he snapped his headphones in place.

Camille shifted and reshifted her feet.

John David shot a dagger toward Camille. She pursed her lips in an I-didn't-know-what-to-do smirk.

"No problem. I can tell you're a pro," Stevie praised Ronald. "She's actually done most of the song. I just need you to get in where you fit in, especially on the hook."

The sinking feeling had descended to her bladder. *Great. Now I have to pee.* Nowhere in any of the screen shots she'd played the night before had it occurred to her that she might actually pee on herself in the middle of all this. But she dared not leave the room at this critical moment. Ronald was about to read the lyrics, hear her singing "On Top of Me" for the first time.

Stevie gave Camille and John David the other two headphones, and they all sat while the opening bars of the song played. Ronald glanced at Camille, smiled. She managed a smile back. His head bobbed to the beat, fingers tapped on his knee.

Stevie and John David joined in the head-bobbing dance, grooving with Ronald. They were all on the same page, the same note.

Camille lowered her eyes and waited for her voice to crank out the first verse. *Baby, I've got the place for you. A place that satisfies.*

Ronald's fingers stopped tapping.

I've got the perfect place for you. Right here between these thighs.

He turned his chair slightly. Bumped knees with Camille's.

Slowly, she raised her eyes to his and read the no screaming from those brown irises. Worse was the disappointment tucked in the corners of his mouth. Camille wished she could literally crawl into a hole and die a slow, painful death. Might as well. She could just as well have been singing "Amazing Grace" because this felt like the funeral of her relationship with Ronald. Actually, a funeral would be better than this torment. She couldn't even look at him anymore.

The music continued. *That place, that space, is here on top of me, baby. Take me ecstasy. Oooh, yeah! On top of me, baby.*

Stevie yelled over the music, "Ronald, I think this is where I'll have you come in. Second verse."

Ronald sighed, took his gaze off Camille as they all

listened to her croon, *Don't make this a one-night stand, baby. We can meet here and do it 'til these sheets are soaked in love. Get over the past. Get over the future, and get on top of me, baby!*

Oblivious to Ronald's disgust, John David and Stevie continued their exaggerated head dips.

"Here's the hook," John David bellowed.

Ronald lasted until she started with the part about "pumping" before he had to take off his listening equipment. The others followed suit. Stevie turned down the volume, thwarting the sounds coming through their collective headsets.

"Lady and gentlemen," Ronald announced, "I'm sorry to disappoint you all, but I cannot sing this song."

"What's the problem?" Stevie asked. "It's a powerful arrangement."

"True," Ronald said, "but this isn't the song for me. I can't lend my voice, my gift to something I disagree with."

"What's there to disagree with?" from Stevie again.

"Look, I know that sex sells. This is your business, you do what you do," Ronald reasoned. "But I have to do what I do, too. I'm a minister; I'm a father. I can't lend my voice to a song that promotes principles I don't believe in."

As though he'd been awaiting Ronald's reaction, John David pressured, "Aw, come on, dude. It's just a *song*. It's not like you're killing anyone. And if you want to make some good of it, just donate some of your royalties to charity."

Bewildered, Stevie threw up his hands. "For crying out loud, this song is about sex, God's best gift to mankind. I don't understand what's wrong with that?"

Ronald shook his head. "I don't expect you to understand. I'm playing by different rules."

"Hey," Stevie barked, "I'm a Christian, too. I know right from wrong. *This* is not wrong. It's art. Music."

Ronald put palms to his chest. "I can't tell you what's right or wrong for you. Only God can judge that. All I know is, *I* don't use *my* talent to oppose the One who gave it to me. Whatever you decide to do with your God-given talent is between you and Him." Ronald pointed toward the ceiling.

Camille watched as though she were a fly on the wall. These men were arguing about her future. She'd been so busy observing, she'd almost forgotten the lines she'd mentally rehearsed all night long. "Stevie, I was thinking . . . maybe we could change a few of the lyrics. Or just have him harmonize with me on a few notes."

She had Ronald's attention now.

"You know 'Nobody Greater' by VaShawn Mitchell? He and the choir sing most of the song, but one lady does a few ooohs and repeats what the choir says. You think that would work. I mean, in light of your convictions?"

"We could try it," John David interrupted cheerfully. "I'm willing to try anything."

Ronald's cheeks dropped another inch, as if that were possible. "I'm not. Camille, I thought you and I had the same convictions."

"We do," she all but whined, "I'm just asking, for this *one song,* Ronald, to get my foot back in the door. *Please.*"

"Camille, believe me—I really wish I could. But I

can't. My life, this voice, doesn't belong to me," he said.

Ronald stood. John David scrambled to his side, grabbed Ronald by the shoulders, and fast-talked. "Okay, Ronald, forget Camille. She's . . . she's a chameleon. How about you? A different song? I've heard you, you're right. You have an amazing gift. Your voice is heavenly. I could match you with a different woman. Same soundtrack, different song. It'll be as innocent as . . . what was that reggae song? 'Don't Worry, Be Happy.'"

Now Camille stood. "Are you kidding me?"

"You can leave now," John David ordered.

She would do no such thing!

But before Camille could speak, Ronald asked John David a question that zipped her mouth, sent her pulse through the roof. "When have you heard me sing?"

John David pointed at Stevie. Stevie unplugged a cord, pushed a button, and the room filled with voices Camille and Ronald's voices.

Mmm, I don't know. I was trying to get to the gym tonight.

You look fine to me.

Thank you, but that's only because I've been working out lately.

It's definitely paying off. But I was really hoping we could grab a bite since Brittney's still in practice..

Cool.

"Sorry. Let me back it up," Stevie said. He stopped the tape, pushed another lever.

Ronald crossed his arms, stared Camille dead in the face. "You were recording our conversations?"

"No," she denied. "I recorded us singing. I just forgot to turn it off."

"That's What I Live For" blared through the speakers now. Soprano and tenor, their undeniable mix, along with background.

"Ronald, you're incredible. You're a force all by yourself, but you'd also make anybody's voice sound like a million dollars next to yours. You *balance*, man, like Billy Ocean. Stevie Wonder."

"Thanks, but I'm not interested," Ronald declined. "I'm gonna call me a cab now so I can go to work. Sorry to have wasted your time."

Ronald excused himself and walked out, just like she'd imagined he would. In fact, watching his backside leave the room in blue jeans and a red shirt was exactly the way she'd pictured this going down. Begging John David, that two-faced, male chauvinist, was out of the picture. John David was straight triflin', right along with three-fourths of the other people in the industry. Ridiculous!

"There went your last chance with me, Camille," John David piled insult on top of injury.

"No," she countered, "there went *your* last chance. I see who you really are. All you care about is the bottom line."

John David crossed his arms, stared down at her condescendingly. "I thought that was all we *both* cared about."

"God made the earth, but money makes it go 'round, sweetheart," Stevie added.

She started down the nearly vacant hallway, her heels echoing so loudly they almost made her ears hurt. "Ronald, wait."

He stopped, pivoted with alarming speed, and tore into her. "What else have you been recording, Camille? What is this all about?"

She sighed. "Ronald, I can explain. I needed a demo to give to John David."

"So you took it upon yourself to record us anyway, without my permission."

"Yes, but—"

"What else have you recorded?"

"Nothing else."

He hung a hand on his neck. "Why couldn't you just tell me?"

"I didn't want you to think that I was . . . I don't know—"

"Using me?" he completed her sentence precisely.

"Yeah, I guess."

"You recorded other people, too. What's your excuse there? For all I know, you could have been recording the choir, making copies, and selling bootleg CDs."

"Don't be silly."

"Am I, really, being silly, Camille? Let me ask you this, why did you join Grace Chapel to begin with?"

Now was her chance to come clean. Even if it meant losing him forever, at least she'd lose him for the truth, not because of this craziness with John David and the recording. She forged ahead, hoping if nothing else that he would at least appreciate her honesty on his way out of her life. "I did join the church, initially, to be a part of the choir. At John David's recommendation. But—"

"So you've been using all of us."

"No. I mean, at first, yes, but not now."

His eyes misted slightly. "Brittney, too? Was she just part of the plan to get closer to me?"

"No, not Brittney," Camille declared plainly. "Brittney's different. We connected before I even knew she was your daughter, Ronald, I swear."

He sighed. "Leave us alone." He took off again.

"Ronald, I'm telling you the truth."

He yelled over his shoulder, "You want a sticker for that?"

She quickened her pace but held her breath as they turned the final corridor and beheld flashes of red, white, and blue bouncing off the walls. *What's going on?*

Up ahead, Ronald opened the exit door. Quickly, he called to her, "Camille, the police are at your car."

"What!"

She pushed past him, rushing toward her vehicle. "Hi. What's the problem?"

"You Camille Robertson?" a female officer in her mid-forties who'd never heard of lip gloss or Chapstick asked.

"Yes."

"First of all, you parked in a handicap spot. One of the tenants of the building couldn't even park, thanks to your inconsiderate actions."

"Sorry about that." In her presunrise rush, she must have missed the faded sign atop the leaning pole in front of her car. Weren't the building owners responsible for making the signs visible? And why did this slight error merit a cruiser with lights?

"Secondly," the officer continued, "we have a warrant for your arrest."

"Huh?"

John David and Stevie appeared at the door now.

"Unpaid ticket."

"There must be some kind of mistake. I paid my ticket," Camille claimed loud enough for everyone, including her former agent, to hear.

"Tell it to the judge, Miss Robertson. Let's go."

"Wait." Camille backed away from the officer.

"Are you resisting me?" she taunted.

"No. I just want to give him my key." She motioned toward Ronald. He stepped forward. Camille removed the vehicle's key from the ring and placed it in his hand.

He took it without a word.

Obviously chomping at the bit to tow Camille's car, the smart-mouthed officer asked, "Not so fast. Is the vehicle insured?"

"Yes. The card is in the glove compartment," Camille stated. She looked at Ronald again. "I've already paid this ticket. This is a mistake."

Again, he held on to his words.

Ms. I-Love-Hating-People flirted with Ronald. "Honey, I wish I had a dollar for every time someone told me I was arresting them for no reason. You and I could run off to Hawaii."

The second officer slapped the cuffs on Camille's wrists.

"Officer, do you really have to restrain her?" Ronald asked.

"Policy," he explained compassionately. "It's not safe for us to escort hostile subjects unrestrained."

Then he led Camille into the backseat of the cruiser and escorted a boo-hooing Camille to the station.

CHAPTER 30

Somehow, she'd managed to convince the nice male officer that there was something wrong. If he'd just open her purse, he'd see carbon copies of the checks she'd written to the county as payment for the ticket. But his partner said she'd heard this story a million times. She confiscated Camille's purse and told Camille to save her story for the judge.

Camille stopped talking and did the only thing she could do . . . pray. She closed her eyes and asked God to intervene and do whatever He had to do to make everything right. Everything, including this situation with Ronald. *God, I'm sorry. I'm going to jail, God! Jail!*

Inside her heart, she heard a whispered rhyme. *Better jail than hell.*

Surely, God didn't find this situation funny. Was this His way of getting her attention? She'd heard about people having to be flat on their backs before looking up. Why did it have to be this way? Why couldn't He just teach her a lesson the easy way?

You wouldn't listen.

Okay, there it was again—this argument emanating from within herself. If she had been pondering, thinking to herself, she might have believed these words were her own. But they couldn't be. She would never accuse her own self of not listening, let alone decide that a trip to jail was preferable to the eternal elevator down. Aside from all that, God's sentences were awfully short.

This was God, speaking to her like a father chastising His child. No hint of condemnation, only an undeniable truth. God was right.

Between God softening the officer's heart and the check copies Camille was able to show the booking clerk, she managed to avoid a cold, hard jail cell and the humiliation of taking a mug shot. She whispered a thank you to God as she waited for the error to be unearthed.

As she waited in what looked like a secured interrogation room, Camille put her head down on her desk, encircled by her arms. She wanted more than anything to wake up from this nightmare. She'd never imagined things could turn out this bad. As far as she knew, no one in her immediate family had seen the inside of a police station. Not even Bobby Junior, for all his shady ways.

How would she explain this to him? His only daughter, downtown. On false premises, of course, but still . . .

nobody wants to have to call someone and say, "Hey, can you come pick me up? I'm at the jailhouse."

His first question, of course, would be, "What did you do?" And all of this would make it back to Courtney. He'd probably have something smart to say, even if, in his heart, he, too, was disappointed in his little sister.

Maybe that's what hurt most. The disappointment. After all her efforts, all her scheming and even praying, nothing had worked out to her advantage. *Why me?* Why couldn't she live her life, sing, and then die when it was all over with? Was it too much to ask to just be happy again?

She'd even lost the handsome guy, which was *not* supposed to happen. He was supposed to love her through all this. Be there for her, have compassion and pity on her. Instead, he'd walked away. Driven, away, actually, in her ticketed, insured vehicle.

Stupid. This whole thing was stupid. Her whole life was stupid, now that she thought about it. Nothing had been right or fair since her mother died. Couldn't God give her a break? If anyone deserved to have a great life, it was her! Hadn't He taken enough from her without taking her dreams and her almost man, too?

Tears leaked onto the table as Camille found herself sobbing again. She had come to the end of herself. There was no way up or down, left or right. This was simply the end.

If her mother had been alive, she would have been the most let down by all this mess. How many times had she prayed over Camille's life? Dabbed blessed oil on her forehead, asking the Lord to protect Camille, guide Camille, and give Camille a heart for Him?

Better yet, if her mother had still been alive, none of these terrible things would have happened. She'd still have her brother, and her father would still be the respectable man she'd known growing up. Sweet Treats would still be together. Maybe. Or, at least, the rest of the group wouldn't hate her so much.

Yes, everything would have been different if God hadn't taken her mother away. Now, for the first time since eleventh grade, she asked aloud, "Why my mother, Lord? Why did you have to take her and leave me without the one person who loved me more than anything?"

No response. It was as though God Almighty decided He didn't need to answer to anybody. He would just do what He wanted, when He wanted, how He wanted, and people could love Him or hate Him, he didn't care. He didn't have to care; He was God.

I love you. I have never left you.

Camille bolted straight up. She looked around the room because, this time, the words sounded like they had come from inside and outside, too. She blinked a few times, examined the four corners of the empty room. Every logical cell within her tried to discount what she'd just heard, but the truth resonated more loudly than anything else that had ever passed through Camille's soul.

The Inner Witness brought to mind Chrisandrea's thoughts about the footprints poem. *When you look back over, like, the sands of your life and see only one set of footprints, that's not when God left you. That's when God was carrying you through the tough times because you were too weak to walk,* the young girl had said.

He loved her and had never left her. If that was true, then He'd been there when her mother died, when Sweet Treats broke up, when she'd moved into that ratty apartment, when she joined Grace Chapel under false pretenses. Even when she met Ronald. If He had been there all the time, why didn't He say anything?

She recalled the words He had spoken in the car. *You wouldn't listen*. She charged, "How was I supposed to listen when I couldn't hear you?"

You couldn't hear because we don't talk.

He had a point.

A flood of scriptures rushed through Camille's mind. From stuff she'd learned in Sunday school almost twenty years ago to things Pastor Collins preached the previous Wednesday night. All of them pointing at one idea: Draw close to God and He will draw close to you.

Only, this time, she realized God had actually taken the first steps in love. He had pulled her into this situation. He had allowed her to sabotage Sweet Treats and live in her own self-imposed wilderness long enough to realize she had to do something to get out. That *something* had drawn her back to church, back to Him. Even to jail, where He wanted to answer her mother's prayers after all these years.

She must have read that verse in the eighth chapter of Romans a hundred times—all things work together. But it never made sense until that very moment, sitting in an examination room in a jailhouse, of all places. Everything, the good, bad, and ugly, had come to this. Because He loved her. Like the old folk said at the old church, it's one thing to have the information. Another thing altogether to have the revelation.

One word from Him makes all the difference.

Suddenly, divinely, she wanted to know God for herself. Not to get a record deal, not to stay out of hell. But if He loved her this much, she wanted to love Him, too, singing contract or not.

"Jesus, I'm sorry I tried to use you." Even though she'd said the prayer of faith when she was twelve years old along with everyone else in the youth choir, she realized now that she hadn't really meant it. Yes, she knew Jesus was God's son, that He had died for her sins. But, like Pastor Collins had preached, even the demons have that little bit of information. The truth was, in the past, she'd wanted him to save her from the consequences of sin, not sin itself.

She'd made that Romans 3:16 confession in hopes of avoiding hell (and not hurting her mother's feelings), but not because she had any intention of making Jesus her Lord.

This time was different. "Jesus, I love you. I can't make it without You. I confess You as my savior, and I surrender myself to You. Thank You for standing in the gap until it all made sense. And thank you for making it make sense to me." And then she thanked Him in tears as she marveled at His Excellency. His grace, which had paved the way and opened her ears to hear God's voice in a way she had never heard before.

Though she felt a lifetime had passed since the officer ushered her into this life-changing situation, the wall clock showed only twenty minutes had passed. Camille wiped her face dry and used her cotton shirt sleeve to clear the table as well. Yesterday was over. Today was the first day of the rest of her life. As soon as these people cleared her name, she'd walk out of the

station, find Ronald, and tell him the whole truth—
including the fact that she liked him more than she'd
ever let on, more than she was willing to admit to herself because that might foil her master plan. Whatever
happened after her confession . . . well . . . she'd leave
that up to God.

CHAPTER 31

Tonya and Courtney waited in the periphery, giving the family choice, covered seating at the military burial grounds. Alexis's father's service in the army resulted in a dignified, proud salute to Alexis, her mother, and her brother. The American flag, presented after two soldiers meticulously folded the symbol of freedom, was the final portion of the memorial ceremony for Mr. Nevils.

The funeral directors thanked the family and allowed the mourners a few moments to comfort the family before corralling Alexis, Mrs. Nevils, and other close relatives back into the limousines and back for the repast.

Neither Tonya nor Courtney had had the opportunity to really embrace Alexis yet. She'd been so crowded by people who were, obviously, closer than the old Sweet Treats gang. Still, they wanted her to know they cared. Since their virtual meeting last month, they'd been in touch regularly. Kyra had wanted to make the funeral, too, but her own father had surgery scheduled. Someone should have called Camille, probably, but no one ever got around to it. The one person who would have made sure it happened was too overwhelmed with grief and funeral plans to concern herself to stop to make contact with Camille.

Mr. Nevils's swift death had caught Alexis by surprise. It was no secret that he wasn't in the best of health. Still, she'd expected some kind of warning. Several days in a hospital, some drifting in and out of consciousness so she would have a clue that it was time to start saying good-bye. But, when she really thought about it, she knew she was only being selfish. Her father had passed away in his sleep. No machines, no needles, no tubes. Everybody wants to go like that. Even the doctor said her father probably felt little or no pain, though she wondered if he was just saying that to make her feel better.

Courtney knew all too well that the hardest part, the days after all the cards and meals subsided, would prove to be the toughest days. Because he knew Alexis would need his comfort more then than now, he'd almost decided to stay home from the funeral and simply contact her in a few weeks. But his wife had convinced him otherwise.

"It means a lot to the family to see an audience full of people," Monique had said. "Even if she doesn't remember seeing your face, she'll see your name in the guest book later."

Since money wasn't a problem, Courtney saw no reason not to buy the airline ticket and skip up to St. Louis for a day to be there for Alexis. A long time ago, neither he nor any of the Sweet Treats would have imagined not attending the funeral. Now that they were about to all get back in the swing of things, he knew this was the right thing to do.

Back at the church, the fellowship hall quickly filled with loud-talking, friendly, famished church folk. Courtney and Tonya waited their turn to pass through the serving line. Courtney smiled at the oversized helpings of mashed potatoes and green beans the hospitality crew piled onto his plate.

"Thank you," he said to a woman who'd done double duty as an usher during the ceremony. He remembered the days when his mother played the piano, transported flowers, and poured punch after funerals. Like these women, she had given her life over to good works in Jesus's name. He'd been blessed to find a wife with the same heart, and Monique was doing a good job of handing down the tradition to their own daughter, Jamia, who took great pride in caring for her dolls. Nurturers, the both of them.

He had been a nurturer, too. Always looked out for his little sister, until she burned him. Alexis and Tonya weren't the only ones who'd been pressuring him to move beyond this thing with Camille. Monique had joined the battle. "One of these days, you're going to realize how much you and your sister need each other," she had predicted more than once. "I just hope you don't come to that epiphany too late."

He hoped the same thing, too. Seeing Mr. Nevils in that casket made Courtney think of his own father. Bobby Junior wouldn't be here forever. Right now, his father was the last good memory leftover from childhood. Momma was gone. Camille estranged. He had his family with Monique, of course, but there's nothing like hanging with the people you played hide-and-go-seek with. If he hadn't spent his young-adult years trying to build his sister's career, he might have a few home-boys. Fact was, he'd given up his early twenties to make sure his sister turned out fine.

Hmmm. Maybe he had something in common with the church ladies after all.

"Dang, Tonya, we probably could have split one plate," he joked as they grabbed cups of tea at the final serving station before returning to their seats.

"I know, right?"

Courtney took note of the fine lines gathering in the corners of Tonya's eyes. Probably from lack of sleep. All that time on the road can age a person prematurely. Coupled with the fact that Tonya had to be at least thirty now, Courtney realized how much time had passed since he'd been in her company.

He wondered how Camille was aging. Alexis had said his sister was broke. Lack of money and health in-surance can wreak havoc on a person's body. Bad teeth, pock-marked cheeks, dark fingernails—all the visible signs of hard living in America.

As the guests dined and left, Courtney and Tonya approached Alexis and her mother at the front table. Flanked by so many comforters, Courtney didn't think Alexis had even seen them in the crowd. However, she fussed at them for taking so long to give her hugs. "I saw y'all come in church! You should have sat closer."

"Naw, girl. That's for the family," Tonya said, pulling Alexis into a full hug.

Alexis released some of her grief on Tonya's shoul-der.

Courtney completed the embrace, holding both girls in place for a moment. "It will get better. I promise," he whispered.

Alexis switched to his shoulder now, drawing on the comfort his experience with losing a parent had to offer. "I'm so glad you decided to bring us back together. Daddy said he didn't want me to put my life on hold anymore for him and Momma. Singing again will help me get through, I think." She collected herself and looked over Courtney's shoulder. "Where's Camille?"

"I didn't get a chance to call her," Courtney stretched the truth.

"You didn't call her?" Alexis scowled.

"No, Lexi. I'm sorry."

"Daddy really liked Camille, you know. He said she was a scrappy something." Alexis laughed.

"He was right about that," Courtney had to agree. No one had ever called his sister timid. "But don't worry. I'll call her soon."

"You'd better," Alexis said. "Life is too short."

CHAPTER 32

An hour later, without so much as an apology, an administrative worker opened the door, handed Camille her purse, and said, "Clerical error. Computers are only as good as the people usin' 'em. You can go."

Camille dried the last drops from her eyes and rose to her feet a new woman in Christ. Before she could even get out of the room good, a negative murmur nagged inside her head. *Don't kid yourself. Everybody gets saved in jail. Now that you're out, you'll go back to your old ways.*

She found herself arguing with the voice internally. *No! I am not the same!*

Yes, you are. You and everybody else who calls on Jesus when they're in trouble.

The same clerk who'd greeted her when she first got to the station interrupted the mental battle. "Here's a printout of your payments, in case someone tries to bring you in again.

"Under the circumstances, I can have an officer transport you home if need be."

She fought the urge to make a sarcastic comment. It was their fault. A ride home was the least they could provide. "I'll take you up on the offer, thank you."

"What's your address?"

Camille answered promptly.

"Did your car get towed?" the woman asked next.

"No. A friend drove it for me."

"Okay. Have a seat. I'll find somebody who's going out to that part of town for you. We've always got people in *your* hood."

Already, people were trying to make her go off. Couldn't they let her get back to her apartment first?

The trip home didn't help. She'd always guessed officers were turning on their lights and sirens so they could speed through intersections for no reason. Now she had proof. Officer McGinnis couldn't have been a better stereotype of a policeman. He had a dirty mouth, a lead foot, and he'd obviously consumed way too many free donuts. Still, Camille felt an uncharacteristic compassion for him. For as much trouble as all these men of the law had been to her, she realized they had a tough job. They'd seen people mangled in accidents, shot as a result of violence. And each of them risked their lives every day.

She bit her tongue about his rogue driving and thanked him when he dropped her off.

"Sorry about that mix-up, ma'am," he said with a belch.

"No problem. Just remember me if you ever pull me over," she joked.

He winked at her, baring a smile she hadn't expected from him. "Sure thing."

Cat made a beeline to Camille upon entrance. *Meow! Meow! Meow!*

"Hey, you." Camille threw her bag on the kitchen counter, slipped out of her too-flat flats, and sat to allow Cat his routine rub. Cat, however, had something else in mind. He stood at the door to her bedroom and bellowed his little heart out.

Camille got up from the couch and made her way to the animal, feeling as though she was having a *Lassie* moment. The way he was carrying on, she honestly wondered if Cat could tell something different about her.

Really, it wasn't that deep. It was that *gross,* however. There, in the space where her feet hit the floor when she got out of bed, was a dead mouse. "Eeew!" Camille shrieked.

Cat looked up at her like he'd done something good.

"Cat! You did that!" She visually searched for traces of blood around his mouth. Nothing. Must have been a clean kill.

"Cat, you can't be killing stuff—"

Then it hit her: Cat never left her unit. If Cat killed a mouse, the mouse must have been *inside* her apartment. "Oh my God," she said, and not in vain, either. She needed God's help for real if there were mice in her apartment. Spiders and ants she could deal with. Mice and roaches, however, were another story.

The spiders had done their job to keep the roaches away. And good ole cat was on duty looking out for mice. Good thing he slept right under her bed most nights, too. "Good job, Cat." He deserved a raise, and God deserved some praise because there was a very good chance she would have jumped out the window and almost broken her neck trying to escape the terrifying jaws of a mouse.

After disposing of Cat's trophy, Camille washed her hands thoroughly, then came back to her room for some more time alone with God. Those negative, doubtful whisperings had scared her. She needed more of Him. She refrained from praying bedside, however. Surely God knew her enough to understand her aversion to getting on the floor for a while. As she curled up with the comforter and closed her eyes, she couldn't help but envision herself snuggled in her Father's arms. Ronald, the church, the choirs, Brittney, her car, her job. All that would have to wait. A sweet peace surrounded her that midmorning, lulling her into a post-drunken-like sleep. And, for the first time in a long time, she slipped into an undisturbed nap.

A late-afternoon splash of sun gently woke Camille. Ravenous, she charged to her kitchen for a bite to eat. After fixing a grilled cheese sandwich and tomato soup, she checked her cell phone. Four missed calls from Sheryl. None from Ronald. Two voice messages, presumably from Sheryl, and a text from Mercedes that there would be no evening rehearsal due to preparations for the ministers' wives conference.

First things first. Might as well call Sheryl and get it over with. If Camille was unemployed, she needed to know so she could mosey on down to her nearest temporary agency as soon as possible.

Camille decided to bum rush with an apology. "Sheryl, let me first say that I am sooo sorry. I had an early-morning appointment at a recording studio. Then my car got towed, I ended up at the police station because—"

"Uh, you can stop now. You don't owe me any explanations. You've been relieved of your duties here at Aquapoint Systems due to job abandonment." She added under her breath, "The way the economy is, you'd think people would want to hold on to a job. But not you, for some odd reason."

Camille had been prepared for the axe and some kind of smart-mouthed commentary from her boss, but job abandonment was not quite the label she wanted to have slapped on her personnel file. A brief gig in a human resources office had opened Camille's eyes to the fact that while employers couldn't legally bad-mouth former employees, they could share the official reason for termination. Job abandonment was as bad as having bad credit. "I did *not* abandon my job," Camille argued. "Don't I have to miss, like, three days in a row for it to be considered abandonment?"

Sheryl huffed. "Oh, now you want to play by the rules?"

"I've been playing by the rules." She'd bent them, yes, but not broken them. And, in the spirit of a good employee, she'd used her earned time off to handle her personal business. Sheryl might not have liked her using all those days off for un-feline-related matters, but they were her days off to use them for whatever she wanted. No different than someone taking off two weeks' vacation.

"Fine," her former boss spat. "I'll make the change, but you're still fired. You'll get a severance offer in the mail. I'll FedEx the contents of your desk."

"Thank you."

"And take care of the cat, for goodness sake," she added with a hint of compassion.

"I will."

Camille hung up the phone and waited for the pang of panic to swing through her body. Any moment now, she'd turn hysterical. Round up all the CDs in her trunk and stake out a corner in the Walmart parking lot so she could sell music until someone reported her to the store's manager.

But the sense of fright never came. The blanket of peace God had spread over her at the police station remained. She would be all right, one way or another.

Directly across from her hung the picture commemorating her first official date with Ronald. The fruit bowl on a pedestal. She giggled at the memory. Hers still looked better than his, but now that she thought about it, Ronald's had more character. Hers was nearly perfect, stroke for stroke. If she recalled correctly, his short pedestal made the picture a bit more curious, called for a closer analysis.

She could only hope now that Ronald would value her imperfections as much as he'd appreciated the variance in their artwork.

"Hi, Ronald," she greeted him on the phone.

"Hey. You all right?"

"Yeah. They fixed the problem and released me."

She was glad to hear him breathe a sigh of relief. He must have been concerned about her. "Thanks for taking my car."

"No problem. I'll have someone follow me to your place after work."

Not exactly what she'd had in mind. She didn't want a third party privy to their impending conversation, assuming that Ronald would listen to what she had to say. "No, I don't want to put you through any more trouble. If it's . . . okay with you, I'd like to come get my car later this evening. At your house."

She had to admit to herself that sounded pretty bold. And imposing. Desperate times call for desperate measures. Even if Ronald couldn't forgive and forget, she wanted him to know how he had watered a seed within her heart. He deserved that commendation. If his lifestyle had half the impact on Brittney that it had on a mere choir member, his daughter would be just fine.

No, a drop-off wouldn't do. He needed to hear her out, for his sake more than hers. "Ronald, I'd really like to talk to you. I need to explain."

"No, you don't. I should have listened to the Spirit when we first met. I let my feelings for you get in the way. That's my fault, not yours."

The *Spirit*? Okay, now she was curious. Flattered that he had feelings for her, of course, but leery of what the Spirit had told him about her. Did He say that she was a Jezebel? A Delilah? A Bathsheba who would cause him to reap a heap of trouble over time? "Ummm . . . what exactly did the Spirit say about me?"

"I don't feel like talking about this right now. Probably never will, really."

Camille's eyes closed as the finality of his words beat against her heart. They wanted in, wanted to quench the glimpse of hope she'd begun to kindle over these past weeks with Ronald. No, they hadn't made any official claims about their relationship. Every couple starts somewhere, though. He'd even called her "babe" just this morning. "Babe" had to count for something.

"Ronald, I *am* sorry about everything. When I first joined—"

"Camille, I have to go now. I'm pretty busy. Maybe another time. I'll drop off your car and leave the keys under your mat. Bye."

So, this was cut-off-Camille day. No-second-chances-for-Camille national recognition, eh? She dragged herself to the couch and took the head seat at her pity party. Cat responded to the invitation, rubbing his head against her side, then curling up into a ball to enjoy the festivities.

Why do bad things always happen to me? Why can't I have a regular life like everybody else? Then she thought about her questions and realized the very thing she *hadn't* wanted in life was a regular life. She wanted a spectacular, superstar life. The champagne, caviar, private jet lifestyle.

In all the day's craziness, her hopes and dreams had changed. *Would a regular life be so bad?* She sank into the cushions, let her head fall back, and imagined what her life would be like if she became complacent with a regular-people life. She would get up every day, go to work, come home, check on Cat, go to choir rehearsal, church on Sunday. If Ronald actually listened to her one day, they might start going out again. A movie here, dinner there, ice skating. Dare she imagine that, one day, they'd get married. Finish raising Brittney, maybe have some kids of their own. Go to soccer games, piano recitals. Cat would eventually die. Ronald would eventually die, right along with everyone else.

Then what? Nothing. No huge funeral, no memorial erected in her honor, no television documentary or *Unsung* special on TV One. Just eighty-something years of sucking up oxygen, blowing out carbon dioxide. She'd be gone and forgotten just like every other person who'd ever walked the planet.

This wouldn't do. She was born to sing, and something deep inside Camille wouldn't let her forget this fact. But she couldn't go back to her old life—hustling and bustling to try to make it happen. If God put her here on this earth to sing, *He* was going to have to give her an outlet for this gift before it drove her crazy.

Camille slumped to the floor and rolled onto her knees. "God, show me your purpose for my life. You know I love to sing, and I know You blessed me with a beautiful voice. Show me how You want me to use it, and I'll do what You say. In Jesus's name, Amen."

It was all up to Him at his point. Somewhere, she'd read a scripture about God finishing what He'd started in His people. Though she had no idea where to find this promise in the Word, she felt certain that she'd heard it before. If not from her Sunday school teacher, definitely from her mother. And now that she'd turned everything over to His capable hands, she had the faith to believe He would come through. No one else had. It had to be His way or nothing at all.

She realized she'd have to do the same thing with Ronald. If the Spirit had impressed her motivations on him initially, surely the Spirit could let him know that she was telling the truth now. That, too, was in His hands.

CHAPTER 33

The severance package would get her through the rest of the month easily. She might even be able to survive on unemployment if she let go of her cell phone, but that wasn't an option. Communication was nonnegotiable. Besides, Camille wasn't quite in the mood for a handout. In addition to purposefully losing control of her singing career and the situation with Ronald, she'd asked God to take the reins in this "regular-people" job arena. Up until her jail day, she'd seen every nine-to-five job as temporary, a means to her extraordinary superstar end.

Now that she was learning to stomach the idea that she was normal, that the world wasn't here to shine the spotlight on her, she'd asked God to give her a job she actually liked so working wouldn't feel like a waste of forty hours every week, one third of every weekday of her life.

A week after getting laid off indefinitely, as Sheryl

had restated in the release paperwork, Camille still hadn't so much as landed a factory gig to tide her over until whatever God had in mind happened. He needed to put His holy foot on it.

Meanwhile, Camille took a break from the choirs. Took a break from Sunday services, too. She knew it wasn't totally the right thing to do, but it was just too awkward being in Ronald's presence in the choir room, too painful seeing him on stage during praise and worship. Truth be told: She couldn't concentrate when she saw Ronald. By no fault of his own, that intensely brown face of his reminded Camille of the self-serving person she used to be. How could she stand in his presence after misleading him?

She also began to wonder if people in the choir knew about what had happened between the two of them. Who had brought him to the apartment to drop off her car? What explanation had Ronald given the person about why he was in possession of Camille's car and keys? He must have told them something close to the truth. What if they'd had a meeting about her and kicked her out of the choir before she had a chance to quietly resign?

Okay, she was getting carried away. It wasn't in Ronald's character to badmouth people. Wasn't like most men period, come to think of it. And if they hadn't kicked Faison's Romeo-wannabe behind out of the choir yet, they still had more than enough room for Camille.

This wasn't about Faison, though. Bottom line, she was flat embarrassed. Yes, God had forgiven her. He'd even changed her. But how could she fix all she'd done wrong to the people she'd deceived?

The second Sunday of church avoidance, Camille

figured that maybe she should just join a different church and start over. Sit in the audience for about a year and just listen to the preacher until she got herself right before she started singing in the choir again.

Leave it to Mercedes to send out a text message to the voluntarily shut-in. **Hey, C! Where you been? Missing you! Mentors and Models tomorrow @ 9. Girls been asking about u. U coming?**

Great. Just great. Now she *had* to go to Grace Chapel again. She'd played church with a lot of folks, but she'd been true to the teens. And assuming none of them had been tainted by whatever rumors might be floating around about Camille, they would still accept her for who she was.

Camille responded. **I'll be there.**

Brittney was the first to nearly strangle Camille's neck in a super-tight hug. "Oh my gosh, Miss Camille, where have you been? I wanted to call you, but my dad's being super mean lately." Her bright, twinkling eyes hinted at no trace of animosity. She obviously knew nothing of Camille's faults.

Next, Shaki slung a million questions, asking why Camille hadn't come to the pastor's wives' conference.

"Uh, because I'm not a pastor's wife." Camille laughed.

"So! You could be like the real housewives of Atlanta. Most of them ain't housewives, but that don't stop them from coming on the show," Shaki joked.

"For real," Michaela cosigned.

"They had, like, a little teen workshop for girls during the conference," Sierra drawled. She stuck her finger in her mouth, pretending to gag. "It was so lame and fake. We were all saying they should have had you up talking, then we would have paid attention."

Like one of the kids, Mercedes flocked into the Miss Camille fan club to share her thoughts as well. "Camille, you gotta talk to them about how they work with us. We need more *real*ness, you hear me? Somebody who's made mistakes, you know what I'm saying?"

"Well, I certainly qualify, if that's what it takes." Camille laughed at herself.

The meeting began with a prayer and some announcements. Then someone fired up the LCD projector and displayed the day's topic: godly dress. Since Camille was modest by nature, she had no qualms with the way the main speakers presented the information. The girls, however, balked as though Mary Poppins herself had flown in under her umbrella and begun singing a childish chant with a British accent.

After a few Bible verses and a quick YouTube video about making first impressions, a slideshow of appropriate attire began. On the left, pictures of low-cut blouses, high skirts, and too tight, midriff-exposing knit shirts. These, of course, were the no-nos. On the right, tents and nun-ish clothing got the thumbs-up from the older sisters.

Whispers of "I ain't wearin' that" and "That's just wrong" spread throughout the audience.

Next, a picture of Beyoncé on stage wearing something equivalent to a bikini. The girls piped up in obvious admiration.

"Young ladies, this is not the way to dress for respect," the leader announced to them all.

Finally, Chrisandrea spoke up. "I'm not tryin' to be

funny, but Beyoncé gets much respect. They pay her, like, millions of dollars even when she's not dressed like that. She was in *Dreamgirls*; she models for Cover Girl. She doesn't always dress crazy."

"That's what I'm saying," Brittney agreed.

"And I feel like the reason some people don't dress better is because they're fat," Shaki added. "I mean, if you've got it, flaunt it. If you don't have it, hide it."

A burst of laughter from the girls sent the leaders into a frenzy, scrambling for even more scriptures to counter the girls' comments.

Another girl Camille didn't recognize added fuel to the fire. "I feel like as long as God knows your heart, it don't matter what you wear."

"That's the problem," one of the larger older women struck back, her face riddled with indignation. "When God *has* our hearts, He teaches us better than to walk around dressed as floozies!"

The girls looked at each other in confusion. Clearly, they had never even heard the word "floozy," let alone been all but accused of dressing like one.

One of the teens yelled out, "But the Bible says come as you are."

"Come as you are, but don't leave as you are. Be changed by the Word of God!" from the grown-up side.

The room rumbled with more dissention. "They tryin' to make us look old."

"I'll bet they didn't dress like that when they were in high school."

Mercedes nudged Camille. "Girl, you betta say something."

"What?" Camille whispered. "Both sides have valid points."

"You know what we're trying to get across, but these girls are taking it the wrong way," she said. Then she stood and called everyone's attention. "Um, I think we should hear what Miss Camille has to say."

Alrighty, then!

"What do you think, Miss Camille?" Mackenzie asked.

All eyes landed on Camille now. She cleared her throat as she tried to think of what her own mother would say and temper the most holy advice with her own experience as an entertainer and a young woman who appreciated an occasional whistle on the streets just to let her know she still had it.

"Ummm. Well, everyone here has some good arguments. I mean, fashion changes from one generation to the next. I mean, where I went to church, women didn't even wear pants like they do here at Grace Chapel. If my grandmother were here, she'd say everyone in the room who's wearing pants or makeup, or who isn't wearing stockings or has the crowns of her shoulders exposed is being disrespectful to the church this very moment."

Camille turned to the adults, seated mostly on the right side of the room. "Raise your hand if you grew up thinking that women who wore pants were on their way to hell."

Reluctantly, a few of the women obediently elevated an arm. "Okay, so you understand where these girls are coming from. What your mother or your grandmother thought was inappropriate, you now believe is okay. Somebody who had your hand up, tell me why it's okay for you now but it wasn't okay for your grandmother?"

Mercedes offered her own explanation. "I think it's because times have changed. As long as the pants aren't tight, they're okay. I mean, a lot of stuff just depends on how you wear it."

She got a few nods from the grown-ups.

Next, Camille turned to the left side. "And how many of *you* know that just because the world says something is okay doesn't mean it's okay?"

All of the girls raised their hands.

"So, give me an example of what's not okay to wear, in church or anywhere, in your opinions."

Immediately, the girls raised their hands. Camille instructed Mercedes to station herself at the laptop and create a new slide that would list all the girls' comments. Quickly, the left side churned out a list of their own self-determined no-nos: pants so low your panties show; breasts hanging out; belly button showing; panty-shorts; panty lines; sagging, transparent shirts without a camisole underneath; bra straps showing.

"That bra-strap thing has nothing to do with church, that's just tacky, period," Shaki remarked.

After they exhausted the list, Camille asked another question. "Now, somebody tell me why you all think these things are a problem."

"Because it shows you have no respect for yourself," Brittney said. "And if you don't respect yourself, no one else will, either."

Agreement from both corners.

"I really don't care what anybody thinks about me," Sierra declared. "If I see something cute and I want to wear it, I'll wear it. The way I act shows I have respect for myself."

"But isn't how you dress a part of how you act? How you present yourself?"

No response.

"Okay. I'm gonna do this because we're all ladies. Watch." Camille hiked her skirt, tied a knot in her knit shirt, and pulled her neckline down so low that her breasts almost spilled out into the crowd. "Look at me. If I walked into a room full of people, what's the first thing they'd notice about me?"

"Your breasts," Chrisandrea noted.

"What else?"

"Your legs, your body. I mean, you look hot," Michaela said.

"Right," Camille agreed. "Everyone in the room would be concentrating on my sex appeal. They would have a hard time hearing the words coming out of my mouth. *Especially* the men, because that's how they're wired.

"All we're trying to say in this meeting is . . ." Camille searched her heart for the right words. Then she blurted out the weirdest line. "If you want people to see Christ in you, don't show them your boobs first."

The adults clapped. Next thing she knew, the original Fly Girls started a chant, complete with a human beat box and chest-pointing: "Show Jesus, not these. Show Jesus, not these."

Mercedes typed in the word "STOP" on the screen, sending the entire group into a fit of laughter. Somehow, in the few moments Camille stood in front of them all, she'd managed to divert the strife, put everyone on the same page, and get both points across in a way that put Jesus front and center.

When she sat down again, Mercedes pinched

Camille's shoulder. "Girl, you must have been to President Barack Obama's charm school, 'cause that was smooth! You really have a gift for reaching young people. You should think about applying for one of those jobs they have listed on the church Web site."

Camille made a mental note to follow up on Mercedes's suggestion. If God blessed her with a job that made a difference, working would be so much easier.

After the meeting dismissed and the girls squashed Camille in good-bye hugs, Mercedes practically begged Camille to join her at a literary fest. "It'll be fun. You need to get out and do something since you obviously haven't been coming to church, ahem, ahem."

"I have my reasons," Camille said without explanation.

Mercedes followed Camille to her car, watching like a detective. "Mmm-hmmm." She hooked her arm around Camille's elbow. "This is an intervention. I am pulling you out of your funk whether you like it or not. Whatever happened between you and Ronald cannot be the end of you and God."

Camille stopped shy of the driver's door. "What have you heard about me and Ronald?"

Mercedes released her arm. "Nothing, but it's pretty obvious. You were a regular at choir rehearsal, now you're MIA. Ronald's back to his same old uptight self. Doesn't take a genius to figure out something happened."

"He's uptight?"

"Ummm, yeah. Nathan told him to take a chill pill the other day. I think you should talk to Ronald, for real," Mercedes suggested. "Y'all gotta work this out, because he's miserable without you."

"I can't talk to him. There's nothing to discuss."

"Yes, there is, and you can. I'll let you practice on me. At the festival. You game?"

Camille sighed. "Okay, okay. I'll go to this thing, but there better not be any weird spoken-word artists sounding all spooky and stuff."

"Hey, they're artists, too." Mercedes laughed.

As she followed Mercedes downtown and into Fair Park, Camille wondered if Mercedes would be as friendly if she knew the big secret Ronald had obviously been keeping from everyone. The fact that he'd been so discreet and protected her reputation made Camille feel even more guilty. If he told them all, then they might treat her with the contempt she figured she deserved after all that lying and using them. But their consistent love, consistent respect only exacerbated the problem.

Mercedes parked several yards away from the bulk of vehicles, presumably to protect her car from dings and nicks. This must have been her secret to preserving her ten-plus-year-old Chevy Malibu. Camille had to give it to her: That thing looked as good as any new car. Probably ran better, too, in Mercedes's care.

From the bottom floor, Camille could see that the artwork and authors must have been on the upper levels. Chunks of people ambled through the booths and displays. On the bottom floor, where they'd entered, the literary festival was more like a food festival than anything else. Vendors teased the book lovers with cakes, barbecue, pies, and even turkey legs. Warming up for the fair, Camille supposed. Though they had eaten a light snack at the meeting earlier, both ladies agreed to eat before exploring the various workshops and readings.

Mercedes had to buy Camille's food because the turkey-leg seller didn't accept credit or debit cards. "I gotcha," she'd quickly offered, whipping out a twenty-dollar bill.

"I'm sorry. I never carry cash," Camille said.

"No worries. That's what sisters are for."

Poor Mercedes. She had been nothing but kind to Camille from the beginning. She, too, needed to know the truth.

"How about right here?" Mercedes motioned toward an empty table in the museum's makeshift cafeteria.

"Okay."

They sat across from each other, blessed the food, and literally tore into the meat like untamed carnivores. There was really no other way to do turkey legs. Plus, there was no need to try to be cute. This was Mercedes, after all. She'd seen Camille up at seven in the morning with no makeup, hair a mess.

"So," Mercedes began, "let's give this a shot. You're you. Imagine I'm Ronald. What are you going to say to him?"

Camille raised an eyebrow. Now was her chance. "I'm going to say to you exactly what I need to say to Ronald. And I want you to react the way you think Ronald will react. So I can be prepared."

"Got it." Mercedes took off her shades, peered into Camille with the same serious expression Ronald would probably have on his face. They both cracked up laughing. "You said act like Ronald!"

"Okay, okay. You're right. Okay." Camille collected herself. Mercedes was about to get more than she'd bargained for. "Ronald, you were right. The only reason I became a member of Grace Chapel was because I wanted to join the choir so I could advance my singing career."

The ever-present giddy smile vanished from Mercedes's face.

"I especially wanted to get on the praise team so I could record myself singing with background and give the file to my agent, who was waiting on it."

"Oh my goodness, are you kidding?" Mercedes asked.

"No. Let me finish. Those were my intentions. And they were wrong. But once I got into the church, met nice people like you and Mercedes, my heart began to change. I started ministering to the girls. People whom I intended to use started loving on me, and before I had a chance to back out, I had fallen back into the person I'm supposed to be, the person my mother raised me to be, the person God has called me to be.

"When I asked you to sing that song at the studio, I was desperate. I should have told you about the lyrics ahead of time, but I was sure you'd say no before I could even get you into the studio, so I kept my mouth closed, hoping you'd just do it for me. But I'm glad you didn't. You showed me what it means to have convictions. Thank you for your example."

Mercedes bit her lower lip.

Camille's voice filled with emotion. "I'm sorry I used you, the church, and the choir."

Mercedes let out a cleansing breath. "Geez Louise. That's a lot to digest." She snatched a bite of meat.

"I apologize to you, too, Mercedes. This was all one big show at first. I was just stupid and selfish."

Tears breached the brims of Camille's eyelids. All she could do now was focus on the turkey.

"Okay, for the record, you were wrong," Mercedes fussed. "I accept your apology. But you're not the first person to join church for all the wrong reasons. Folks join church to find a husband, receive from the benevolence fund, get their company name in the church business directory.

"And *plenty* of women have joined the choir in an attempt to get next to one brother Ronald Shepherd. Jesus knew why you were here, but He let you stay anyway. It's kind of like what Joseph told his brothers— you meant it for evil, but God meant it for good. I'm not saying what you did was right. I'm just sayin' God used it anyway, 'cause He's sovereign like that."

Camille held up her greasy hand. "This is you, Mercedes, not Ronald. What is *he* going to say about all this?"

She shrugged. "Ronald's not stupid. He's been in choirs all his life. He has to know that people join choirs for various reasons. In college, some of us joined the gospel choir so we could get a free hot meal after church Sunday.

"But here's the thing that I know about being in God's service with people who truly have a white-hot passion for Him. That fire will either draw you in or push you away. You can't stay around it too long without being affected one way or another. Sounds to me like you got pulled inside."

"Yeah. I guess I did," Camille had to agree.

Mercedes credited, "By the grace of God."

Over the next several, silent chews, Camille pondered Mercedes's summation. If she hadn't joined the church, she never would have met Ronald. Never would have been sitting under Pastor Collins's poignant preaching. Never would have been there for Brittney and the rest of the girls.

Though this whole thing had begun as a selfish endeavor, maybe she was exactly where she was supposed to be this very moment. And she owed Him all the thanks.

"So what do I do about Ronald?"

"I don't know. All I know, Ronald is the best kind of man."

"What's the best kind of man?" Camille quizzed. "I mean, Ronald hasn't said he loves me or anything. I don't even know if the relationship was going anywhere, so how could he be the best man for me?"

"The best kind of man is a man who loves God more than he loves you," Mercedes clarified. "He has to forgive you, be faithful to you, love you, and treat you well, because when he doesn't, he can't stand in the presence of his true love, Christ."

"Hmmm. I'm thinking a man like that deserves a woman who loves God more than she loves her spouse, too," Camille said. After all, given her past, she'd probably be nothing more than a thorn in Ronald's side.

"I agree. And if you want to be the type of woman who loves God more than anything, you needs to get your behind back in church, back in the arc of safety, as the church folk said back in the day," Mercedes teased. "Not for Ronald, but for God. If Ronald's not the one ordained for you, whatever. You've got to run on anyhow."

"Enough with the old-school church clichés," Camille warned.

Mercedes continued, "Ninety-nine and a half just won't do."

They both squealed in laughter.

"So, Mercedes, tell me. You've been at Grace Chapel for a long time. Why didn't you and Ronald ever get together?"

She shook her head. "Girl, please. Ronald is, like, my third cousin on my daddy's side. Illegal in all but a few backwoods counties."

CHAPTER 34

Bobby Junior had given Courtney the number three days ago. "'Bout time one of you got a lick of sense."

He couldn't argue against his father. Bobby Junior was right.

Now, as he entered the numbers, adrenaline rushed through his veins. The last time he spoke to Camille, he had said some pretty ugly words. She deserved them, but still . . . his mother would have been ashamed to hear them coming from his mouth. He prayed for the right words this Sunday morning.

In her bedroom, Camille propped herself on pillows, turning on her phone to see if she needed to address any important e-mails before getting ready for church. Surely people reviewed and responded to job applications over the weekend. She hoped.

Her screen lit up, showing three e-mail messages she'd received overnight. Two were spam. One was a generic note from Ronald, addressed to the list for the young-adult choir, reminding her of practice Tuesday night. She hadn't heard anything personal from him in over a week now.

She'd heard about men's cave mentality, that they had to go somewhere to think for a while before they could address problems. She wondered if he would ever come out of the cave, or if she should knock on the rock and see if he'd answer. Maybe it was just over between the two of them, period, despite Mercedes's promptings for Camille to give Ronald a call.

The other day, she'd gone to the recreation center and searched an online Bible for the key words "apologize" and "regret." Ronald was a man of God. He'd probably already forgiven her. Didn't mean he had to go out with her again, though.

If she'd been the superstitious type, she would have asked God for a sign. Maybe her lights would flicker. A cereal box might topple from the counter inexplicably. Such things happened only in cheesy novels and Lifetime movies with people who didn't have this inner voice whom she knew would speak again whenever it was absolutely necessary. Too bad He didn't deem the situation with Ronald dire.

Cued by Camille putting her feet on the floor, Cat crawled from under the bed and stretched himself. Lately, he'd been acting strangely. Scratching at the windowsill, acting all territorial like he didn't want her to come into the restroom. Then sometimes he didn't want to be around her too much, which suited Camille just fine. Cat liked his space, and so did she.

Camille fixed herself a bowl of instant oatmeal and plunked herself in front of the television screen. Early-

Sunday-morning television consisted of political shows, pre–sporting event shows, and preaching. She settled on a Joel Osteen broadcast. In the past couple of days, she'd been listening to him preach positive messages. The kinds that helped people who'd ruined their lives muster some kind of hope. When she listened to him, that nasty old accusing voice within her had to shut up for a little while.

After pumping herself up with the Word, she actually began to entertain the idea of going to church. If she got there late, they'd seat her in the balcony. The video cameras never took shots of the late folk. And when they dismissed, she could sneak out one of the less-traveled side entrances farthest from the choir room. She'd be in there and out of there.

Yes. I'm going to church.

She flicked a blouse and skirt off the hanger and dressed before she had time to change her mind. When doubts arose in her thoughts, she said aloud, "I *am* going to church today." She knew she'd better leave and get in her car quickly. Her last order of business was to pocket her cell phone. She noticed the blinking message light. The voice mail icon sat in the status bar. *Who would be calling me this early in the morning?* She checked the call log and noted the unfamiliar area code. Next, she listened and nearly felt all the blood drain from her face as her brother's voice addressed her.

"Hi, Camille. It's your brother, Courtney. Dad gave me your number, I hope you don't mind. I also hope you're well and everything's fine with you." He cleared his throat. "It's been a long time. We need to talk and I don't know where to start, really, so if you don't mind, could you please give me a call back?" He'd left his number, then signed off with, "Call me as soon as you can. Thanks."

Mouth wide open, Camille stood in her bedroom trying to process what had just happened. *Courtney called me?* And he didn't even sound angry. Immediately, she called Bobby Junior's last known number in an attempt to make sure her father was still alive. *Why else would he be calling me?*

She put her fears aside when her father answered the phone. "Hey, Cami."

"Hey, Bobby Junior. How are you?"

"Oooh, you right on time! You got ten dollars I can hold 'til next Friday?"

"No, I do not. I don't even have a job right now, Daddy. We're both broke, all right?"

"If you say so." He moaned.

"What are you doing up this early anyway?"

"I'm on my way to church."

"When did you start goin' to church?"

"Well"—he lowered his voice—"it's this woman I'm with now. She's retired. Drives a nice car, got a house, but she lives at church, that little one on Mohawk Street. She just like your momma used to be, there every time the doors open. Say she ain't gon' let me lay up here in her bed while she's gone. When she leave, I leave. Most the time, she on her way to church. And since I ain't got no car to go nowhere right now, I gotta go with her.

"You know what, Cami? These preachers are makin' a killin'! All they do is get up there and read a few scriptures, start hollerin', and the people go crazy. What you think about me becoming a preacher?"

"No, Bobby Junior, that is not a good idea." Camille

had to leave it alone. At least she knew where she'd gotten her conniving ways.

"Hmmm. You probably right. This woman would want me to marry her then and I shole ain't 'bout to jump no broom with nobody treatin' me like I need a babysitter. Shoot, I'm a grown man."

"Alrighty, then. I'll talk to you later."

"Hey, your brother call you?"

"Yes."

"Pretty good news, huh?"

"What good news?" Camille asked.

"You didn't talk to him?"

"No. He left a message."

Bobby Junior laughed slightly. "I'll let him tell you. Call him back."

"I will. Have a good time at church, and *listen* to the preacher."

"I would if he'd stop all that whoopin' and hollerin'."

"Bye."

"Bye, Cami."

Talking to Bobby Junior could nearly drive Camille to need a strong drink.

Hands shaking, she pressed Courtney's number in her call log. No answer from Courtney. Unsure of what to say, she kept her message short. "Courtney, it's Camille. I got your message. I'll try you again later."

Camille slid the phone into the top pocket of her shirt dress. With keys in hand, she reached for her door's knob and barely had the door cracked when Cat squirmed between her feet and darted out the front door like he was on his way to collect a check from Publisher's Clearinghouse.

"Cat!" Camille screamed as she watched him amble down the staircase and across the parking lot before he

disappeared under an SUV. "Cat! Come back here!"
Then she saw the problem. Another cat, which led the
way across the courtyard and into a set of bushes.

Cat had a friend. A friend with benefits, which
would explain why he'd been clawing at the windows
and acting like he was running things. *Mmm-mmm.* It
was time for Cat to get fixed, 'cause all this running out
the door chasing female cats in heat was not going to
work.

She stood on her balcony for a few minutes. Should
she wait until he . . . finished his business? What if a
dog found Cat? Or a mean serial killer in training?
What if he got run over by a car? Cat might instinctively know what to do with another feline, but he had
absolutely no experience with humans or vehicles.

"Cat! That's enough!"

When did he get like this anyway? He was too little
to be mating, wasn't he? That other cat was grown.
What if she didn't like Cat snooping around? What if
another male cat beat Cat up?

All thoughts of church slipped Camille's mind as
she followed the trail to the bushes, hoping Cat would
be finished by the time she reached him. But when she
approached the spot where she thought they'd be, they
were gone. She glimpsed the tip of Cat's tail in a water
draining hole.

"Cat! Why are you doing this?"

She didn't bother to answer the question for herself.
She knew *why*. But why *now*? Of all the hundreds of
times she must have walked out the door, he chose the
one morning she was about to return to church to run
off and act uncivilized.

Immediately, the tail disappeared. Camille got down

on hands and knees, peering into the opening between the street and sidewalk curb.

"Oogh!" Camille shrieked in frustration, beating the ground with her hand. That's when her phone slipped out her pocket and landed within centimeters of the drain. Without considering the momentum of the device, Camille reached for the phone. In her haste, she managed to shove it over the edge and into the underground abyss. "Aaah!"

Fearlessly, she extended her hand into the unknown and felt a slickness she wasn't even sure she wanted to identify. A four-letter word as intense as the horror of losing a cell phone in such an absurd manner escaped her lips. "Lord, forgive me," soon followed. He must have forgiven her a hundred times now since she walked out of the jailhouse. And that was just for the stuff she remembered to ask pardon for.

The phone was gone. Courtney's number, gone. Bobby Junior had it, surely, but come to think of it, she didn't even know Bobby Junior's number by heart. *Mohawk Street.* He'd said the woman attended a little church there. Not far from her apartment. She'd have to run by there as soon as she was dismissed from Grace Chapel.

A few months ago, she wouldn't have dreamed of risking her knees, let alone her phone, to chase down this cat. Cat gone, off in the free world, doing catly things with his cat buddies, would have been a dream come true. Now . . . now he was hers. He had a bowl and a nice spot under the bed. Had his own kitty litter box, for crying out loud. Why leave at this point, after she'd invested all this money and they'd been through all this mess together?

Camille stood, but her shoulders slumped with her next thought. *What if Cat never comes back?* Some people might find him, take him in. He probably wouldn't even miss her.

She was tempted to go back to the apartment and drown her sorrows in television while waiting for Bobby Junior's church to dismiss. Maybe she should try getting in touch with Sheryl. She would know what to do. And even though their parting hadn't been friendly, Sheryl would do anything for an animal.

Against all pride, Camille scuttled to the 7-Eleven, asked the attendant for a phone book. At first, he looked at her like she was crazy. Then she looked behind the counter and saw the subject of her question. Poor boy didn't even know what the white pages were. Camille looked up Sheryl's number and jotted it down, certain that there weren't many Sheryl Finkowichs listed. She grabbed a quarter from her coin bag and made the most unsanitary call she'd made in a long time. Public pay phones should have been banned a long time ago.

This time, the emotion in her voice came from within her chest rather than feigned from her throat. "Sheryl, I'm sorry to call you but my cat ran away. What do I do?"

"Oh my gosh, oh my gosh. Where did he go?"

"He chased another cat."

"A female cat?"

"I guess," Camille wondered. "Maybe she was in heat?"

"Has he been acting weird? Trying to get out of the house?"

"Yeah. He's been scratching at the windows."

"You're right. The female cat was probably in heat.

He got a whiff of her and had to chase her down. Don't worry. I mean, you *can* worry because of traffic, but you're in an apartment complex. They'll probably just go do their business and he'll be back in a while.

"But you've got to get him fixed or else he's going to drive you crazy. Has he sprayed your furniture yet?"

Camille guessed, "No. I don't think so."

"Oh, if he did, you would know. No human can stand the smell of a cat marking his territory while he waits for a female cat to mate with. Get him neutered before he starts spraying, or you're gonna be in huge trouble.

"Don't you know this stuff already?" Sheryl questioned.

"No. I don't."

"Hmmm. Fluffy must have been fixed when you got her."

"I never actually owned Fluffy," Camille said.

"Well," Sheryl slipped on her empathetic tone, "I guess you're right in a sense. God only lends us our pets for a little while."

Never mind. "Thanks, Sheryl."

"Anytime."

With Sheryl's assurance that Cat would most likely return when he was good and ready, Camille drove on to church. Courtney's call, too, still frazzled her nerves. What did he want? Bobby Junior had said there was good news. She should have pushed her father until he spilled the beans. If she didn't get hold of Courtney immediately after church, she'd get Bobby Junior to talk.

The main lot was packed, so Camille had to file in

with the overflow and take a five-minute hike to the sanctuary with the rest of the stragglers. Most of them had kids and babies. They had some kind of excuse for being late. All Camille had was a cat who might not even come back.

Ushers pointed her in the direction of the balcony, but Camille snuck off down a different hallway. If she sat where they were telling her to sit, she was sure to run into a smorgasbord of off-week choir folk. They always sat near the front on the left side so they could stand up and support whoever was singing.

She peeked down the right hallway. The coast was clear. No ushers watching. Camille dashed down the hallway. As she neared the less-used entrance, one of the classroom doors swung open, nearly bopping her in the face. "Woo!"

"Hey! You're back. Girl, get in your choir robe," Mercedes ordered. "We're singing your song."

"What song?"

"The one Ronald rehearsed last month—'All Things New.' Remember?"

Of course she remembered. She and Ronald had practiced it only once, but it was a simple, pure praise. Totally beside the point. "No, I'm not singing this week. I haven't been here in forever."

"Camille, get over yourself. We want you back. Ronald texted you this morning. Didn't you get it?"

"No. My cat got out and my phone slipped into a drain hole."

Mercedes frowned. "Ewww. That's nasty. I hope you didn't retrieve it."

"I couldn't."

"Good. So go get your robe on."

"Mercedes, I feel—"

"Haven't you learned anything in all this mumbo-jumbo you've gone through? It's not about you, Camille. It's about Jesus. Do what will bring Him the most glory. And hurry up, they're about to pass the buckets."

Mercedes gently shoved Camille in the direction of the choir room. *They want me back? Who's they?* Mercedes and Ronald or Mercedes and the choir? While she slid the robe in place and snapped the bib with the church's initials into place, Camille warmed up her cords. "La-la-la-la-la-la-la-la-la." The notes soothed more than just her diaphragm. She was about to sing. In church. With Ronald.

She was home again.

Mercedes appeared from nowhere and yanked Camille from the choir room and directly onto the center platform. The band had already played the introduction. One of the media ministry workers thrust a microphone in Camille's hand.

"You make all things new," Ronald sang. "You make all things new."

Camille joined in, "By Your grace and Your mercy, You make all things new."

The choir repeated Camille's line. Camille and Ronald's voices then mingled, yielding a sweet spirit of peace and surrender in the sanctuary. The congregation picked the song up, sang it with conviction as Camille added her own personal thank you.

She raised her hands toward heaven as tears trailed in the opposite direction.

She was home, indeed.

Unintentionally, Camille caught Ronald's eyes and sang the final couplet, hoping he would get some sense of how sorry she was about everything, how much the words to this song meant to her now. "When I gave my life to You, You made all things new."

"When I give my life, when I give my life," he improvised, returning Camille's heartfelt gaze.

Together, they reconciled in song. "When I gave my life to You, You made all things new."

CHAPTER 35

Back in the choir room, choir members drowned Camille in hugs, questions, and warnings. "Don't get ghost on us like that again, you hear?"

Their love for her nearly caused her second public meltdown of the day.

Mercedes must have sensed Camille's emotions overflowing. "Y'all give her some room." She swatted them away, and the girls exited. Mercedes grabbed Camille's arms. "Okay. I'm going to leave you two alone now." She winked and nodded her head toward Ronald.

Camille looked to her left and saw Ronald standing at the doorway. He must have been the reason the room cleared so suddenly. These people were conspirators for love . . . or at least for a good romance story.

Finally, they were face-to-face. "I'm sorry."

"Me too."

She waited, unsure if he was sorry that *she* was

sorry, or if he was sorry for something he'd done, whatever that could be.

"I'm sorry I wasn't there for you," he explained. "You were in jail and I was like whatever. I wouldn't have treated any other choir member or brother or sister in Christ that way, and I certainly shouldn't have done it to you. Especially considering your condition."

"My condition?"

"Your *heart* condition."

Snap! She'd forgotten all about that lie. "Oh, yeah, about that. I don't have a pacemaker. That lump you felt was actually the digital recorder I used to record our song. Sorry."

"Okaaay. Is there anything else you need to reveal?"

"No. No more lies."

"Good. I don't want to have to lug a polygraph machine around everywhere we go."

Her stomach twitched. This was good. He planned to spend time with her in the future. "Ronald, I can't begin to tell you how awful I feel about what happened. I mean, I couldn't even come to church without thinking about—"

"Mercedes told me."

"What?"

"Yeah."

Camille huffed. "I wanted to tell you myself."

"Well, she wasn't the only One who beat you to the punch. I knew it. Inside."

"There's something else I want to tell you. Something Mercedes couldn't and the Holy Spirit probably didn't.

"Ronald, being around you has changed me. You make me think about what God would want and what the Bible says before I make decisions. You make me question everything I thought I believed, reevaluate what I thought was important. I mean, I know God was working through the pastor and even Brittney and the rest of the girls. But you . . . you made this walk *real* to me. Thank you."

"You're welcome." He laughed. "I have to admit, though, you're not the only one benefitting from our . . . friendship, relationship, whatever you want to call it—"

"I want to call it a relationship," she staked her claim.

A full smile ripped across his face. Those gorgeous teeth peeked out.. "Okay. This *relationship* brought joy back into my life. Taught me that God is not only righteous and true and sovereign, but He's also compassionate. Merciful. And He never gives up on us. That's what I see in you.

"Aside from the fact that your face is almost one hundred percent symmetrical."

"What?"

"And beautiful."

Pop-pop-pop!

"We'd better get out of here"—he chuckled—"before we start kissing."

They finished what they'd started about two blocks from the church at a stoplight. The van behind them honked and the driver yelled, "Get a room!"

Camille yelled back, "Sorry!" She drove them back to her side of town, trying to remember exactly where this street was.

"What was it again, babe?" Ronald asked again while consumed with his phone.

"Mohawk," she repeated. "You looking it up?"

"No. I'm texting Brittney to make sure she made it home. Telling her I'm out."

"She's home alone again these days?"

"Yep, but I never tell her how long I'll be gone so she should expect me when she least expects me."

He slid the mini-keyboard back in place and began reading off the street names as she passed them. "Seahawk . . . Blackhawk . . . Redhawk. Somebody downtown must have been smokin' somethin' when they came up with these street names! There it is. Mohawk."

Camille hooked a quick right, since there was no other way to turn. They cruised down the narrow residential roadway. Finally, as the street dead-ended, a makeshift steeple appeared. "Must be the church."

By the number of vehicles still parked along the curb, Camille figured they were still in service. She and Ronald grabbed their Bibles and approached the entrance. On the driveway, she asked, "You got twenty dollars?"

"Yeah, why?"

"'Cause Bobby Junior's probably gonna ask for it."

"Who's Bobby Junior?"

"My daddy."

"But . . . this is my first time meeting him. Why is he going to ask me for twenty dollars?"

"Your guess is as good as mine. My Daddy is kinda throwed, all right? I'm only trying to prepare you."

"If you say so."

Ronald opened the door for her. The heat from the house-turned-sanctuary nearly pushed them right back outside, but Ronald gently placed his hand on the small of Camille's back and whispered, "Go in. You know what they say, it's gonna be hotter than this in hell."

"I ain't goin' to hell," she whispered back, stifling a giggle. Ronald could sure bring back some good memories.

The sanctuary itself consisted of what probably used to be a living room and a dining room, only the dining room wall had been torn down. Four rows of chairs flanked the main aisle. Camille spotted Bobby Junior on the front pew. He was sitting conspicuously close to a woman in a hot pink three-piece dress suit and a humongous matching hat.

He nearly jumped out of his seat when he saw Camille, and waved at her like a child flagging down the ice cream man. The other twelve members of the audience smiled, but the lady in pink frowned and began talking to Bobby Junior. Camille waved back, then sat down next to Ronald. The preacher must have been nearing the end of his sermon because the piano player had begun steering him in for the landing, which consisted of nothing more than age-old clichés he'd probably heard all his life.

Suddenly, Miss Hot-Pink was up dancing, amening, and sho-nuffin' the preacher on. Camille had to consciously make a decision not to judge the woman, especially knowing that she was shackin' up with Bobby Junior. After all, Camille should know better than anybody the pain of acting one way and living another. And Bobby Junior was no great catch by any means. *Grace and mercy. Grace and mercy. God's not through with us yet.*

Bobby Junior stood up and announced his visitors just before the pastor dismissed. "Well, all right. Let's give these young people a hand. We sure appreciate you coming by."

Applause and up-and-down stares from the congregation. After the benediction, Camille introduced Ronald to Bobby Junior. Then Bobby Junior introduced them both to Miss Beverly Deveraux. She'd probably been a New Orleans beauty back in her day, but now her face spoke of too many hours spent in the sun.

"How y'all doin'?" She shook Camille's hand vigorously. "Your daddy told me about your new singing career. I sure do hope you and your brother do well."

"Oh, thank you," Camille said, glancing at her father.

"Honey, I'll meet you at the car," Beverly told Bobby Junior. Ronald followed suit.

"What's this Courtney wants to talk to me about, anyway?"

"Well, I wanted to let him tell you. Didn't you call him back?"

"No. My cat got out and I lost my phone while I was looking for him."

"You have a cat!"

"Yes. It's a long story. I didn't want him, but now he's mine and I'm keeping him."

Bobby Junior shook his head. "I raised you better than that."

"Daddy, it's a cat, not a criminal record."

Still disturbed, Bobby Junior proceeded to answer her initial question. "It's like this, Cami. Courtney and some of the girls did some songs together a few years back. They're doing pretty good in London or somewhere."

"They're singing without me?" Camille could hardly breathe.

"Yeah, but a couple of 'em decided they wanted you back in. So they finally broke Courtney down and made him agree to let you back in. Now he's got a deal to rerecord some of the Sweet Treats songs somewhere overseas." *No! No! No!* She couldn't sing those songs now. Not after the surrender and all. Bobby Junior flipped open his ancient cell phone. "Here. Let me call him for you."

Camille put her father's phone to her ear and waited for her body to just split in two, half going with Jesus, the other half back to fame and fortune. "Hey, Bobby Junior."

"Courtney, it's me."

"Hi, Camille."

"Ummm . . . Daddy said you had some kind of recording contract?"

He moaned. "I told him I wanted to be the one to break the news."

"You know Daddy can't keep a secret. Momma had to hide the Christmas presents from him more than us."

They shared a laugh.

"Yeah, Alexis, Tonya, and I have been in contact. Kyra, too, as much as possible. One of her sons has special needs, so it's kind of hard for her right now. We do have a date in the UK to record."

Why, Lord? Why would you show me what I want when You know I can't take it? "That's great news, Courtney. I'm thankful, I'm touched, I'm excited and everything."

"I hear a 'but' coming on," her brother said.

"But I'm a Christian now. That part of my life— booty shakin', provocative lyrics—I don't want to do those things anymore. That's not *me* anymore."

"Apparently, it's not Alexis or Tonya, either. They're on the same page with you. We'll have to make it a dance mix. Something people can move to without getting suggestions. I'll make it work."

She relaxed now. If Courtney said he would make it work, he would make it work. "Okay. I trust you."

"Do you, really?"

"Yes. Yes, Courtney, I trust you now and I should have trusted you all along. I was wrong, I was greedy, and I was just plain stupid, and I am so sorry I kicked you out of my life." The blabbering released a steady stream, so much so that Bobby Junior had to comfort his daughter with an embrace.

He grabbed the phone from Camille and put the call on speaker. "The girl said she's sorry, Courtney. Give her a break, shoot. You ain't been perfect all your life, son."

Camille remembered now why she'd kept in touch with Bobby Junior despite his constant begging. He'd saved her hide from many a whippin', always standing in the gap and pleading her case with Momma. There was a time when Camille could do no wrong. Maybe that was why Bobby Junior refused to believe she was broke. He still thought his baby girl was responsible for the stars shining at night.

"Tell Cami I forgive her. I'm not glad about what happened, but she's still my sister and I love her. Always have, always will.

"And tell her to call me tomorrow so we can talk money."

He called me Cami. And he loves me.

"Your brother says he loves you."

"I heard."

Bobby Junior gave her another squeeze. She thanked him.

"You two 'bout to make another run for the money, huh?"

She couldn't concur. "No, Daddy. I'm not the same person I was back then. I'm running a different race."

"Mmm. Sound just like your momma."

She smiled. "That's the best thing you've said to me in all my life."

"Glad you like it. You got twenty dollars on you?"

EPILOGUE

Camille, Alexis, Tonya, and Kyra stood in that order behind their separate microphones, with chins bobbing and headsets clamped to their ears. Camille took the lead in one of their lesser known hits, "Keep Moving Ahead." Once again, Courtney had worked his magic and convinced the executives to work around their beliefs. Kyra didn't care one way or another, but Camille hoped one day she would. She remembered what Mercedes had said. If Kyra hung around them long enough, she'd come into the light, too.

This was their last song to record. They might not see each other again until next summer's tour. Kyra vowed she'd lose thirty pounds before then.

"Don't sweat it, girl. You got kids," Tonya assured her the night before as they sat in their hotel room doing a group Bible study.

"You can have kids without rolls of fat hangin' over

your belt buckle. Got me looking like a can of exploded biscuits around my waist."

They had all cracked up, giggling like teenagers again. Kyra always did have a way with words.

"I wish you could stay longer," Alexis said to Camille again.

"Mmm-mmm. I gotta get back. I'm already landing at DFW late Friday as it is. It'll take me all day to recover from this jetlag so I can be ready to sing Sunday morning, get my mind right to go to work Monday and create a presentation for the mentees." Between working with the girls at church and groups at the Medgar Evers center, Camille's time was stretched to capacity. But she loved every minute of it and prayed that the church would be in a position to renew the grant they'd obtained to pay her salary and reimburse her travel.

"Besides, my cat is going to be so crazy when I get back. Seriously, he's a spoiled brat with whiskers."

"You got a cat?" Tonya grimaced.

"Yes! I have a cat! Why is that so hard for everyone to believe?"

Alexis snorted. "Because you are not the cat type."

"Whatever. I am kind, I am patient—just like these verses we were reading! I am love, people!"

"That's what this is all about," Kyra smacked her lips. "You ain't gotta sing that bad. And cats take care of themselves. There's gotta be a man somewhere up in here."

"Well"—Camille squirmed—"yeah. I am seeing somebody. His name is Ronald; he's the minister of music at the church. And he's fiii-iii-iiine!"

Alexis grabbed a brush and kicked off Salt-N-Pepa's

"Whatta Man." The Sweet Treats's harmony was perfect. Camille added her own lyrics. None of them rhymed, of course, but they were true.

She had a mighty good man. And a mighty good God.

Don't miss Michelle Stimpson's

Someone to Watch Over Me

In stores now

CHAPTER 1

I crossed my fingers in hopes of being named Top Quarterly Producer for my department. I mean, every single one of my clients had experienced Web site traffic and sales above the projected estimates, and I had even received two letters from pleased customers. "Tori's expertise made all the difference in our product launch," one had commented. "We'll be using NetMarketing Results for a long time to come!" Planning and implementing online advertising and marketing campaigns came with its own sense of fulfillment. After all, depending on who you asked, the Web pushes America's economy even more than a good old-fashioned mall.

But even as we stood around the conference room waiting for the announcement, I felt queasy. What if they didn't name me? One look around the room sparked another dose of apprehension.

Lexa Fielder was recently hired, yet she'd already managed to land a pretty impressive list of new customers for the company, though it was rumored she did quite a bit of work on her back.

Brian Wallace was one of the older marketing representatives, but he still had a few tricks up his sleeve. Every once in a while, he pulled off a last-minute record-breaking month for one of his clients and caught management's eyes.

There were only four eyes I wanted to catch, and all of them belonged to Preston Haverty. Okay, he really only had two eyes, but he did wear a set of insistently thick glasses that took on a life of their own at the center of his slight facial features. Every time I saw him, I felt like I was in a scene from *The Emperor's New Clothes*. Like, why won't somebody tell Preston those glasses are ridiculous, that we do have technology to free us from such spectacles? Probably the same reason no one talks to Donald Trump about that comb-over.

Anyway, Preston was good people, glasses and all. I appreciated his "hands off" management style. He didn't really care where or how we worked, so long as we got the job done. I only hoped that I'd done a good enough job to add to my collection of blue and green plaques given to outstanding employees. Lexa and Brian aside, I appreciated being appreciated. And God knows I'd put in enough woman-hours to earn this recognition.

"And the top producer for this quarter is . . ."—Preston announced as everyone in the room beat a drum roll on either the sixteen-foot table or some spot on the surrounding walls that wasn't covered with a motivational poster—"Tori Henderson!"

My cheekbones rose so high I could barely see in front of me. *Is this what it's like to be Miss America?*

Everybody applauding, confetti flying, the runners-up on the sideline clapping wildly to distract themselves from their jealousy and impending mental meltdowns following the show?

Okay, maybe it wasn't that serious, but I sure felt like a pageant queen. My fellow coworkers, probably twenty-five people or so, cheered me on as I walked toward the head of the table to receive my plaque. "Good job, Tori!" "You go, girl!" Their affirmations swelled inside me, feeding my self-esteem. *If only my mother could see me now.* Maybe then she'd forget about 1996.

I shook Mr. Haverty's hand and posed for the obligatory picture. In that moment, I wished I'd worn a lighter colored suit. Black always made me look like a beanpole. Gave no testament to all my hours at the gym and the doughnuts I'd turned down to keep the red line on my scale below one hundred and twenty-five.

I wasn't going to pass on the sweets today, though. Jacquelyn, the lead secretary, retrieved a towering pink and white buttercream frosting cake from somewhere and brought it forward now to celebrate my achievement.

Preston offered, "Tori, you get the first piece."

"Get some meat on those bones, girl," from Clara, the Webmaster.

But the mention of meat and the sight of the cake suddenly made me nauseous. To appease the group, I took the first piece. Then Jacquelyn got busy cutting and distributing pieces as everyone stood around milking the moment before having to return to work.

I sat in one of the comfy leather chairs and took a bite of my celebratory sweetness. Almost instantly, my stomach disagreed with my actions. My hand flew to my abdomen, lightly stroking the panel of my suit. People were so busy devouring the cake they didn't notice me catching my breath. *Whew!*

I pushed the plate away from me, as though the pink mass possessed the power to jump onto my fork and into my mouth. This was clearly not the cake for me. I thought for a moment about how long it had been since I ate something so densely packed with sugar. Maybe this was like red meat—once you stop consuming it, one backslidden bite tears you up inside.

No, that's not it. I'd eaten a candy bar the previous week, before my monthly visitor arrived. Renegade cramps? I rubbed my palm against the aggravated area again. No. The pain was too high in my torso for female problems. This had to be some kind of bug. Whatever it was, it didn't like strawberry cake, so I quietly tossed my piece in the trash on the way back to my desk.

An hour later, I felt like I could throw up so I sat perfectly still at my desk because . . . well . . . any movement of my torso sparked a pain in my side that might trigger this upchuck. I just didn't *feel* like I wanted to go through the process of throwing up. I would never tell anyone this, but I find vomiting an altogether traumatic experience. Such a nasty feeling in one's throat. And the aftertaste, and the gagging sounds. Not to mention getting a close-up look at the toilet seat. It's just not humanlike and should be avoided at all costs, in my opinion.

Thank God I made it all the way to my apartment before I finally had to look at the inside of a porcelain throne, only this time I hadn't even eaten anything. Bile spewed out of me, splattering in the toilet water. The pain in my side shot up to 7 on a scale of 1 to 10.

Now that I'd done the unthinkable and temporarily lost all self-respect, perhaps my body would relent. I could only hope the worst of whatever this was had passed (albeit out of the wrong end).

I managed to thoroughly brush my teeth and gargle a great number of times, assuring myself it was safe to swallow my own spit again. The image staring back at me in the mirror was normally me after a good workout— kinky twists dampened slightly at the base by my sweat, light brown face glowing in the accomplishment of burning hundreds of calories. Today, however, my sagging eyelids told the story of a woman who'd . . . vomited. I tried smiling, elevating my cheekbones even higher. No use. Maybe my mother was right when she'd told me, "You're not that pretty, Tori, but you can keep yourself skinny and, when you turn fifteen, I'll let you wear makeup. Fourteen if you're *really* ugly by then."

I closed my eyes and pressed fingers onto my temples, reminding myself that people told me all the time I was cute. One time, I went to this women's empowerment event my client was hosting, and I won a T-shirt that read I'M BEAUTIFUL with some Bible verse on it about being beautifully and wonderfully made. I wore that shirt to Walmart and a total stranger walked up to me and said, "I agree." So why did the only voice ringing now belong to my ever-beautiful mother, the timeless Margie Carolyn James, who bragged of still being carded at age forty?

My side still ached enough for me to call off the evening's kickboxing class. Good thing Kevin was out of town working. He probably would have called me a wimp and dared me to run at least two miles with him. And I probably would have at least attempted to make

Kevin eat his words, despite the pain now radiating through my stomach.

After downing a dose of Advil, I trudged to my bedroom, changed into a nightshirt and gently lay across the bed. I didn't have the energy to answer my landline when it rang. I could only listen for the message.

"Hey, I'm gonna lay over tonight. My flight comes in at seven, I leave out again tomorrow morning at eight. See ya."

I was hoping that by the time he got home, I would have awakened from a refreshing nap, totally healed and ready to finish up some of the work I'd had to bring home with me in light of the unproductive afternoon I'd endured. Yet when Kevin returned, he found me hunched over the toilet seat again.

"What are you doing?"

"What does it look like I'm doing? Uuuuck!" The wretching produced another plop of bile into the commode.

"Are you okay?"

"Perfect."

"What's going on?"

"I'm pregnant," I quipped, though the hint of mockery escaped my tone thanks to the reverberating bowl.

"Oh my God, Tori. You're kidding, right? You know how I feel about kids," he yelled. "How could you—"

"Stop freaking out. I'm joking."

He balled up his fist and exhaled into the hole. "Don't give me a heart attack."

"I ate some cake today at work and got sick."

He backed out into the hallway. "Let me know if you need me."

I rested an elbow on the toilet seat and looked up at Kevin. Six foot one looked even taller from my bathroom floor perspective. His deep sandy skin contrasted perfectly with his ivory teeth and hazel eyes that, according to him, had won over many women back in the day. I wasn't one of those eye-color crazy girls, but I was definitely a sucker for track star legs, and Kevin had those for miles and miles. Watching him unveil those limbs when he undressed was definitely the greatest benefit of moving into his condo eighteen months earlier. Well, the legs and the free rent. And the sex, when my mind cooperated.

Kevin was the modern, metrosexual type when it came to clothes, but he had some pretty old-fashioned ideas about finances. Who was I to argue with him? He paid the major bills. I handled groceries, the housekeeper, dry cleaning, and all things communication related since I needed high-speed everything for my job. I often wondered if he was being chivalrous or if he never obligated me to a substantial bill because he still thought of the condo as *his* place.

At first glance, our living quarters still resembled a bachelor pad. Simple furniture, mix-and-match bath towels. Not one picture of us on display, though I had plenty on my computer and stored on my camera waiting to be downloaded someday.

Either way, I'm no fool. Thanks to our financial arrangement, I had a growing stash of rainy-day money I'd earmarked to start my own business after an early retirement.

My stash was chump change compared to Kevin's anyway. I'd seen a few of his pay stubs lying around the condo from his work in telecommunications sales. Made my college degree seem like a huge scam to keep the masses from getting rich.

Thoughts of my master plan to retire well and get

rich later compelled me to hoist myself from the floor to a semistanding position and shuffle back to bed. Sick or well, there was work to be done.

Kevin did check on me, but only by default as he changed into his running clothes.

There went those strong, milk chocolate legs again.

"I'm going for a jog at the track. Might head over to Cameron's after to watch the game."

I gave my best big-brown-doe-eyes routine. "But you're leaving again first thing in the morning. Can't we spend time together?"

He held up a cross with his fingers. "I don't want to catch whatever this is you've got. You looked pretty distraught in that bathroom there a minute ago."

"Thanks so much, Kevin."

"Any time, any time," he smirked. "I do feel bad for you, if that helps."

"It doesn't."

"You need me to get you anything while I'm out?"

"A new stomach."

"No can do, babe. How about Pepto-Bismol or Sprite? That's what my mom gave me when I was sick."

I scrunched my face. "Didn't your mom also make you swallow Vicks VapoRub?"

"Yeah," he supported the madness. "Makes you cough the cold up. Worked every time. If you're getting a virus, you might want to give it a shot."

My stomach lurched at the thought. "No. I don't want anything else coming up out of me tonight. Just . . . call and check on me."

He detoured to my side before walking out of the room. A gentle kiss to my forehead was his first affectionate gesture, despite more than a week's passing since we'd seen each other last. I suppose it would have been hard for him to kiss me since I was engulfed in the commode earlier. Still, I wanted him to rub my back or something. What I really wanted was for him to stay home and . . . I don't know, watch me suffer. Hover like they do when women are giving birth in those old movies. Put a damp towel on my forehead and encourage me, "You can do it! You can do it, Tori!"

Who was I kidding? Kevin would hire a birthing coach before he'd subject himself to *my* labor. Not that I'd ever find myself in a position to give birth so long as Kevin stubbornly refused to father a child. I held hope, however, that things would change after a few of his friends settled down. Sometimes guys are the only ones who can convince other guys to grow up. It's a sick reality.

I decided to put the suffering out of my head for a moment. The Advil had taken the edge off the pain, so I carefully reached onto the floor and pulled my laptop bag onto the bed. The sweet challenge of work carried me into a trance that dulled the pain for a while.

I tapped on the mouse to wake my computer and then resumed toggling between the open programs on my computer desktop, making sure my client's newsletter matched the updated blog content precisely. Next step was to update their social media networks with useful information about the company's new products.

With reviewing several press releases still on my agenda, I really didn't want to stop working. But the pain in my midsection returned with new vigor, biting into my concentration. I powered down my computer for the night and made my way back to the restroom for another bout with bile and a double dose of Advil. If the pain wasn't any better by tomorrow, I'd have to miss work so I could visit the doctor.

Kevin rolled in a little after eleven to assess me again. He slipped a hand beneath the comforter and rubbed my backside. "You all right now?"

"No," I groaned.

He nibbled on my ear, a sure indication of his intentions. "Mind if I make you feel better?"

"That won't help."

"Marvin Gaye says sexual healing is the best thing for you."

"Marvin Gaye never felt this bad. Besides, I might have germs."

Kevin tried again, lapping my neck with his tongue. "I don't care. I miss you."

Now he doesn't care about the germs.

His hand moved around to my stomach, warranting a stern rejection. "Kevin, I cannot do this tonight. Move your hand."

He jumped up from the bed. "Fine. Fine. I understand. I'll be on the couch."

CHAPTER 2

"Maybe it's because you haven't eaten anything," my secretary speculated when I told her I felt like I'd been kicked by a horse. "You tried crackers?"

"Yes, but they wouldn't stay down," I confessed. Jacquelyn had never seen me so miserable—in fact, no one had ever seen me so miserable because I'd never *been* so miserable in my whole life. I hurt so bad I was close to crying, which is the only reason I decided not to hang around the office another hour before my eleven o'clock semiappointment with Dr. Lightfoot.

His receptionist had assured me, "You may have to wait a bit when you get here, but we'll try to work you in as soon as possible."

I figured if they were going to work me in some way, I might be able to get the ball rolling sooner if I got there earlier. I grabbed my laptop bag and purse, and stopped by Preston's office on my way out the door. By this point, I was nearly doubled over in pain.

"Tori, can I get someone to take you to the doctor?" he asked. "You really don't look well."

Truth be told, I would have preferred a ride. I'd even considered calling Kevin, but if he came home, he probably wouldn't be able to reschedule his flight and make it to Chicago in time for his next presentation. Still, the logistics of having a coworker take me—leaving my car in the parking lot, getting someone else to pick me up when this was all over—was too much to ask. Plus there was always the possibility I might barf upside someone else's door panel before they could pull over, like I'd contaminated my car only three hours earlier.

"No, I'll make it. I've got my unfinished work here in my bag, in case I don't get to come back this after-noon." I raised the black leather satchel for him to see.

To my surprise, he didn't seem impressed. Then again, who could really tell with those glasses?

"Well, let us know if you need a day off or some-thing."

I frowned and shook my head. "Oh, no. I'll be back at my desk tomorrow for sure. There's way too much work to be done."

Now it was Preston's turn to frown. "Take care, Tori."

"Okay. See you tomorrow."

I treaded lightly down the hallway, stabilizing my midsection. Movements were the enemy. Movements and food. Even liquids were suspect.

The beauty-queen wave would have to do as I floated down the hallway saying good-bye to the few coworkers who happened to be looking up from their screens as I passed by. Our gray cubicle partitions defi-nitely prevented outside distractions.

Once down the elevator (which nearly did me in),

through the parking lot, and sitting in my shiny red Cadillac SRX mini-SUV with the lovely lingering aroma of throw-up, I carefully snapped my seat belt and took off for Dr. Lightfoot's office. My only saving grace was the weather. February in Houston is still quite cold, thus the odor from this morning's puke hadn't been baked in yet. The detail shop would have to work me in, too.

Why are there so many lights? I was down to one hand driving now. The other was practically glued to my midsection, attempting to protect myself from this invading pain. The act itself was impractical because the pain came from inside me, but I couldn't help myself.

I began to doubt whether I could step out of my car if I ever made it to Dr. Lightfoot's office. Agony elicited little animal noises from deep within me. Now, I was thankful for the stoplights. They gave me a chance to catch my breath, refocus myself and gain my wits again. I promise you, the road to this office was turning into that long, ever-extending hallway in *The Shining*.

I think I had maybe two more intersections to go when I decided there was no way I could make it in. I should have taken Preston up on his offer because, at the moment, tears blurred my vision. "Oh my God!" I finally cried out, followed by a long string: "Oh my God, oh my God, oh my God." And I wasn't just saying His name jokingly, either. I felt as though I was, maybe, ten minutes from meeting the Big Man Himself if this pain didn't cease.

Then came this sudden, unquestionable realization that I needed to make a quick right into the hospital's emergency room, which was directly across the street from the physicians' offices. I knew I couldn't sit in Dr. Lightfoot's office and wait to be seen after someone with a mere stuffy nose. I needed someone to see me stat.

A gloriously close spot opened up just as I was pulling into the emergency room parking lot. Couldn't have asked for better without being in an ambulance. I swerved between the white lines and parked, waiting for a moment of diminished pain. No such luck. No reprieve in sight.

I opened the car door and found footing on the nice, steady concrete. Now to push myself up and out of the car. I rolled down the window to get a good grip on the door's frame with my right hand. I'd just grabbed hold of the headrest with my left and was attempting to tilt forward when this band of torture wrapped itself around to my right side and dictated in no uncertain terms: *you ain't goin' nowhere, Tori!*

Yes, Pain has a voice. He sounds like Freddy Krueger and he minces no words. The excruciating fire in my stomach had spread.

"Help!" I whimpered desperately. "Help me!"

The lot was completely void of all human life. Eyeing the building's glass windows, I saw why no one inside the building had noticed me. The shades were pulled down to block out the high sun. Only the patrons' legs were visible.

But wait! A little girl. On the floor. I waved my hand and finally managed to lock gazes with her. She gave me a snaggle-toothed smile that, at that moment, was the sweetest vision I'd ever beheld.

I motioned for her to touch the nearest grown-up and get me some help—or at least I thought that's what I'd motioned. In restrospect, I'm sure I must have looked like I was doing the chicken dance.

The little girl turned away from me and continued

playing with some toy on the ground. But a second or two later, she gave me her attention again. This time, I mouthed the word "help" and folded my hands in a pleading gesture.

She laughed, apparently amused. This little girl was not *even* trying to help me. I had to go mean-church-usher on her. I'd never been so glad that 90 percent of communication is body language. Through gritted teeth and flared nostrils, I ordered her with words I'm sure she couldn't hear, "Get your momma! Get your momma!" I wagged my finger angrily toward her. "Get her now!"

The child's face wrinkled with fear and she tapped her mother's leg, then pointed back at me. Seconds later, the bottom of the blinds lifted and a woman's face peeked out at me.

"Help me!"

Nurses came scrambling out with a wheelchair. Thankfully, they had the wherewithal to secure my car and grab my purse. I was transported straight to an examination room. They asked me a ton of questions that I couldn't answer because I was in such agony I couldn't even think straight anymore. Their faces blurred by tears, their words overshadowed by my wailing. I just wanted them to knock me out and do whatever they had to do.

"Who can we notify for you?"

I cried, "Nobody! I came by myself!"

"Have you taken any drugs, Miss Henderson?"

"No!"

"Is there a possibility that you could be pregnant?"

Home-training aside, I managed to say, "No, no, no to everything, all right? Just help me!"

After covering every possible topic—including my

insurance—and prolonging my pain to the full extent legally allowable, a doctor finally entered the room. She asked me two questions about my symptoms, had me lie flat on my back, and pressed one area on my stomach that made me want to slap the judge.

I didn't have to tell her she'd hit the spot.

"Looks like it's your appendix. We'll have to operate right away." She glanced at my chart again and ordered the nurses to prepare me for surgery.

"Miss Henderson," the pesky nurse drilled me again, "we have to notify someone before we can proceed. Don't you have *anyone* we can call? Grandparents? Cousins?"

Surgery? I shook my head violently as, now, a fresh batch of tears spewed from my eyes. These, however, came from a different well. *I don't want to die.*

"How about coworkers or a friend or a boyfriend?"

"He won't answer—he's on a flight."

"It doesn't matter. We can leave a message. We just have to let someone know you're going under sedation. It's the law."

"Kevin Walker." Then I gave her his number and someone whisked me off for surgery. "And call my job for me, okay?"

"We'll do that later."

The last thing I remember was a woman saying, "I'm gonna stick this needle in your arm and you'll be on your way to la-la land."

I remember thinking, "Lady, you can stick a needle in my *eye* if it'll get me out of this misery."